DOMESTIC GODDESS

Regina Hale Sutherland

WARNER
VISION
BOOKS

NEW YORK   BOSTON

Cover design by Diane Luger
Book design by Stratford Publishing Services

ISBN 978-0-7394-7811-0

Warner Vision is a trademark of Time Warner Inc. or an affiliated company. Used under license by Hachette Book Group USA, which is not affiliated with Time Warner Inc.

Warner Books
Hachette Book Group USA
1271 Avenue of the Americas
New York, NY 10020

Printed in the United States of America

R^{The}ed Hat Society's

DOMESTIC GODDESS

Chapter One

"I hate the word housewife; I don't like the word homemaker either. I want to be called Domestic Goddess."
—*Roseanne*

Feeling like the rabbit in *Alice in Wonderland,* Millie Truman pulled her gray Taurus into the driveway of her condo and impatiently pushed her garage door opener. Late. She was running late. But like the rabbit, at least she looked good. She spared a quick glance into her rearview mirror, admiring the new 'do. Cinnamon. Since she loved the flavor so much, she'd taken a chance on the color.

And it had paid off. Of course, now she would have to hear her friends, Theresa and Kim, say, "I told you so." They'd been bugging her for a while to stop being so old-fashioned and get a dye job. She had to admit they were right; she looked much younger than fifty-five.

Except . . . had the beautician missed a gray hair? She reached up for the offensive strand, but it dissolved between her fingers like gossamer. A cobweb.

From cleaning Mitchell's apartment. It figured. Her youngest son was responsible for all the gray hair she'd just gotten rid of, too.

She'd stopped at his place after the beauty parlor, expecting only to have to do a quick dusting and vacuuming. But she'd found his loft apartment totally trashed, as her granddaughter would say, like the frat houses he and his brother had lived in during college. The big mess had probably not been the result of a party, though, just his usual fast-paced lifestyle.

While she was there, he'd rushed in to pack a suitcase for a business trip for the automotive firm where he worked. Except *she* had wound up packing the suitcase, after she found it shoved under his bed.

She didn't want to think about what else she'd found under there. She brushed her hand through her cinnamon curls again, dislodging another cobweb and shuddering.

What had happened to Heather, who'd actually made an attempt to keep the apartment neat? Millie had asked, but Mitchell had just grinned and shrugged and made some smart remark about Suzy Homemaker types liking boring nine-to-five men like his brother, Steven, the insurance agent.

Suzy Homemaker indeed, Millie sniffed. She preferred the term her fellow Red Hatters used: *Domestic Goddess.* Millie had reigned as one throughout thirty-one years of marriage, and she'd loved it. Like she'd told her dear husband, it was her *job.*

But Bruce had died five years ago, and she should have been able to retire her tiara and spend less time cooking and cleaning and more time with her friends. But she'd still had Pop to take care of; he lived with her then . . . and Mitchell, the confirmed bachelor. At least she hadn't had to worry about Steven, who was happily married with a beautiful daughter. Then. She was a little worried about his marriage now.

But she didn't have time to worry. She had to clean up, bake her snack contribution for Movie Night at the community center, and meet Kim, a neighbor and fellow Red Hat Society member, for dinner.

Resisting the urge to check for more cobwebs, she tore her gaze from the mirror and noticed that the garage door was up. But there was no room for her car in the single stall of her end unit brick condo. Another car was already backed into it with the trunk lid lifted. She pressed the brake, stopping an inch shy of its front bumper.

"What in the world . . ."

A robber. That should have been her first thought, and she should have been fumbling in her purse for her cell phone to call 911 while backing away. But the black car looked vaguely familiar, or as familiar as the grill of a vehicle can look. She'd feel pretty silly if she called the police on someone she knew, especially if it was, as she now suspected, her oldest son.

Of the few people who had a key to her place, Mitchell was probably on a plane by now. Pop was in Arizona with his new wife, or at least he had been when they'd talked a few nights ago. Process of elimination left Steven, but as Mitchell had just pointed out, Steven worked nine to five. And it was only four o'clock.

Her hand trembling slightly, Millie shifted the gear into park but left her car running as she stepped out. For a quick getaway? From her own house?

Maybe the cinnamon dye had leaked into her brain. Or she spent too much time with Kim. Kim was the daughter of a retired police chief; she suspected everyone of something. The scary part was that she was occasionally right.

Remembering that, Millie opened the back door of the Taurus and reached for something to use as a weapon. Her fingers closed over the handle of the vacuum, but the muscles in her shoulder protested as she started to lift it out.

She couldn't blame Mitchell for her cramped muscles, though; those were courtesy of the aerobics class Kim had started at the condo community center. Millie couldn't very well not attend since it had been her idea for Kim to start the classes after school budget cuts had cost her a Phys Ed teaching position. *But push-ups? Really?* Kim had a tendency to treat her new students like her old ones: teenagers.

Millie released the vacuum handle and reached for something else, pulling out a hot pink feather duster. Not very lethal. But from all the dust left on it from Mitchell's place, it might make a burglar sneeze hard enough for Millie to escape . . . if the need arose.

She drew in a quick, fortifying breath, then walked into the garage. The car parked in it was the same make and model Steven drove. While the trunk was open, the contents inside hadn't been taken from *her* house. She didn't own a laptop or a set of golf clubs, so unless her robber had a Robin Hood complex, she was safe.

And if he did . . . she preferred jewelry to golf clubs and computers. Rings and necklaces. Tiaras she could do without.

The door between the house and the garage creaked as it slowly opened. Millie ducked behind it and lifted the duster, hoping that her exercise-weary joints didn't creak as loudly as the door hinges. Her heart beat hard and fast against her ribs as a dark shadow emerged from the house.

Broad shoulders, thinning dark hair, expanding belly . . . he was not exactly her image of a cat burglar. He was her son. Steven caught sight of her and gasped, "Mom!"

Millie's heart rate subsided, and she breathed a sigh of relief.

Steven sneezed and gestured toward her weapon. "What the heck are you doing? Dusting the garage? You take this neatness thing a little too far."

"Steven?" It wasn't like she didn't recognize him; what she questioned was what he was doing at her house, at four o'clock.

"Did you have a golf outing?" she asked, waving the duster at his clubs in the trunk. The insurance company for which Pop, Bruce, and now Steven worked their boring nine-to-five jobs often sponsored them. "It's a great day for one." Not that she had spent much time in the gorgeous, warm weather, which was unusual for such an early spring day in Michigan.

Steven didn't answer her, brushing a slightly shaking

hand over his thinning hair instead. He had his father's hair, or premature lack thereof, as his younger brother relentlessly teased him. Maybe it was the hair loss, or his growing waistline, but he always looked older than his almost-thirty-six years. Today he looked even older, his face set in lines far too grim for a man his age.

"Bad game?" she teased, though he wasn't dressed for golf. He was wearing suit pants and a dress shirt. The jacket lay across the front seat of his car and his tie hung from the rearview mirror. Her heart started beating fast again.

"Mom . . ."

"Steven, what's going on? You're here in the afternoon, with the garage door down—"

"I shut the garage door because of your nosy neighbors. I already had a run-in with that crazy lady—"

"Crazy lady?"

"The neighbor who's packing."

He probably didn't mean luggage or a can of mace, either. Besides being Hilltop Condominium's aerobic instructor, Kim was the unofficial neighborhood watch captain. Nothing and nobody got past her. "That's Kim."

"Dirty Harriet."

"Actually, Harry's what she calls the gun," she said. If Kim had brought it out, she'd really been concerned. But since she'd left, she must have ruled Steven out as a burglar, too.

"She named her gun?"

Millie smiled. You really had to know Kim for a while before you realized she wasn't crazy. Just a little intense. "It's not real."

"Could have fooled me," he said, brushing that hand through his hair again. It was shaking even more.

But Millie didn't believe it was his run-in with Kim that had him so upset. "It's an air gun, kind of like the BB guns you and Mitchell had growing up."

That they'd used to shoot each other with before claiming the resulting welts on their skin were chicken pox. Millie might have fallen for it, too, had they not both already had the chicken pox.

"Those can really hurt," Steven said. He would know.

"She didn't use Harry on you?" Millie asked, horrified. Because he looked like he was hurt. His brown eyes were dark and wounded, his mouth tight and devoid of his usual easy smile.

"No," he assured her, "but I could have done without meeting him today."

Somehow she knew he was talking about more than the uncomfortable sensation of looking down a gun barrel. As she glanced again toward his partially unpacked trunk, she had that uncomfortable sensation herself. "Steven, I'm sorry about that."

He shrugged, his broad shoulders bobbing slowly up and down as if they carried a burden too heavy for him to bear. His gaze kept sliding away from hers. He couldn't meet her eyes, like when he'd been a little boy and had, on the rare occasion, done something naughty. Unlike his younger brother, he'd never wanted her disapproval or disappointment.

"It's not a big deal," he said. "It's good to know someone's looking out for you."

"Hey, *I* look out for me!" She brandished the fuchsia

duster, leaving a trail of cobwebs across the garage floor that she'd just swept that morning. Now she *would* have to dust it . . .

One half of Steven's mouth lifted in a half-hearted smile. "So now *you're* Dirty Harriet."

"I do feel pretty dirty," she admitted, letting him stall for time.

Unlike Mitchell, Steven had always confessed his misdeeds to her. She'd only had to wait until his conscience got the better of him and then he would spill all. He'd been the one to tell her what had really caused the welts on his and Mitchell's skin. BBs.

"I just finished cleaning your brother's apartment," she explained her dirtiness, hoping there were no more cobwebs in her hair.

Steven's face twisted into a disgusted grimace. "I don't know how he lives like that."

Millie knew that if it weren't for Steven's wife, Audrey, his house would look the same way. "I love it when you drop by, but I'm surprised . . ."

"It's so early," he finished for her, his voice thick with emotion, "and that I've brought luggage."

She hated to ask, afraid of what he might answer, so she just nodded.

"Audrey made me come home for lunch today. I thought . . ." He sighed, a ragged gust of air full of resignation. "It doesn't matter what I thought. I came home to my bags packed. She threw me out."

"Audrey threw you out?" Millie couldn't digest it; like the half-eaten pieces of pizza left in the boxes on Mitchell's coffee table, the thought made her queasy.

Steven and Audrey had met in college. While he'd finished, she'd dropped out to marry him. They'd been together seventeen years, married almost fifteen; they had Brigitte, who was just starting her teen years.

"No . . ."

He nodded, his brown eyes filling with tears. "I don't understand it, Mom," he said, blinking furiously before lifting a box from his trunk and heading into the house with it. In the foyer, at the top of the stairs, which led to Pop's old apartment in the walk-out basement, he turned back and said, "And really I don't want to talk about it."

"But you and Audrey . . . you need to talk," she protested. "The *last* thing you should do is move out."

"It's what *she* wants, Mom. She doesn't want me around anymore."

Panic pressed heavily against Millie's heart, stealing her breath away much more than any of Kim's outrageous exercises ever did. Steven, Audrey, and Brigitte were the perfect family. Well, maybe not perfect. They had their arguments, but that was normal.

Except that things hadn't seemed normal for them lately. They'd been strained. But Millie knew from experience that marriage was like a rubber band; it could get stretched to the limits but snap back tightly, not even showing any traces of how far it'd been stretched. Unless . . . it broke. The divorce rate proved how many times that happened.

"Steven," she said, reaching for his arm as he started down the stairs. "You're not giving up, not like this, not after so many years together."

He sighed and bowed his head, refusing to turn toward her. "Mom, it's not that simple anymore."

"Marriage isn't." Not that she could complain about hers. All her memories of Bruce were happy ones; at least the ones she'd kept alive were. Maybe there'd been others, but so few and far between that they weren't worth remembering.

"But it shouldn't be this difficult, either," Steven said, running a slightly shaking hand over his hair yet again.

"What's difficult?" Millie asked, desperately wanting to understand. Despite noticing the strain, she hadn't wanted to ask about it. From the minute her sons had been born, she'd vowed not to become one of *those* mothers, the kind who interfered in their children's lives. She'd trusted them enough to let them live their own lives. "What's changed? You were happy together."

"Until . . ." he started, his voice thick with emotion, "she went back to school."

Audrey had recently gone back to college to finish up the nursing degree she'd started so many years ago. Millie had applauded her determination and been so inspired by it that she'd gotten serious about retiring her own tiara. Now a horrible thought occurred to Millie, turning her stomach as if she had eaten Mitchell's leftovers. "Oh, no, she met someone else."

He laughed, a short bitter sound. "No, but I almost wish she had."

"Steven!" She fought the temptation to whack him with the duster; her son was already hurting.

He jerked his hand through his thin hair again. His whole body was shaking now . . . with frustration and shock. While Millie had noticed the strain in their marriage, she wondered if *he* had. His next words confirmed that he hadn't. "If she'd found someone else, then I could actually understand why she threw *me* out."

"You need to talk," she maintained. "We'll go back to your house. Brigitte can come stay with me while you and Audrey work things out."

He shook his head and squeezed his dark eyes shut, probably trying to hold in the tears she saw glistening in them. "No, Mom, it's too late. Or it's too soon. I'm not sure what it is anymore."

It was not fair to him or to Audrey but most especially not to Brigitte. *That poor girl . . .*

"Oh, Steven . . ." She squeezed his arm, trying to express her love, support, and willingness to help any way she could. The phrase *too little, too late* taunted her. She refused to accept that it was too late. "You have to try."

He nodded. "I know. But not now. It . . ." One tear fell, sliding down the hard line of his taut jaw. ". . . hurts too much, Mom."

The shock, the pain, it was too fresh. She understood that. "But you will."

"After we've given it some time. But I have to ask you something, Mom."

"Of course you can stay here." But it was a little late to ask that since he'd apparently already brought some stuff down to Pop's old apartment. It consisted of a bedroom, a bathroom, and a family room, with a little kitchenette in one corner.

Steven blinked, surprised again. "Well, that, too. I didn't think . . ."

"It's okay." That he hadn't asked her first. "Don't worry about it."

Obviously he didn't think she had a life. But she did and she actually needed more time for it. She'd thought she'd only had Mitchell left to marry off before she could retire her tiara and take that time for herself.

There was someone else she'd flirted with the idea of making time for, though, but it was definitely too soon for him. And Millie was so old-fashioned, she'd never actually learned to flirt. Was it as easy as getting a dye job?

"Mom? Are you okay?"

She nodded, pushing the crazy thought from her mind. She didn't really need anyone or anything else in her life. Even with Pop married and moved out, it was too full now for her to fit in all the things she wanted to do, like shopping and gambling excursions with her Red Hat Society chapter, The Red Hot Hatters of Hilltop. She'd always wanted to travel, but Bruce had been such a homebody, and they'd had Pop and the boys to take care of then, too. She really wanted to take a cruise like several members of her Red Hot Hatters often did. She blew out a resigned sigh before assuring Steven, "I'm fine, just tired."

He snorted. "From cleaning Mitchell's place. I would have moved in with him, but I couldn't stand his mess."

Which multiplied by Steven's would have given Millie nightmares. She would have had to beg Mitchell to hire a maid.

"I'm happy to have you here," she insisted. But she hoped it wouldn't be for long. While she wouldn't mind his company, Steven belonged home with his family. The connection between a mother and child as strong as ever, she could *feel* his heart breaking, and hers ached, too.

He let out another ragged sigh. "Thanks, Mom. I need to ask you for another favor, though."

"Anything."

"I need you to go . . ." he drew in a quick breath, "to my house."

He couldn't call it home. He'd only been gone a few hours, but he couldn't call it that anymore. Panic pressed on Millie's heart. She refused to believe it was too late, though. Maybe she could still help.

But how could she, who had never interfered before, interject herself into the middle of a battle between a husband and wife when she had no real idea what their problems were?

"Steven, I don't think it's my place . . ."

"I just need you to pick up my briefcase. I've looked through the boxes I brought downstairs."

Boxes? He'd already moved *boxes* of his stuff from his home to the basement?

"And I checked the trunk again. I can't find it. I brought it home with me to do some work this afternoon. Can you go get it for me? I can't go back there."

"Steven, you're going to have to . . . for Brigitte."

"I can't go back *because* of Brigitte. It's too soon. We all need time to adjust."

Millie worried that he was adjusting pretty quickly, then she saw his eyes and the tears he couldn't blink away. He was hurting, and he didn't want his daughter to see him in that kind of pain.

Millie hated seeing him in that kind of pain.

"Of course." She blinked fast, pushing back her own tears. "I'll go right now." And give him a chance to pull himself together. *She* needed one, too.

She'd conveniently left the car running for a quick getaway. Hands trembling, she opened the door, then tossed the duster into the backseat. She rammed the Taurus into reverse, then glanced into the rearview mirror *after* she'd already started moving. Too late.

A man stood behind the car, his outstretched arm clutching a leash. But she couldn't see the dog he usually walked at the end of it. She slammed on the brakes, the seatbelt biting into her sore muscles, but she didn't care about that. She cared about him. He couldn't lose his dog, too. He'd just buried his wife not that long ago.

She threw open her door. "I'm so sorry. Are you all right?"

She couldn't look down. She was too afraid to see whether or not a furry, gray body lay beneath the tire of her car.

# Chapter Two

"I only like two kinds of men: **domestic** and foreign." —*Mae West*

*M*illie held her breath until she heard an indignant yip. Then she let it out in a relieved sigh, glancing down at the small, bearded dog. "Oh, thank goodness. I thought I hit him."

"No, you didn't," a deep voice assured her though it didn't sound particularly relieved. Actually, it sounded a little disappointed. "You seem to be in a hurry, though, so I can hang onto this. . . ."

She forced herself to meet Charles Moelker's amazing blue gaze. Instead of feeling relief that she hadn't harmed the dog, her heart rate accelerated more. It was silly, this giddy little rush she experienced whenever she saw her handsome neighbor. She wasn't a teenager anymore, hadn't been one for a long, long time. Though now, with her new hair color, she didn't *look* like it had been that long. She reached up, patting her hair to surreptitiously check for more cobwebs, then she looked down at her yellow velour sweatsuit, which was smeared with streaks of dirt.

Charles, even in faded jeans and a gray sweatshirt, looked like he'd stepped off the cover of *GQ*. His bright eyes made her think of the carefree summer days of her youth and Pierce Brosnan, her personal favorite, although Charles' slightly graying beard made him look more like Sean Connery. While Kim had teased that he was starting to look like his dog, a miniature Schnauzer, Millie understood why he'd grown it. He didn't care about his appearance right now . . . or much of anything else.

She'd gone through a rough patch after Bruce's death. But with the support of her friends, and the comfort of her memories, she'd never really felt as if she'd lost him. They'd been too close for too long for him to ever completely leave her. From that first night Pop had brought him home from the office, they had been inseparable, marrying the summer right after Millie graduated high school. That was old-fashioned, getting married that young, but she didn't regret a minute of their time together.

Realizing she had been silently staring at Charles for some time, probably with her mouth hanging open, she said, "I'm sorry."

"Your hair—I mean, your bowl." He lifted an orange casserole bowl in his leash-free hand. "I was returning it."

When she had nearly run him and his little dog over. "I'm sorry," she said again, inwardly grimacing about sounding like an idiot.

Oh, she hoped Kim wasn't anywhere around, lurking behind the trees and shrubbery, watching and laughing about this; Millie would never live it down, as Kim would be sure to share it at their next Red Hat Society chapter get-together. Millie peered around, but as short as she was, she could barely see across the evergreen shrubs lining her drive to the next door unit, let alone to Kim's, which was another building down and across the street. The complex fit its name; all the buildings were carved into a woodsy hilltop with the dark brick walls and green slate roofs blending into the surroundings.

Millie reached out, taking the bowl from Charles's hand, nearly dropping it when their fingers brushed and a funny little current traveled up her arm. Probably just another muscle twinge courtesy of Kim's class. She hoped.

"Thank you," he said, "for the casserole."

"No problem." She loved cooking; that was why she'd probably never be able to permanently retire the Domestic Goddess tiara no matter how tarnished it got. "I always make too much." Considering she lived alone. Like he now did.

The dog yipped again, dancing around, eager to resume their walk, and reminding Millie that Charles wasn't as alone as she was. Maybe she should get a pet; she wouldn't have to worry about how to talk to one of them. Even Kim had a cat, although she swore she wasn't keeping it; she'd recently inherited it from the elderly lady who had lived in the unit next to hers.

But Millie didn't need a pet; she had Steven now. Flustered over her near-collision with Charles, she had almost forgotten.

"You don't need to keep doing this," Charles said, his gaze on the dog, not her. Above the beard, she noticed a slight reddish tint to his skin. *He* had nothing to be embarrassed about.

"It's what neighbors do," she insisted. Especially at Hilltop. Despite the vast acreage it covered on the hill overlooking Grand Rapids, Michigan, the condominium complex was a tight-knit community. She'd certainly gotten her share of sympathy casseroles after Bruce had passed away. While she hadn't always appreciated the tastes since she was a critical cook, she had always appreciated the gesture. But it was too bad everyone hadn't used recipes from the Red Hat Society cookbook, like she always did.

He shrugged. "Maybe. But—"

She reached out, touching his arm much like she had Steven's earlier. She meant it as a reassuring gesture. Instead she felt that disturbing little electrical charge again. "It gets better," she assured him. "It takes time, but eventually it won't hurt as much."

He sighed. "It's not as if I didn't see it coming. Guess I just didn't want to face up to it."

His wife's death?

It had happened while he and his wife were in Arizona. Although Charles was young, probably the same age as Millie, he'd already retired, and he and his wife had split their time between condos: summer and fall in Grand Rapids and winter and spring in Phoenix. But this year he'd come home early, in spring, and alone.

Millie hadn't even known that his wife was sick, but then Mrs. Moelker hadn't exactly been an easy woman to get close to. And Millie had rarely spoken to Charles; they'd exchange hellos when they'd bumped into each other at the community center but that was all.

"I'm sorry," she said. Now that he had started talking, she didn't want him to stop. Steven could wait for his briefcase.

"We weren't married that long, you know," he confided, with a resigned sigh. "I've been a bachelor most my life. I can survive being a bachelor again."

"That's a good attitude," she said.

"Just wish she would have taken the dog," he added.

To her grave?

"But there's nothing wrong with the dog!" Millie had *read* about some people having their pets cremated with them. There were all kinds of eccentrics in the world; apparently Charles Moelker was one of them.

"There's nothing wrong with Ellen's new husband, either. I don't believe he's allergic to dogs."

"What?" Millie asked. "Ellen's new husband?"

"Yes," he said. His brows, untouched by gray unlike his beard, arched in confusion. "Where did you think she was?"

"Dead."

She felt like a fool the minute she admitted it. Here she'd been thinking his wife was dead and instead she'd just divorced him. Served Millie right for listening to Mrs. Ryers, Hilltop's grapevine.

It didn't help Millie's embarrassment that Charles was laughing so hard tears streamed from the blue eyes that had apparently addled whatever sense Millie had.

"You thought she was dead," he finally managed to

gasp. "That explains the casseroles. They were pity casseroles!"

"Sympathy casseroles," she insisted, hating to think of them the way he had. But he'd only just dubbed them that. What had he thought they were before?

Heat rushed to her face. Oh, no, he had probably thought she'd been trying to impress him with her culinary skills, that she'd been hitting on him. Her stomach churned with dread. And when he'd made the bachelor comments, had he been warning her off?

She'd thought the worst thing she could have done was run over his dog; she'd just found something worse, or at the very least, more humiliating. But she didn't know which was more so: her thinking his wife was dead or his thinking that she'd used her cooking skills to make a pass.

Yes, she was way too old-fashioned to even attempt flirting. After Steven returned to his family, she'd see about getting a pet. She could always put it in a kennel when she traveled.

*G*randma, I'm so glad you're here," Brigitte said as she opened the door and threw her arms around her. Her auburn hair tickled Millie's nose as she squeezed tightly, sobs shaking her slender body. Already Brigitte was much taller than Millie, but then most people were.

She patted her granddaughter's back. She wanted to offer words of comfort, things like, "Everything will be all right. They'll get back together." But there was no way Millie could make promises that she had no control over keeping. That wouldn't help anyone.

"You'll do something, right?" Brigitte asked, sounding like a little girl instead of the mature fourteen-year-old she was. "You'll fix this."

"Honey, I'd love to fix things, really I would, but this is between your mom and dad. I really shouldn't interfere," Millie said, her voice breaking as surely as her granddaughter's heart was. "I'm sorry."

Brigitte sniffled; her sadness tugged at Millie's heart. "That's what Mom said. That it's between her and Dad, then she locked herself in her bedroom. But I can still hear her crying."

If Millie listened hard enough, she would probably be able to hear her, too. They stood in the back hall, from which the utility room, kitchen, and the master bedroom branched. Oak wainscoting covered the bottom half of the walls, cheerful green and gold wallpaper the top half. Millie had helped Audrey hang that wallpaper when she and Steven had first moved in ten years ago.

Millie squeezed her granddaughter's shoulders, holding her closer. "Brigitte . . ."

"I want to know why, Grandma. Why did Dad have to move out? What's going on?"

Millie shook her head, which had first begun to pound when she'd found Steven moving into her condo. Her embarrassing encounter with Charles Moelker had compounded the pain. "I don't know either, honey."

Brigitte pulled away, swiping at her damp eyes and cheeks with trembling hands. "This is about me, too,

Grandma. This is *my* family." Her dark eyes were wide with fear.

Millie nodded. "I know."

"And yours, too. If they don't want to tell me because they think I'm a kid or something, they should still tell you. Did Dad?"

Millie shook her head. "No."

"This is so stupid."

Millie wanted to wholeheartedly agree, but she held her tongue. "Honey, I'm sure they have their reasons." A couple wouldn't throw away fifteen years of marriage without a reason. She hoped.

"What reasons?" Brigitte cried. "I have a right to know what they are!"

"Maybe you already do," Millie pointed out, not that she wanted to pump her granddaughter for information.

Brigitte shrugged slender shoulders. "I don't. I'm gone a lot for practice . . . for band and cheerleading." Her bottom lip quivered, and guilt flashed through her dark eyes.

"It's not your fault," Millie assured her. "Your parents are very proud of you and everything you do."

The lip stopped quivering, tugging up into a brief, beautiful smile that quickly dimmed again. "Maybe it's because Mom went back to school."

"Your dad supported her decision."

"The decision, yeah," Brigitte agreed. "But Mom complains that he doesn't support anything else."

"Your dad has a great job."

"No, not with money. He doesn't help her, you know. With dishes. With laundry. He doesn't pick up after himself. That's the only thing I've ever heard them fight about."

Millie thought about this for a moment. Audrey had lived with Steven's messy ways for a long time. Why get sick of it now? Unless Steven was wrong and she had met someone else.

"Please, Grandma, you have to help them get back together," Brigitte begged, her big, dark eyes full of tears.

"Honey—"

"Come on, Grandma, you always fix everything."

Millie wished she could.

A door creaked open, and Audrey stepped from her bedroom into the hall. "I thought I heard voices," she said, sniffing back tears.

"Just me," Millie said. Despite all the years she'd known her daughter-in-law, she felt awkward, like when she met Audrey for the first time and didn't know what to say to this strange girl that her son loved but who Millie was afraid might break his heart.

"I should have known he'd send you—"

"For his briefcase," Millie broke in to explain, just in case Audrey had been about to say something ugly.

Millie had always thought of Audrey as the daughter she'd never had, the one she'd been given later in life, after the angry adolescence, when they were able to enjoy each other. And they had. They'd shopped, baked, and had thoroughly enjoyed all the time they'd spent together. Millie didn't want that to end now . . . even if Audrey and Steven's marriage ended.

"I saw that he left it," Audrey admitted, nodding. "Brigitte, can you get it for Grandma? I put it in the den."

Brigitte stared hard at her mother, and Millie tensed, afraid that the girl, hurt and confused, was about to lash out at Audrey. But then the teenager sniffled and shuffled down the hall toward Steven's den, leaving her mother and grandmother alone.

Millie shifted uncomfortably. Despite how many times she'd been in her son and daughter-in-law's house, she felt like a first time visitor, as if she were a stranger selling magazines or candy bars and not entirely trusted beyond those few feet from the back door.

Audrey looked just as uncomfortable, shifting her gaze anywhere that it wouldn't meet Millie's. So Millie studied her with the same intensity her granddaughter had. Audrey's swollen eyes were hollowed and underlined with dark bruises of exhaustion. Always slender, she was even thinner now, so much so that she looked frail. Breakable.

Millie couldn't hold in the concern that clenched her heart. "Audrey, why didn't you come to me?"

"Mom, this isn't something I felt I should talk to you about."

"You can talk to me about anything," Millie insisted. "But more than talking, I wish you would have let me help you." She cleaned Mitchell's house. She could have cleaned theirs, too. "You're running yourself ragged. You shouldn't have been doing everything by yourself."

Audrey lifted her chin, her dark blond hair brushing her shoulders. "I know. That's what I tried telling Steven."

"You should have told me. I'd have been happy to help. I'll help you now."

and she surreptitiously glanced around to see if Charles was sitting somewhere in the dark, too.

"Let her watch the movie," Theresa said, slipping out of her chair and gesturing for her friends to follow. "I'm sick of staring at a TV. That's all Wally does since he retired." She led the way down the wide corridor to the center's kitchen, turning back to Millie and Kim to add, "With his eyes closed, snoring louder than Mr. Lindstrom in a deep sleep."

"And she wonders why we don't date," Kim said with a snort. The friends knew why Kim didn't. She was so adamant about maintaining her independence that she'd left two grooms at the altar. With her reputation of being a runaway bride, there probably weren't too many men brave enough to take on her . . . and Harry.

Millie would like to pretend she didn't date out of loyalty to Bruce's memory. But Bruce wouldn't want her to be alone. She didn't date because no one asked her, and she was too old-fashioned to do the asking herself. Of course she'd been too old-fashioned to dye her hair, too.

"Wow," Kim said, letting out a low whistle, as they stepped into the brightly lit kitchen. "Look at you with the new hair! Hot, very hot!"

Theresa clapped her approval. "Gorgeous, which we knew you would be. I love the color you picked."

So did Millie. But the excitement of finally dyeing her hair had been eclipsed by more important things. Still, she had been a little disappointed that no one in her family had noticed.

She could always count on her friends.

Audrey reached out, her hands closing over Millie's shoulders. "Please understand when I tell you this, that I love you, but I don't want *your* help."

"You want Steven's." Millie nodded. "I understand, honey. And I'm not making excuses for him." But then, helpless to act as anything other than a mother, she did. "He works hard."

Audrey's hands dropped from Millie's shoulders as she said, "So do I."

"I know that, honey."

"I'm not giving up school."

"I'm sure he doesn't expect you to."

"But he expects *me* to do *everything*."

Shame washed over Millie because she should have realized, probably would have if she hadn't been preoccupied with trying to "retire." It should have occurred to her that Audrey had too much to do.

But when she'd been Brigitte's age, she'd helped her mother. She'd learned how to be a domestic goddess from her mother before that goddess had died . . . too young. But Brigitte was busy, her school activities only added to Audrey's responsibilities.

Audrey went on, "He expected me to be *you*."

"Me?"

"Despite my working and going to school, he expected me to clean and cook and do everything by myself . . . as if I have some magical powers." Her eyes welled with tears, her bottom lip quivering as she continued. "I don't have any magical powers."

"Neither do I, sweetheart." Just that darned tarnished tiara. But if she did have magical powers, she would have found some way to make everything right between Audrey and Steven, some way to erase all the pain and frustration they were both feeling. "I'm so sorry."

Audrey nodded, then turned and fled back into her bedroom. As the door shut behind her, Brigitte appeared in the hall, tears streaming down her face.

"Grandma, please . . . do something."

Millie choked back her own tears. Despite not wanting to make promises she might not be able to keep, she nodded. "I'll think of something."

And if she couldn't come up with anything on her own, she'd ask the advice of her friends.

*W*here've you been?" Theresa asked as Millie walked into the back of the darkened recreation room at the community center. The expansive area, with its big windows and soft carpeting, was also where they held many of their Red Hat Society chapter get-togethers. "The movie started a while ago."

Millie glanced at the big-screen television in front of the easy chairs they'd commandeered for the room when they'd first started Movie Night. Leonardo DiCaprio's youthful face filled the set. She'd never been able to see him as the heartthrob others did. She would have felt like a cradle robber if she even tried.

"I have company," she whispered as she slid into the chair next to Kim, who had obviously not shared anything with Theresa yet. Not that she knew everything. But besides catching Steven moving in, Kim also knew that Millie had had to run an errand for him; Millie had

called on her way to his house in order to cancel th[ ] dinner plans. She hadn't been sure that she'd make i[ ] the movie either but had decided she should just po[ ] and quickly explain why she couldn't stay. She figur[ ] was okay to leave Steven alone for a little while sinc[ ] had his briefcase now.

"Company?" Theresa asked.

Kim leaned across her to tease, "*Male* company[ ]

Millie couldn't help but laugh at Kim's teasin[ ] the memory of Steven's run-down of his confro[ ] with Dirty Harriet. "Well, yes, it *is* male company[ ]

Someone from a row closer to the TV shushed[ ] maybe it was Mr. Lindstrom snoring. When he w[ ] a really deep sleep, air whistled through the ha[ ] nostrils.

"Where is he?" Theresa asked, twisting he[ ] peer around Millie.

"Unpacking." She hoped, but she had a sus[ ] task would be left for her to do. While she'd[ ] Audrey and Brigitte he hadn't done anything[ ] off the cookies she'd baked a few nights a[ ] been a back-up, in case she hadn't had time t[ ] thing for Movie Night. Well, she hadn't had t[ ] now the back-up snack was gone, too.

The shush hissed again, louder than st[ ] out of an overheated iron. Only one person[ ] loud, Mrs. Ryers, and she was probably jus[ ] they weren't talking loud enough for he[ ] Just thinking of the misinformation she[ ] about Charles caused heat to rise to Mill[ ]

"So Millie's found a man," Theresa said, dragging stools back from the kitchen's industrial-size-granite island where an assortment of snacks and liter bottles of pop had been arranged. The white cupboards and stainless steel appliances complemented the gray granite.

"Shall we put her out of her misery?" Kim asked, nodding her platinum blond head toward Theresa as she scooped up a handful of pretzels from one of the bowls on the counter.

"Misery?" Theresa scoffed as she unscrewed the top of a Sprite bottle, the hiss of escaping carbonation sounding a lot like Mrs. Ryers. "I wouldn't call it that. But my friends holding out on me . . ."

"It's my son," Millie said, before Theresa was led any further astray with Kim's teasing.

To think that Millie would have—what did they call it now?—hooked up with a man! She hadn't heard that phrase from her granddaughter or Kim; she'd picked it up from reading *Cosmo* at the beauty parlor. And that was about as likely to happen as Steven unpacking his own bags, especially after her humiliation with Charles Moelker.

She reached for the bowl of M&Ms and glared at Kim before the fitness expert could warn her about the caloric intake of the colorful candies. She needed chocolate right now more than she needed to lose her few extra pounds.

Kim lifted her hands, backing off. "I wasn't going to say a word."

Theresa snorted this time, or made a sound as close to a snort as she could get. Theresa was the most ladylike of them, with her silk blouses and pressed slacks. And her blond hair, in her chin length bob, was always perfectly straight, not a fine hair out of place.

Of course Kim never had a wayward hair either. The brash platinum strands were cut too razor short to fall out of place, as if anything on Kim would dare. She bore an uncanny resemblance in appearance and attitude to that "Stop the insanity" woman who'd had her fifteen minutes of fame some years back.

Millie reached up, tucking a curl behind her ear. Only *her* hair was out of control, despite the beautician's efforts to tame it, in a million cinnamon-colored curls that went every which way. Right now her life felt like that, out of control.

"Millie?" Theresa's smooth brow puckered, and her blue eyes clouded with concern. "Everything all right?"

She shook her head, hopelessly tousling those curls. "No, no, it's not."

"Mitchell's moving in?" Theresa asked, perching daintily on the edge of a stool. She did everything daintily, even sipping on the rim of her plastic cup of Sprite.

"I wish it was Mitchell," Millie said, emotion choking her voice. She hooked a stool with her ankle and dragged it closer, struggling to hoist herself up to the seat while tall Kim effortlessly settled onto the counter, pushing the bowls and bottles aside with her denim-clad bottom. Like Kim, Millie wore jeans with a lightweight, celery-colored sweater. "It's Steven," she admitted. "His wife threw him out."

These were her best friends, her most trusted confidantes. They wouldn't share her family gossip with anyone. But still she hesitated a moment. This wasn't her life she was talking about; it was Steven's and Audrey's. She drew in a deep breath, then spilled the bits and pieces she knew about their marital woes.

Her friends were silent for a moment, then Theresa said, "Wally and I would have never made it to our first anniversary if I'd thrown him out for not doing housework."

"Are you sure that's why?" Kim asked Millie.

"That's what Audrey said. I knew there was a strain in their marriage. I just had no idea . . ."

Theresa sighed. "The mother is always the last to know." Her comment wasn't a flip generalization. One of her daughters had gotten divorced, and Theresa hadn't known about the marriage trouble until the ink was already dry on the decree.

Millie reached out and squeezed her friend's hand, regretful that she'd brought up Theresa's pain but grateful for her support. "I just hope it's not too late for Steven and Audrey."

"As long as no one's filed yet, there's hope," Theresa assured her.

Kim laughed. "If there's one thing Millie always has, it's hope."

Millie's heart warmed, as she took more pleasure in that compliment than the ones over her hair. But she wasn't exactly sure Kim intended her remark as a compliment. Her friend confirmed this when she added, "Or should I say 'hopeless,' as in hopeless romantic?"

Millie tipped up her chin with pride. "Guilty," she

admitted. And unrepentant. "If Pop can find love again at eighty years old . . ."

"So is Mitchell married off yet?" Kim teased.

She shot Kim a mock-fierce glare, as she scooped up another handful of M&Ms. "No."

"We're not talking about Mitchell," Theresa reminded them. "We're talking about Steven."

Millie would rather talk about her baby, though. It was a little less depressing. "I'd thought he might be getting close. But his latest girlfriend dumped him."

"Was this Heather?" Theresa asked.

Millie nodded.

"Well, at least they weren't going out long."

"He never goes out with any of them very long," Kim pointed out, not that she was in a position to call the kettle black. Her crooked smile acknowledged this before Millie could say anything.

"He's such a good looking young man," Theresa said, shaking her head in disbelief. "I don't understand it."

"He says it's because women want the nine-to-fivers, not someone who travels as much as he does."

Theresa lowered her gaze, staring at her hands folded on the counter, as she shared, "I miss those times when Wally had to travel for business."

"If I'd ever gotten married, I would have preferred a traveler to the nine-to-fiver," Kim admitted, "always underfoot." She shuddered. "It's easier to understand Audrey getting sick of Steven not helping around the house."

Not for Millie. "It is?"

"Sure, I'd hate living with a slob—"

"Kim!" Theresa interrupted their outspoken friend.

Millie dismissed Theresa's concern with a dismissive wave. She couldn't get offended at the truth. With just the few boxes he'd brought to her condo, Steven had already made a mess in the basement. Nothing like Mitchell's apartment, but she had a queasy feeling that in time it would be just as bad.

An incredible realization came over Millie, churning the M&Ms in her belly. "Oh, my, it just occurred to me why Mitchell's still single."

"Because he's smart," Kim said with a quick laugh.

"No," Millie said, "because he's a slob just like his brother."

That was why Mitchell kept getting dumped. Not because of his long hours, but his big mess.

Chapter Three

"The male is a domestic animal which, if treated with firmness and kindness, can be trained to do most things."
                                                    —*Jilly Cooper*

*M*y sons are slobs," Millie said again, feeling none of the mother's pride she usually felt for them. Instead she felt as if she were attending a support meeting and was confessing her most humiliating weakness. It was only right that it would be her children; they're always a mother's biggest weakness.

"Millie . . ." Theresa said with a soft, sympathetic sigh.

Kim laughed. Of course she could be smug. She had no children. "All men are slobs. That's why I could never bring myself to marry one."

"You should have realized that *before* you got as far as the altar," Theresa said softly, with a teasing glint in her blue eyes. "Heck, before you accepted the rings . . ."

Kim shrugged, totally unrepentant. "Yeah, but I kept

thinking I could housebreak one. Then I realized it wasn't worth the effort."

Millie laughed despite herself. "Housebreak? I don't know if I would call it that. But maybe I should have taught my sons to do some housework."

Then she dismissed the thought. Women hadn't taught their sons those kinds of chores back when Mitchell and Steven were young. And she had seriously considered taking care of the house, and all the men living in it, *her* job. Until now she hadn't realized it was the type of career from which it was hard to retire. If she'd known then . . . she might have chosen another profession. No, she'd loved it and hadn't wanted to share her responsibilities with anyone.

"How old is Steven?" Kim asked.

"Thirty-six next month."

"And he's been married how long?"

"Fifteen years."

"Don't worry about it. His wife had fifteen years to housebreak him. She should have been able to train him in all that time."

Theresa shook her head. "I've had Wally thirty years and I haven't managed to train him. He still hasn't figured out how to lift the lid on the hamper and put his dirty clothes inside instead of leaving them on the bathroom floor. The man made a fortune teaching others how to run their businesses, but he can't learn how to pick up his stinky socks." Color flooded her cheeks when she glanced up and caught her friends staring at her. "Sorry . . ."

"You're not packing Wally's bags, are you?" Kim asked.

Theresa's blush deepened. "And send him where? *His* mother only has a tiny apartment that she's already sharing with her sister."

Millie wondered if she was joking. Ever since Wally had sold his business to the consultants he'd trained, Theresa had been frustrated with having a prematurely retired husband constantly underfoot. She hadn't said that much about it, but it was clear she wasn't happy.

Kim must have sensed Theresa's frustration, too, because she sounded serious when she suggested, "He could live with one of your daughters."

"And they would never speak to me again." Theresa sighed. "No, I'm stuck with the dirty clothes and the old black and white westerns . . ."

"You're only stuck if you want to be," Kim advised as she picked up a water bottle and twisted off the cap.

Theresa frowned at their friend. "Weren't you listening? My daughters would disown me."

"I'm not talking divorce," Kim assured her.

"Murder?" Theresa asked, her blue eyes twinkling with amusement. She obviously thought Kim was joking.

But one never knew with Kim.

Millie had another idea—like she'd had when school budget cuts had cost Kim her job. She only hoped she wouldn't wind up regretting this idea like her aching muscles made her regret her earlier one. "Classes."

"What?" Theresa asked.

As the idea formed, Millie's excitement grew. It was perfect. She'd promised her granddaughter she would try to think of something. And she had.

Or maybe she'd picked up on Kim's brainwave. "Classes. Isn't that what you were thinking?"

Kim shrugged. "I was kind of leaning toward murder."

Millie laughed. "C'mon."

"I don't know about *official* classes," Kim said, "but I really believe they can be retrained, if someone's willing to put in the time and effort. You're never too old to learn something new."

Theresa snorted, a little ladylike expulsion of air. "You have met Wally, right? He's the ultimate old dog. He won't learn any new tricks."

"Tricks?" Millie considered the word. "I suppose we could teach some of those. Cooking shortcuts. Laundry tips, that kind of thing. They have so much to learn. We'll have to meet more than once a week."

"Here?" Kim asked.

"Yes, the kitchen's great." Millie coveted all the counter space and the industrial-sized appliances. "It's the perfect place."

"You're serious?" Theresa asked, her blue eyes brightening with interest.

Millie nodded. "We'll concentrate on cleaning skills. Or maybe cooking. We'll have to cover grocery shopping, too. Spring cleaning." She sighed at the enormity of the task. "We'll have to work up a lesson plan."

She glanced at the clock hanging above the industrial-sized kitchen sink. Since she hadn't planned on staying for the movie, she'd put a pie in the oven before she'd left for the community center. She'd thrown it together, using frozen crusts, while she'd made Steven a quick dinner. "But we'll have to do that another time."

"I like the idea," Theresa said. "But I really doubt I'll be able to get Wally to join. He'd have to actually leave his old easy chair."

Some of Millie's excitement dimmed. What if Steven refused to participate in classes? Mitchell was her baby; she'd be able to talk *him* into it. Maybe he could goad Steven. He had certainly done enough of that while they were growing up.

"I'm not so sure Steven will go for it either," Millie admitted. "Otherwise, he would have let Audrey or Brigitte teach him." She leaned toward the counter and grabbed another handful of M&Ms, munching on them as she mused aloud, "But there's got to be a way . . ."

"Do what you do best, ladies," Kim snorted, nothing ladylike about it. "Manipulate them."

"Manipulate?" Millie asked, getting a little nervous from the intensity of Kim's brown-eyed stare.

"Yeah, you know how. Manipulate them like you did me." She batted her lashes. "Oh, Kim, you'd be helping us, truly you would, if you taught an exercise class at the community center. You'd be helping us get in shape and stay healthy. Do it for us, Kim, for our health," she imitated the argument that had precipitated her starting up the aerobics classes. Then she dissolved into laughter.

"You knew?" Theresa asked, a wide smile spreading across her face.

"Neither of you are exactly Mata Hari."

Millie laughed, too. "Then how will we manipulate the men?"

"They're men. They won't realize what you're up to," Kim said with a derisive laugh. "Play them the same way you did me. Then we'll have at least a few students for our class."

Our class.

The problem was really Millie's: trying to get Steven and his wife back together and trying to get Mitchell trained so that someday he'd stop scaring women away and get married. But just like that, Kim and Theresa had made her problem theirs.

"I don't know if Wally will fall for it," Theresa cautioned.

"Try."

Because maybe the solution to Millie's problem would also fix the one Theresa wouldn't admit she had, the frustration of dealing with a husband who Millie suspected was more depressed over selling his business than he was messy.

"Can we think of anyone else to join?" Theresa asked.

Bright blue eyes came immediately to Millie's mind. He'd been a bachelor before and survived. He would again. Isn't that what he'd said? Maybe he'd like a little help this time. Her face heated up just thinking about bringing it up to him. He would probably assume she was making another pass.

Maybe she should. If she could teach some old dogs new tricks, she should be able to learn some herself, like how to flirt. She wasn't as old-fashioned as she'd once thought. She wrapped a wayward curl around her finger to admire the color. She really loved cinnamon.

"We can put up a sign-up sheet on the bulletin board." And maybe he'd see it and sign up. Or she could mention it to him . . . if she could keep her foot out of her mouth.

"We can also bring it up at our next Red Hat luncheon," Theresa said. "I'm sure some of our friends have domestically inept men in their lives, too."

"If we get a good turnout, maybe we can keep it going," Kim said.

"I thought men weren't worth the effort," Theresa reminded her.

Kim shrugged. "It's not like I'll be doing it alone. I'd only be helping you two."

"Be warned," Theresa said to Millie. "If she thinks about getting married again, she's going to want us at the altar with her, saying some vows."

Kim shuddered now. "The only vow I'm making is to *never* get married. Teaching is entirely different . . ."

It was in Kim's blood. It wasn't in Millie's. She'd never taught anyone anything; she'd always figured it was easier to just do it herself. But that was probably what had gotten her sons into this mess, literally.

"So what are we going to call this class?" Kim asked, she and Theresa both turning to Millie.

Millie laughed at her friends' expectant faces. They turned to her just like her granddaughter had.

"We'll call it . . ." She paused, thinking of those blue eyes again as the perfect name came to her. "A Bachelor's Survival Course."

You didn't have to rush back home," Steven said as he lifted a spoonful of steaming apple pie and vanilla ice cream into his mouth, dribbling some across the usually sparkling white surface of the Corian countertop as he did so. A few other drops landed on the white v-neck T-shirt he wore with gray sweatpants.

Millie had popped the pie into the oven before heading to the center. And thank goodness she had; it had saved her from any more humiliation with Charles Moelker. Just as she'd been leaving the center, he'd stepped out of the TV room and into her path.

"Going to run me over again?" he'd asked, deep voice vibrating with amusement.

"I am in a hurry again," she'd said, willing the blush from her face. "I have a pie in the oven." She'd talked longer to Kim and Theresa than she'd planned, so she'd been worried it was about to burn.

"Pie? What flavor?" he'd asked, leaning against the wall of the wide corridor and folding his arms across his chest. He didn't need Kim's class; there wasn't an ounce of fat on his trim body. He wasn't as tall as her sons, or as her husband had been. Leaning like that, his face had been quite close to hers.

"Apple," she'd said, a bit breathlessly.

"My favorite."

"Mine, too . . ."

She'd almost invited him back for a slice. If not for her houseguest, she might have. But Steven had been through enough for one day; he didn't need to be subjected to his mother's first attempts at flirting. No doubt she'd be as clumsy as a toddler first trying to walk, so she did *not* want an audience.

"No," she said to Steven, blinking the image from her mind of Charles's face so close to hers. "I didn't plan on staying. I just dropped by to tell my friends."

"It's good you came back when you did," he said, sounding eager for company.

She hoped he was ready to talk; then she could convince him to fight for his marriage, to help his wife out like she wanted. To be there for the poor, overworked woman.

"I was afraid the pie was going to burn," he explained, nodding toward the double ovens built into the polished hickory cabinets of the kitchen.

"You don't know how to take a pie out of the oven?"

He shrugged. "I wouldn't know when it's done."

"But if it were burning?" Would he have let the house catch fire before he opened the oven door? That little hammer started pounding at Millie's temple again. The situation was much worse than she imagined; she and her friends definitely had their work cut out for them.

"I wouldn't know it was burning till it was too late," he said, around a mouthful of pie. Some juice dribbled down his chin and onto the front of his already stained T-shirt.

For a moment, Millie felt like running, like Kim had from her weddings, but then she remembered her granddaughter's tear-streaked face, her dark eyes wide and hopeful that Grandma could fix her family for her. Obviously there were other things, besides burning pies, that her son didn't notice until it was too late.

"Have you talked to Brigitte yet?" she asked softly.

Steven jerked as if she'd jabbed a fork in his arm. "Mom—"

"Have you?"

"She called," he admitted, his voice raspy with emotion. "She's upset her mother threw me out. She wants me to come home."

Millie wished it was that simple, but after talking to Audrey, she knew it wasn't. "Brigitte doesn't understand."

He sighed. "She's not the only one."

"Did you talk to Audrey?"

He shook his head, then passed a hand, probably sticky from the pie, through his thinning hair. "She's made up her mind."

Millie *tsk*ed her disapproval of his defeated attitude. "So get her to change it."

"Mom . . ."

"Or better yet, *you* change."

"Change what? I'm the same guy Audrey married. She's the one who's changed, who doesn't love me anymore," he pointed out, his dark eyes dull with misery.

"I'm sure she still loves you," Millie insisted. "She's just exhausted. She needs some help around the house."

He nodded. "I know. I offered to bring someone in, to hire a maid service to come a couple times a week."

Pride warmed her heart. Her son wasn't entirely clueless then. "You did?"

"Yeah, this afternoon, when she was throwing boxes of my stuff into the garage," he shared, staring at the design he was making on his plate by dragging the fork tines through the pie filling. "She called me lazy."

"She wants you to make more effort," Millie said, drawing in a quick breath before pitching the Bachelor Survival Course. "I could help you—"

He shook his head. "It wouldn't matter what I did or

how I changed," he argued. "She doesn't want me anymore. I can't make her love me, Mom."

Knowing how stubborn her oldest could be, Millie resorted to Plan B, the idea she'd first considered at the center when Kim had urged her and Theresa to manipulate the men into joining the class. Sibling rivalry. Nonchalantly she asked, "You know whose favorite pie this is?"

"Mitch's," he mumbled around a mouthful of pie. Even talking about his marriage problems hadn't curbed his appetite.

Besides household skills, Millie also had to teach her children some manners. But first things first. "Yes, he loves it," she agreed. "Too bad he wasn't here, too."

"That's what he said," Steven said, a devilish gleam flitting through his red-rimmed eyes.

"You talked to him?"

"He called from Mexico. I made sure to let him know what was in the oven."

Oh, yes, her sons still loved to goad each other. It didn't matter that they were grown men in their thirties; they were still as competitive as they'd been as kids seeing who could raise the most BB welts on the other one. Plan B relied heavily on that rivalry. Millie counted on them challenging each other to join the class, then competitively try to outperform each other.

When the phone rang, Steven jumped, and hope brightened his dark eyes. Obviously he wasn't entirely certain Audrey wouldn't change her mind. Then he glanced at the caller ID.

"It's Mitch again," he said, disappointment heavy in

his voice as he handed the cordless phone to her. "I'll take my pie downstairs, so you two can talk about me."

Her gaze followed his path from the kitchen, his shoulders stooped like those of a man much older than thirty-six. She let out a shaky breath before hitting the talk button on the receiver.

"You're going to save me a piece of pie, right?" Mitchell asked before Millie even said hello.

She laughed. "I can't make any guarantees. You didn't tell me how long you're going to be gone."

"It was supposed to be a few days, but I'm cutting it short."

"For the pie?" She knew why. He'd talked to Steven; he knew his brother was having problems. Despite their good-natured rivalry, they still looked out for each other. She was counting on that, too.

"Well, it *is* my favorite." Then he sighed and let his concern show when he asked, "Is he okay?"

She'd never lied to her children. "No."

"How about you?"

Her dear, sweet boy. Mitchell had always been so sensitive. Yes, he would have already been married if he weren't such a slob.

"This isn't about me."

"Mom, I know you. You've got to be upset, too. And you're going to try to 'fix' this."

She couldn't help but smile. "Well . . ."

"Mom . . ." Mitchell drew in an audible breath, as if bracing himself. "You have a plan already?"

"Yes," she admitted.

"Why do I have a feeling that I'm not going to like it?"

Learning to clean, shop, cook, and do laundry? She was pretty sure he was going to *hate* it. "I'm going to need your help."

He sighed. "Of course."

"So you'll help me?"

He sighed louder, his breath rattling the phone. "Of course."

She laughed. "Mitchell . . ."

"I'll be home day after tomorrow. Save me a piece of pie. Or better yet, make me a whole one."

Maybe she'd have him make it himself.

She hung up smiling and was still smiling when the doorbell rang a short time later. Since it was eleven, it had to be Kim or Theresa. They'd stayed for the movie and clean-up. She owed them for filling in for her, especially as it had been a three-hour movie.

If she hadn't suspected it was her friends, she might have hesitated to open her door after dark. She might have reached for the feather duster again . . . or called Kim and had her look across and down the street to see who was at Millie's door. Like Steven had surmised, Kim looked out for her. Not that she needed anyone looking out for her.

She wasn't alone now, though. Selfishly she had to admit it had been nice to come home to a house aglow with lights and alive with sound. As she crossed the foyer to the front door, she heard the blare of the TV drifting up from the basement. Her heart eased. She was comforted to know that she could call out to Steven, not that he would hear her above the nightly newscast, but it was nice all the same.

To not be alone.

She drew open the door, then stopped. It wasn't Kim or Theresa. As she glanced at her watch, she realized the movie probably wasn't over yet. But apparently Charles Moelker had left, maybe when she had. He and his little dog now stood on her front walk right beside the welcome sign she'd posted among her flowers.

Her heart rate accelerated . . . as if she had opened the door to a dangerous stranger. Maybe Charles was. She didn't know him well despite the years they'd lived in the same complex, just a street apart. So he *was* a stranger, and the way he made her heart race and infiltrated her mind, he was certainly dangerous.

"Returning another bowl?" she asked, inwardly cringing about the amount of casseroles she had left with him. She truly hadn't realized what she'd been doing, that she'd been using her food to flirt with him.

He shook his head. "No. I feel bad about that."

"About my cooking?" She lifted her chin, perversely insulted. She took great pride in her culinary skills; she was definitely a *goddess* in the kitchen.

"No, no. I really enjoyed your cooking. I hope you didn't think otherwise this afternoon." He chuckled. "I still can't believe you thought Ellen had died . . . although I guess she is hanging out with a stiff now. That guy she married . . ."

He dragged in a deep breath. "It doesn't matter. They're happy together—that's the important thing."

"What about you?" The question slipped out before she could censor it.

"Am I happy?" he asked, dark brows lifting about the

eyes that were so bright they even glowed in the faint illumination of her porch light.

It was too personal a question, something strangers or even neighbors wouldn't ask each other. Maybe her sons got their lack of manners from her. Because she still wanted to know. "Yes."

He chuckled with more nerves than humor this time. "Define happy."

That was the most personal question, someone's definition of happiness. She knew hers. Family. She'd do anything for her boys, Audrey, and Brigitte.

Since Charles had confessed to being a long-time bachelor before his marriage to Ellen, she suspected he didn't have any children. The two of them really had nothing in common.

She shrugged. "Happiness is something different for everyone, I guess."

"You're not going to tell me what your happiness is," he concluded with a smile.

"You're going to tell me yours?"

"I'm a simple man. I can be happy with a slice of fresh apple pie."

Her heart tripped over itself, seeming to stumble inside her chest. "You came by for a slice of pie?"

"I was hoping . . ." he admitted, his bearded face creasing into a hopeful smile . . . like a little boy wishing his mother would let him keep the turtle he'd found.

Her nerves increased, causing her fingers to tremble, so she knotted them together. She hadn't had a man in her house who wasn't a blood relative since Bruce had died. Inviting him inside seemed too intimate. But it wasn't like they were alone; Steven was just downstairs.

But if he came up, he'd have a lot of questions. He'd want to know who Charles was .... and more than that, what he was to Millie. She wasn't prepared to answer any of those questions.

She glanced down at his little dog; he had fallen asleep at Charles's feet. "Don't disturb him. I'll just put a slice in a container for you."

"Don't worry about it. I was just teasing." His blue eyes twinkled at her.

Millie's heart beat harder now than it did during Kim's exercise class. "I won't be but a minute," she said, her voice breathless even to her own ears. Then she rushed toward the kitchen, needing distance from him more than she needed to give him any pie. The slice she cut was almost too large for the plastic container she shakily dropped it in. Her fingers trembled as she placed warm apple slices over the pie and popped the cover onto the container.

After she handed it to him, she licked her fingers, removing the sticky cinnamon filling. When she glanced up, she caught him staring at her.

"See, it was no trouble," she said, fighting the nerves that had her hands shaking again.

"No . . . no trouble," he said, but his deep voice suggested otherwise. "This was probably a bad idea."

She chuckled. "You haven't signed up for Kim's aerobics class, have you?" She'd already surmised that he didn't need it. "She advises against pie, too many calories and too much cholesterol."

"No."

She smothered the sigh of relief. The class was hard enough for her without worrying about him being in attendance, possibly watching her, as she struggled through the simple exercises. Not that she was all that out of shape. For a woman who loved to cook, she was surprisingly close, except for a few stubborn pounds, to her target weight. She probably owed that to cleaning Mitchell's apartment. She definitely worked off some calories with that chore.

"We're starting another class you might want to sign up for," she said nonchalantly. She would have tried for coy, but she had no idea how.

"What kind of class?"

"Cooking will be part of it."

"I have to admit I'm pretty impressed by your cooking." He ran his finger around the rim of the bowl, where filling still oozed, then licked it. His blue eyes closed, as he savored the taste.

Millie's heart rate kicked into a higher gear.

"I'd like to learn how to cook like this," he said.

"But you'd said you were a bachelor a long time," she reminded him. "You must know how to cook."

"Nope. Just how to dial for takeout. And that gets old."

She nodded in agreement even though she never got takeout. Maybe she would . . . once she retired. "Well, it's going to be a bachelor's survival course on how to maintain a household. Kim O'Malley and Theresa Shearer are going to help me teach."

"I *should* learn how to do more things around the house," he admitted.

She clenched her hands together behind her back to hide their trembling, but she heard it in her voice as she replied, "Then this could be the class for you."

He laughed. "You wouldn't mind?"

"Mind what?"

"My joining the class. After what happened this afternoon . . ."

When she had nearly run him and his dog over? "My thinking your wife was dead?"

"Yes, I hoped there wouldn't be any awkwardness between us over that misunderstanding."

Awkwardness? No. Embarrassment. Humiliation. Yes. "Of course not," she lied. "It'll be great to have you in the class."

He nodded. "I think so, too. Sign me up. I'm looking forward to it."

With a giddy little rush, she acknowledged she was, too. "It'll be great," she promised. "You'll learn a lot." And hopefully so would she, about flirting.

"Oh, and I meant to tell you earlier today," he said, reaching out with his free hand to touch a curl at her cheek. "I like your hair. A lot."

"Uh . . . thanks . . ." His touch had been fleeting, just the briefest brush of hard knuckle against her cheek, but the feel of it lingered, long after he moved his hand away.

"Thanks for the pie," he said, gesturing with the container as he nudged the dog awake and turned to leave.

She stood there, watching him walk away. Why did

he really want to join the class? To learn to cook or for another reason? That little giddy rush coursed through her veins, setting her pulse to race. Maybe flirting would be easier than she'd thought, if it were all she had to learn.

She also had to learn how to teach; something she'd never done before. Nerves churned the apple pie in her stomach. Maybe she'd bitten off more than she could chew by inviting Charles to take the class. How would she teach the boys *and* flirt with Charles . . . without making a fool of herself?

She could have called him back and told him that she'd rather he didn't take this class, but she wasn't even tempted to back out. If she didn't at least try to kill these three birds with one stone, then she'd really be a fool. She watched Charles until he was gone from sight, then she closed the door with one hand as she cradled her cheek with the other.

Chapter Four

"The important thing about women today is, as they get older, they still keep house. It's one reason why they don't die, but men die when they retire. Women just polish the teacups." —*Margaret Mead*

Thanks for picking me up," Theresa said, surprised that Wally had actually walked instead of bringing the car. She fell into step beside her husband. He was much taller than she was, his strides longer, but he walked slower than she did so they managed to keep perfect rhythm.

Walking.

Life was another matter. Or it was now that he'd retired.

He lifted a hand to his mouth, smothering a yawn. She couldn't fathom why he was tired. He slept all day. Every day.

"I didn't want you walking home in the dark, alone," he said gruffly.

With the street lamps and the lights from the city below them sparkling in the night, it was hardly dark.

But still his concern was sweet, reminiscent of the chivalrous man she used to know. Her heart softened at his thoughtfulness, which alleviated some of her irritation at the mess he'd left in their bathroom earlier in the day: toothpaste smeared over the mirror, his socks on the floor, as well as other unmentionables. And the basement family room, where she'd banished the easy chair he seldom left, was an even bigger mess with newspapers and DVD sleeves spread all around the floor, covering the carpet.

"You didn't need to worry about me," Theresa assured him, although she was pleased he'd left that chair even if just for a short walk. "Kim and I would have walked home together. Nobody messes with Kim and Harry."

Wally laughed. "She's something else."

Most men said that about Kim. Most women called Kim *something else,* with jealousy not admiration. But Theresa loved her and Millie. She'd been fortunate to find such wonderful friends.

She wished Wally would do the same, find some people that were just *his.* Find a life, like Theresa had since they'd moved to Hilltop.

"You really should come to Kim's aerobics class in the morning," Theresa urged. She'd been trying to get him to join the class since it started, hoping that the exercise would give him more energy and that he might make friends there.

"A lot of men come, too," she added. To watch Kim, probably. Even Mr. Lindstrom stayed awake for the sight of her in her leopard print leotard.

"Men can't bend like that, Theresa."

"We're starting up some more classes," Theresa said, as they followed the sidewalk uphill toward their condo. Thanks to Kim's class, she wasn't even winded, but she could hear Wally breathing. Maybe now was the time to manipulate him, when his brain was oxygen-deprived. Any other time she wasn't likely to fool the man. He was too brilliant a businessman to be manipulated. Or at least, he had been . . .

"More exercise ones?"

She shook her head. "No. No bending required. We're going out on a limb with this one. Mrs. Ryers was already mocking us after we put the sign up on the bulletin board."

"Old busybody."

Theresa laughed. "That's a lot nicer than what Kim calls her."

"Don't let her get to you." It wasn't a flip comment. His tone was too serious. By nature men were problem solvers, and Wally had taken this penchant to the extreme when he'd built his consulting business.

She just might be able to manipulate him yet. Theresa forced out a shaky sigh. "Well, she could be right this time." She worked on adding a little catch to her voice when she continued, "I'd hate to fail. She'd never let us forget it."

Wally's fingers brushed over her hand. "You won't," he assured her. "You always pull off whatever you try, Theresa."

"I don't know. We came up with the idea to help Millie. A Bachelor's Survival Course." She filled him in on the situation between Millie's son and his wife. "This might be the only thing to save their marriage. But we have to have more than one student sign up, or he'll figure out what Millie's up to . . ."

"And his pride will get the best of him, probably like it did when he left his wife." He sighed. "You're doing a good thing. All of you, trying to save a marriage."

Wally was still upset over their daughter Judy's divorce. He always wished he'd done more to help. Theresa accepted that there were some times when nothing could help. She really hoped that this wasn't one of them, though.

"Help us," Theresa appealed, wrapping her fingers around his hand as it swung at his side.

"How?"

"Join the class," she beseeched him.

"I'm not a bachelor."

"Neither is Millie's son. Yet."

He turned toward her, stopping on the sidewalk, just outside their end unit. There were three in their building, with arched windows and doors, shining bright in the street lamps. The moonlight shone on Wally, caught a question in his shadowy green eyes. He wondered if that *yet* applied to him, too.

She looked hard for the young man he'd once been. The one who, like a gentleman, would walk her home after their dates and steal kisses on her front porch. Maybe it was darker than she thought because she couldn't see him. All she saw was an old man with graying hair and tired eyes, a man who'd given up, not just his business, but the life he used to lead. A stranger.

She squeezed his fingers, and maybe he felt her desperation because he nodded.

"All right. I'll be one of your pupils."

And Theresa couldn't help but wonder if the marriage they were trying to save was *theirs*.

Sweat dripped from Kim's hair and slid down the back of her neck. Theresa called it "perspiring" but she never admitted to actually doing it. Kim snorted. No matter the intensity of the class, Theresa barely glistened. On the other hand, she and Millie sweated. They weren't classy ladies, not like their glistening friend.

Kim was a little irritated with Theresa. She'd skipped her class to play welcome wagon lady to some new Hilltop resident. Maybe Kim's new neighbor. The SOLD sign had been up in front of the unit next to hers for a while now.

Kim really hoped her new neighbor wasn't allergic to cats because that old fleabag was going to be Kim's welcome-to-the-neighborhood gift. Heck, the cat had lived there first; it was only fitting it should live there again.

It.

Was it a male? Probably. That would explain why it hogged the whole bed and why, no matter how many times she told it not to, it kept climbing onto the kitchen counter. The thing couldn't be trained, so it had to be a male. And when Kim was leaving the house, it wound between her legs, leaving cat hair all over her pants. Marking its territory. Definitely a male.

Kim bent over, digging a towel from her duffel bag. She had just hooked it around her neck when she felt holes boring through her gray yoga pants and white leotard, into her backside. The feeling was familiar since Mr. Lindstrom spent more of the class staring at her rear end than attempting any of the exercises.

But the class was over; Mr. Lindstrom and everyone else was gone. Millie was off working on Plan B to get her sons to join the Bachelor Survival Course, and she'd had to go grocery shopping before the lunch they'd scheduled with their Red Hat chapterettes. Kim had thought she was alone in the community center basement, but for the wide assortment of exercise equipment arranged around the area where she conducted her class in front of a wall of mirrors.

She was not alone.

She was being stared at. She could actually feel it. Hot. Another trail of sweat dribbled down, this one between her breasts. She put her hand back in her duffel bag, feeling around for Harry.

"Kim," Theresa's soft voice called out, "I thought you were gone since class was over. But I see Mr. Fowler found you."

As she straightened up and turned, she looked first to her friend. From the twinkle in Theresa's eyes, she knew what Kim had been reaching for. Then Kim turned toward Mr. Fowler of the hot stare.

She hadn't minded missing last night's movie. Leo was not her thing, nor was she into Pierce Brosnan like Millie had once confessed she was. Kim was more into George Clooney. Okay, she was *really* into George

Clooney, and Mr. Fowler, with his thick head of dark brown hair finely threaded with silver and his warm brown eyes, crinkling at the corners with a grin that involved his whole face, was a dead ringer for George.

"It *is* you," he said, his voice as deep as the amusement in his eyes. He chuckled. "I can't believe it. Miss O'Malley."

"I'm sorry, do I know you?" she asked, although she already knew she didn't. She sure as heck would have remembered him.

"He's your new neighbor, Kim. He bought Mrs. Milanowski's place," Theresa informed her.

She'd forgotten Theresa was still there, watching from the last step of the wide stairs leading down to the basement. She was *not* glistening while Kim sweated all over the place in front of this handsome stranger.

"George Fowler," he said, extending his hand.

His first name was *George*.

Kim wiped her hand on the towel before putting it in his. Maybe she got the sweat off her palm, but she couldn't tell as her skin heated and sizzled in his firm grip.

"Should I recognize your name?" she asked, still having the impression that *he* knew *her*.

"I don't expect you to. It was so long ago when we met. In high school."

Despite the silver in his hair, she doubted he was fifty . . . like she'd turned just a few months ago, graduating from a pink hat to a red one. He was probably only early forties. "I don't think we went to high school together."

"No," he chuckled again. "*I* was attending high school. I was in the first class you taught."

A former student. Usually she remembered them. But then she'd been teaching a long time. That was why she'd been let go when they'd had to cut a physical education teacher from the payroll.

"You made a man out of me."

Some odd sound emanated from Theresa. Not a giggle. Not a snort. Something.

But Kim couldn't worry about her. Spots danced across her field of vision. She was having enough of a struggle keeping her wits about her. Had she worked out too long? Maybe she was having a stroke? She blinked and cleared her head. Then she was able to see his face more clearly. And the amusement heating his brown eyes.

Belatedly she realized he still had her hand, and she withdrew it, with some regret. He had great hands. Big. Wide. Strong.

"I'm sorry I don't remember you." She really was. Just how early could a person get Alzheimer's? She had to have it to have forgotten *him.* He looked just like George . . .

"I was a scrawny kid. Real nerd. Not an athletic bone in my body." He laughed. "Or a muscle either."

His comments invited her to check him out now. So her gaze scanned him from wide shoulders down over a well-muscled chest, lean hips and heavy thighs, clad in a dark T-shirt and jeans.

"Until you got a hold of me," he added. "You made me love working out."

If he owed that body to her, she had certainly done something right in all her years of teaching.

The amusement faded from his eyes as they darkened with solemnity. "You helped me pick my career, too."

"You're a gym teacher?"

He shook his head. "No, a cop."

"I—"

"When you invited your dad to talk to the class."

She'd done that every year, even after he'd retired. The visits had meant a lot to both of them and not being able to do them anymore was the hardest thing for her to accept about losing her job.

"I was so impressed, I decided I wanted to be just like him," he said. "When I first got out of the academy, I worked under him for a while. Everybody still misses him around the department. How is he?"

"Stubborn as a hound dog with a treed possum."

Theresa laughed clearly this time. "Colorful, Kim."

"You've met my father," she reminded Theresa. "Am I wrong?"

Theresa shook her head. "That you're not."

"How old is he now?" George Fowler asked.

"Eighty-three. But don't tell him that. He doesn't have a clue."

He laughed again, a deep laugh that had warmth spreading through Kim's midsection. "That's good, though," he said, "that he's still going strong."

"Well, he's still going," she amended. "So you're my new neighbor?"

A former student. And a cop. She didn't like her

chances of getting him to take Mrs. Milanowski's cat off her hands.

He nodded. "Just a wall between us."

She resisted the urge to shiver. Had to be the vent blowing air on her sweat-slick skin. That was all it was. Not the mention of only a wall separating them. That didn't bother her at all.

"Ask him," Theresa said.

About the cat? "What?"

"About the class."

"What class?" George asked.

"We're teaching a Bachelor Survival course right here at the community center," Theresa answered, probably sensing that Kim couldn't.

"You're teaching it?" he asked Kim, those brown eyes full of warmth.

Warmth that overheated Kim again. She dabbed the damp towel against her skin. "Yes. With Theresa. And our friend Millie. We're actually starting it for—"

She stopped herself from talking about Millie's problems. Or her son's problems, as it were.

"For bachelors," he finished, lifting one seductive graying brow.

Theresa laughed, probably enjoying seeing Kim flustered. "Do you qualify?" she asked. She might look like a classy lady, especially in her smart, ivory-colored, welcome-lady suit, but sometimes she had no manners.

Kim ignored her friend's nosiness and held her breath, waiting for his answer. Then she mentally smacked herself for doing that. It meant nothing to her. Really it would be better for her if he were married. She'd have a better chance of pawning the cat off on his wife.

"I've got a divorce decree that says I do," he admitted.

"Is that why you bought into Hilltop?" Kim found herself asking. He was younger than the usual condo dweller. But then she'd been younger when she'd bought her unit, too. It was the smartest thing she'd ever done . . . if only because of Millie and Theresa.

"I've been divorced for a few years and living in an apartment. That's not the ideal place to live, lots of noise and traffic, but I was too busy to house hunt. So I knew I was too busy to have a house. A condo seemed a smart decision. I assume you'll be quieter than my previous neighbors."

She nodded. "As a mouse," she swore, using her fingers to cross her heart. A gesture he seemed to follow a little too closely. Then she added, "I'm sure you'll get used to the howling."

He lifted that brow again, probably totally aware of how darned sexy it made him look. Probably. "You howl?"

"Not me. The cat." Then she mentally smacked herself again. She shouldn't speak badly about the cat, not if she wanted him to keep his welcome-to-the-neighborhood gift, the one she intended to drop on his doorstep the minute she got back to her place. Well, maybe not the minute. She'd shower first.

And probably feed the cat, too. She wouldn't want it howling at George first thing.

"So it's just you and the cat?" he asked, his brown gaze strangely watchful.

Theresa made that sound from the doorway again, but Kim could barely hear it over the thumping of her heart, which had to be a delayed reaction to the exercise. She was *not* reacting to her new neighbor, no matter how much he resembled George Clooney.

"Yes," she answered finally, a little breathlessly. "Just me and the cat." And that was how she intended to keep it. Well, except for the cat.

He would wind up keeping the cat.

"So should we sign you up?" Theresa dropped her question into the long silence that had fallen between them while George stared at Kim and she stared at him.

"When is it?"

Whenever he couldn't make it, Kim decided. "What shift do you work?" she asked.

"Second."

Kim had heard that shift had killed many a marriage, so it could be the reason for his divorce. But Kim didn't want to believe it was something as simple as his wife getting sick of his shift. It made more sense that she'd gotten sick of him, as Kim would probably even George Clooney if she had to live with him.

"That's too bad," she said, not even trying to sound as if she meant it. "We need to hold the class after five . . . to make sure Millie's sons can make it."

He stepped closer to her and lowered his already deep voice as he said, "Well, since I'll be living right next door to you, maybe I can talk you into private lessons."

If he kept talking to her like that, that close and that deep, Kim had a moment's concern that he might be able to talk her into anything. And that wouldn't do at all.

She started pumping her arms and jogging in place. "Well, it was nice meeting you. But I have to run now . . . before I cool off. . . ."

As she passed Theresa in the doorway, she ignored her friend's highly amused chuckle and her muttered taunt of, "Chicken."

Chapter Five

"The average man has a carefully cultivated ignorance about household matters—from what to do with the crumbs to the grocer's telephone number—a sort of cheerful inefficiency which protects him."   —*Crystal Eastman*

So what's the plan?" Mitchell asked as he passed through the door Millie held open. His dress shoes squeaked against the hardwood floor of her foyer, as a light rain was falling outside.

"Honey, I'm so glad it's you." Although she wouldn't have minded too much had it been Charles. "Why'd you knock?"

He wrapped an arm around her, thumping his briefcase against her hip. "Yes, it's me, your partner in crime. Since the door was locked I had to knock. It was easier than finding my keys."

With a laugh, Millie pushed him away, then closed the door. He dropped his briefcase on the floor; the dented metal case clunked hard. Millie winced, hoping it didn't scratch the hardwood. So *that* was what was responsible for the gouges in the floor of his apartment.

"Kim must have locked the door on her way out."
With the picnic basket she'd borrowed with no clear explanation why; Kim definitely wasn't the picnic type.
Millie was sorry she'd had to leave right after exercise class that morning and hadn't had a chance during her Red Hat lunch to talk to Kim. She might have been able to figure out what her friend was up to.

"Sorry I missed her," Mitchell said. "She's a trip."

"Well, you'll be seeing more of her," Millie promised.

Mitchell's dark brows dipped as he furrowed his forehead. "Why?"

"She's another partner in crime."

Mitchell sighed. "The real crime is Steven and Audrey breaking up."

"Yes," Millie agreed. "He won't talk about it. I've tried." Each time she'd made an attempt during the two days he'd lived with her, Steven had shut down, either leaving the room for the basement or refusing to reply.

"Has he talked to Audrey?"

She shook her head. "He won't call her. Brigitte's called here, and he's talked to her then. But he won't go home to see her."

"Man, this sucks," Mitchell remarked, shaking his head. "That poor kid."

"Yes," Millie said with a sigh. "And your poor brother. He's miserable."

"We'll do something about that," Mitchell promised.

She reached up on tiptoe—all the men in her life were taller than she was—and pressed a kiss against his slightly stubbled cheek. He'd appreciate that more than the "good boy" comment that was burning the back of her throat with pride.

As she stepped back, Millie studied her baby. Like his brother and father, he was over six feet tall, but he was lean where Steven was . . . not.

He shrugged broad shoulders out of his dark suit coat, which landed on the floor near his briefcase. His tie was already askew; his hair, thick and curly like hers, was a little too long. But with his big, dark eyes, the unconventional haircut made him look boyish, more like twenty-three than thirty-three. Catching her staring, he shot her a dimpled grin. Millie couldn't help but smile back.

Yes, the only reason the boy was still single was because he was a slob. She had no doubt now. "I'm so glad you're going to help me," she said with a smile.

"Uh-oh," Mitchell said, narrowing those big eyes. "I'm not sure I like the way you're looking at me. Whatever Steven said I did, it was really *him*."

"What's he blaming on me now?" Steven asked as he came in the door behind them. His briefcase dropped, too, glanced off Mitchell's metal one and spun in a half circle on the floor.

Millie swallowed an impatient breath and struggled to resist the urge to pick up behind them. They were not her little boys anymore; they were grown men who needed to pick up after themselves.

"Any reason we're all standing in the doorway?" Steven asked as he stepped over the briefcases and headed toward the kitchen. "Let me guess, too busy talking about me to even go sit down?"

Millie hated the bitterness that twisted Steven's once-smiling face into a grimace. "Honey—"

"Hey, we just want to help, man," Mitchell said.

"I don't need any help," his older brother insisted. "I did a pretty bang-up job on my own."

"Steven," Millie said, beginning her pitch, "if you'd meet Audrey half-way—"

"I told you. I tried. She doesn't want *me* anymore." His voice cracked with emotion and his face mottled with red color. "And I don't want to talk about this anymore."

Mitchell lifted a hand, reaching out for his brother's shoulder, but Steven pulled away. "C'mon, Steve—"

Steven drew in a deep, steadying breath and pasted on a fake smile. "Mom, dinner smells great."

It should after all the time she'd spent cooking it. But if it made her boys happy it was worth all her effort.

"Too bad you can't stay, Mitch," Steven teased, obviously trying to put his relationship with his brother back on their usual lighthearted footing.

Mitchell forced a laugh; he must have instinctively known what response his brother wanted. "Oh, I'm staying. The only thing I ate today was airport food." He shuddered and added, "You better not have eaten all that pie. I flew back early for a piece."

"Yeah, right," his older brother scoffed. They all knew why Mitchell had flown back early.

Millie's palms itched even though she'd fisted them. She couldn't follow them into the kitchen. She bent down and picked up the mess, setting the briefcases into the closet in the foyer and hanging up Mitchell's coat.

"Mom, aren't you coming?" Mitchell asked, stepping back into the foyer. Then he lowered his voice. "So how are we handling this?"

"Follow my lead," Millie whispered. "And remember," she added, reaching up to pat his cheek, "you agreed to help me."

He narrowed his eyes again. "I have a feeling I'm not going to like this."

"Good," Steven called out from the kitchen. "If you don't like it, there'll be more for me."

When he joined Steven in the kitchen, Mitchell patted his brother's belly, which spilled over his belt and strained the buttons on the bottom half of his shirt. "Looks like you could stand to skip a few meals, bro."

For a minute when Steven had walked in the door, Millie had worried that Mitchell might be overly solicitous and make him uncomfortable about his marital problems. But she needn't have worried. As brothers they cared about each other, but they were rarely nice to each other. Fighting a smile, she opened the door of the side-by-side fridge to hide her amusement.

"Mom, can you grab me a pop?" Steven asked as he settled into a chair at the small dinette table. He'd just walked past the refrigerator. Millie realized that if he'd wanted something, he could have gotten it himself.

"I'll take one, too," Mitchell said, sitting down beside his brother, shoulder to shoulder. He could have gotten his own as well.

But they expected to be waited on. They were spoiled. And Millie had no one but herself to blame. It was a wonder Audrey hadn't thrown him out sooner, or at least thrown Millie out of her house sometime over the years.

"Make Steven's a diet," Mitchell added, pushing his brother's shoulder with his.

She sighed and brought each of her boys a glass of cola; she'd opened the cans and poured the contents into glasses before she could catch herself. Although she worried about it, teaching *them* might not be the hardest part of the class. Teaching *herself* not to keep doing everything for them would be the real challenge.

"You're both getting diet," she said. "It's all I have in the house."

Mitchell exaggerated a face as he took a sip. She chose that opportunity to add, "Have you told Steven about my class?"

Mouth still full, he shook his head; his dark eyes watchful as he obviously sought to follow her lead. It reminded her of how she'd taught him to dance for his prom. She'd forced him to watch her face instead of her feet. He'd stepped on her toes a few times, but he'd finally picked up the rhythm well enough that after the prom he'd complained about how much dancing the girls had forced him to do.

Steven took the bait. "What class? Not that aerobics thing Dirty Harriet teaches?" He chuckled, shooting his brother a challenging grin. "She'll wipe the floor with you."

"Kim's not teaching this class," Millie said, as she set bowls of salad in front of them. "*I* am." Her stomach fluttered nervously even as she said it. She had absolutely no teaching skills. "Kim and Theresa are helping me, though. In fact, we're working on the lesson plan after dinner, at the community center."

"So what's the class?" Steven asked again, his interest increasing.

Mitchell floundered. "Mom can describe it better than I can," he said, gesturing toward her as he took another sip of his drink.

"A Bachelor's Survival course."

Mitchell's cola sprayed out of his mouth, droplets spattering the lettuce and Millie's white tablecloth, as he coughed and choked. Steven thumped him on the back, a little too roughly, and laughed. "So you've finally given up on marrying him off?"

Millie nodded. "Heather was my last hope."

"Heather dumped you?" Steven asked, still chuckling. But even though his mouth curved in a smile, his eyes remained dark with the sadness weighing so heavily on him.

Mitchell opened his mouth, probably to point out that Steven wasn't in any position to criticize him, but he closed it before saying a word.

"He's been telling me he doesn't want to get married," Millie admitted, forcing a resigned-sounding sigh. "I've finally accepted it and decided to help him."

"You already clean his apartment and cook most of his meals. What else can you do?" Steven wondered aloud, probably thinking about himself as well, about what else he could have done for Audrey.

After talking to his wife and living with him for a few days, Millie could tell him: a lot.

"I can *really* help him now. I can give him the skills to do all that stuff himself," Millie pointed out.

Mitchell narrowed his eyes at her. He didn't have to say anything for her to know that he didn't like her plan. At all.

Steven glanced from Millie to his brother, and his eyes narrowed as well. It was one of many traits they shared. Like competitiveness. "So is he your only student?" he asked, his voice full of skepticism.

"Not at all. Mr. Lindstrom signed up, probably to stare at Kim some more. Then during lunch with my chapter of the Red Hat Society, some friends enrolled their sons and a few their husbands." But there was one more student, the one she hoped would be teacher's pet. She stammered over his name, "And Mr. Mo—Moelker."

"And who will Mr. Moelker be staring at?" Steven teased.

She hoped it would be her. Just the thought had her face heating as if she'd stepped too close to the stove. And she couldn't meet her sons' probing gazes.

"Hey, Mom? Mom?" Mitchell called out, waving the hand holding his salad fork around to catch her attention. Thick, red Catalina dressing dripped from it, spattering the white cloth like his cola had.

"She's been doing that a lot," Steven said around a mouthful of lettuce. "Zoning out."

"Well, she is getting to be *that* age, you know," Mitchell teased, his dark eyes dancing with amusement. And a little vengeance. He hadn't missed how she'd manipulated him into the class.

"You're right," she agreed. "In fact, I just may forget that I made another apple pie."

"Another one? He eat all of the last one?" Mitchell asked, reaching for his brother's belly again as Steven slapped at his hand. The glasses of cola teetered on the tabletop.

Millie flashed back to all the mealtime fights she'd refereed over the years. Too many. "Boys . . ."

"I didn't eat all of it," Steven defended himself. "She gave some away the other night. To a *man*."

Mitchell choked, and he hadn't even taken a bite. "A man?" he gasped.

"Were you spying on me?" Millie accused. And here she'd made a point to never interfere in their lives. She should have made them promise the same about hers.

Steven laughed. "No, he dropped the bowl back off while you were shopping yesterday. I believe . . . yeah, he said his name was Charles Moelker. No wonder he signed up for the class. He's already tried some of the goodies."

"Steven!" Millie said, her face so hot now that it had probably turned bright red, which would clash horribly with her new cinnamon-colored hair.

"So I'll meet him," Mitchell said, then with a devilish glint in his eyes added, "Good."

"At least you'll get something out of the class," Steven said with a derisive snort.

"He'll get plenty out of it," Millie insisted. "Mitchell's very bright. He'll catch on fast." She hoped. She gave her youngest a pointed stare and nodded toward his brother.

"Yeah," Mitchell said, watching her eyes. "I'll catch on fast. Faster than you would. You're hopeless."

"Yes," Steven said, rising from the table as all humor fell from his face. The haunted, sad look was back, aging him ten years, with lines of stress and fatigue. "It's hopeless. You two aren't going to fix my marriage with some little class. Audrey threw me out!"

His frustration and pain hung in the air even after he fled from the room, his footsteps falling heavy on the stairs as he descended to the basement.

Millie blew out a ragged breath. "I must be getting forgetful. *Steven's* the one who catches on fast."

Mitchell sighed too. "I thought he was acting too normal."

"*Acting* is right," she heartily agreed. "He won't talk about it. He comes home, eats, and heads downstairs to do paperwork."

"You really think this'll help? A few cooking classes?"

"It'll be more than that."

"But you think it'll make Audrey take him back?" Mitchell asked, his voice deepening with frustration.

Millie shrugged. "I don't know. But I promised Brigitte I'd try to help."

Mitchell nodded. "Okay, I'll work on him. Save me some pie."

"There's a casserole in the oven, too," Millie said as she stood.

"You're leaving already?"

"Of course." The truth was that she was still full from

lunch, and too nervous over the thought of teaching, to think about eating again.

"Mom, who is this Moelker guy?" Mitchell asked, his dark eyes softening with concern. "Is it serious?"

"It's a joke, honey. There's nothing going on between us. We're neighbors. That's all."

Mitchell's eyes narrowed as he studied her.

She couldn't resist teasing him as she dished up a helping of the pie into a plastic container. "I love having a new stepmother. You'd get used to a stepfath—"

"Mom!"

"I'm kidding," she promised. After his recent divorce, Charles wasn't likely to want to marry again anytime soon, if ever, no matter his reason for joining the class. "I'm just bringing this to the community center where Theresa, Kim, and I are working on lesson plans. I know you two won't save me any."

As she hoped, mention of the class distracted Mitchell. "You really signed me up for this thing?"

She nodded.

"It better work," Mitchell said, as he headed down the stairs to convince his brother to attend the classes.

Millie watched his curly head disappear from view and silently agreed. It had better work. For him and Steven.

With Steven, she had a family to reunite. With Mitchell, she had a tiara to retire.

*S*o where do we start?" Millie asked Kim as they waited for Theresa to join them in the community center kitchen.

"Start what?"

"To teach me how to teach a class." But she had a feeling Kim was starting something else. Through narrowed eyes, Millie studied her friend. Kim's face was flushed, nearly as pink as the fuchsia tracksuit she wore. Her brown eyes sparkled, and her breath came fast and hard. If Millie didn't know better . . .

"So just how close are you getting to your new neighbor?" she teased, as she settled onto a stool at the island. She pushed up the sleeves of her green knit shirt and propped her elbows on the granite counter, her jean-clad knees bumping against the white cupboard below it.

Kim grabbed a water bottle from the stainless steel fridge, twisting off the cap and taking a swig before answering. "A wall away . . ."

"And he's got you this flustered." Too bad he wasn't able to attend their class. Millie would love to meet the guy who could fluster Kim, especially since Theresa swore he was really good looking.

Kim shook her head. "It's not him. It's the cat—"

"Your cat?"

"*His* cat. I just dropped it on his doorstep, rang the bell and ran like—"

"Kim!" Theresa exclaimed as she joined them in the kitchen. "You didn't!"

"I felt it was the neighborly thing to do, giving him a welcome gift." She laughed. "I left it in your basket, Millie, with a bow on top."

Now Millie knew why she'd borrowed the picnic basket, and she wondered if she'd get it back. She might need it . . . someday . . . for a picnic. Once she retired her tiara, she'd have time for stuff like that.

"I thought he worked second shift," Millie said.

Kim nodded. "But he has tonight off."

"So you know his schedule already?" Millie asked, trying to control a smile.

Kim's face flushed with bright color, totally matching her tracksuit now. "No . . . he mentioned it this afternoon . . . when he caught me coming back from a run. He just got done with a long shift and has the night off."

"So he's probably sleeping, and you left the cat in a basket. What if he didn't hear the bell?" Theresa asked, obviously concerned about the cat.

Millie wasn't so sure she wanted the basket back anymore.

"Then he'll hear the cat," Kim said. "That thing loves to howl."

Theresa laughed. "Boy, Kim, I guess it has been a long time since you've flirted with a man. You've forgotten how it's done."

"I'm not flirting," Kim protested. "I'm getting rid of that fleabag." But her hand trembled so much she could barely screw the cap back on her water bottle.

Millie took it from her and completed the task. "Oh, no," she said, catching herself. "I can't stop myself from doing this."

"From doing everything for everybody else. From taking care of everybody else," Theresa said, adding a sigh of her own.

Millie nodded. "Steven doesn't even make his bed. Heck, I don't know how he gets to his bed. He just drops his clothes wherever he takes them off. Stairs. Family room floor. And I keep picking up after him."

She might have enjoyed his company the last couple of days if he hadn't been so miserable, but she didn't enjoy the additional work his living with her had brought her.

"I think I need to attend a how-not-to-mother-your-children-for-the-rest-of-your-life class."

"Add husband to that title and sign me up," Theresa agreed with a heavy sigh.

"A lot of stinky socks today?" Kim asked.

Theresa shook her head. "I didn't even look. No, it was a *Gunsmoke* marathon today. The early shows, the black and white ones. That was all he did, watch them and snooze, wouldn't even let me open the blinds in the family room. Can we start the class *this* week?"

"We have to get the curriculum figured out first." Kim, ever the teacher, reminded them of the reason they'd arranged to meet. She undoubtedly wanted to distract them from her new neighbor; it was obvious he distracted her enough.

"*We* have to get the most important student enrolled," Millie reminded them.

"*You* couldn't manipulate him?" Kim asked, obviously shocked. "Stubborn, huh? Wonder where he got that from . . ."

Millie ignored the twinkling in her friend's eyes. "Must have been his father."

"*Men* are the stubborn ones. They're born stubborn," Theresa backed up. "Kim's an anomaly."

"Hey," Kim said, lifting her hands, palms up. "Why are you bringing me into this?"

"Why not?" Theresa quipped, her mouth quirking into a challenging smile.

"Ladies," Millie said. She was used to playing peace-maker between the two strong women.

"Do *you* want to bring me into this?" Kim asked. "I could talk to Steven for you and try to convince him to join the class."

Millie considered the possibility a minute, amuse-ment tickling her. "You might actually be able to intimi-date him into doing it."

"Fearsome Kim," Theresa agreed.

"Dirty Harriet," Millie shared her son's nickname for her friend.

Theresa's laughter sputtered out with the sip of Sprite she'd just taken. "It's perfect."

"Please," Kim said, passing a strip of paper towel to Theresa. "Clean yourself up. You're such a mess." Then she laughed as she pointed out the pop stains on Theresa's cream-colored silk blouse.

Theresa stuck out her tongue but grabbed the paper towel. "So are you going to sic Kim and Harry on him?" she asked Millie, as she dabbed at the damp spots on the silk.

"I already sicced his brother on him. But I'm not so sure that was a good—" Before she could finish the thought, the theme song from "Thoroughly Modern Mil-lie" pealed out from her purse, which sat on the counter. She reached for it and fumbled inside for her cell phone. "Hello?"

"Mom."

"Steven?" Her heart did a little hopeful flip.

"Sign me up."

She held in the victory shout burning the back of her throat. "For what, dear?"

"Cute. You know for what, this class you and your friends are starting."

She was tempted to ask if he meant Kim's aerobics class, especially after all Mitchell's teasing about his weight, but she didn't want to push her luck—or her stubborn son—any further than he'd already been pushed. "Thanks, Steven. You won't regret this."

"But Mitchell might. I'm going to kick his butt," Steven promised.

She smiled and teased, "So you're going to turn into a regular Martha Stewart?"

"Don't push it," he advised. "So where'd you put that casserole you made? We don't know where to look."

"It's being kept warm in the oven," she said. After she hung up, she turned to her friends. "I hope he knows how to open it. Maybe that'll be our first lesson."

"So I take it we have another student?" Theresa asked. She and Kim were waiting expectantly.

"It's on," Millie said, expelling a huge sigh of relief. "Thanks to sibling rivalry."

"Lucky for you," Kim said.

"Well, if Mitchell had failed, I would have sicced Brigitte on him. I doubt he could have said no to her."

"Wally can never say no to his little girls either," Theresa said with a smile.

Millie wanted to point out that he never said no to *her* either. But Theresa wasn't willing to see Wally's good points right now. So Millie focused on their sign-up sheet instead. "So that's Mitchell, Steven, and all the guys our Red Hat chapterettes are going to coerce into joining."

Theresa patted Millie's shoulder. "You did a great job pitching the course at lunch today."

Millie shrugged. "The pitch had nothing to do with it. Our chapterettes would help us no matter what." The chapter was just as supportive as Theresa and Kim. She'd been relieved to learn that she wasn't the only mother who'd raised domestically helpless sons.

Millie returned her attention to the list of students on the clipboard on the counter in front of her. With satis-faction, she wrote down Steven's name.

"And don't forget Wally," Theresa added. "And Mr. Lindstrom."

"He's on here." Millie checked off the list, her pen shaking as it hovered above the name at the top, the first one who'd signed up.

"Mr. Lindstrom?" Kim sighed. "I'll have to wear Teflon pants."

"You forgot someone," Theresa reminded her.

"Who's that?" Millie asked, playing dumb by widen-ing her eyes in feigned innocence.

"You've forgotten all about Charles Moelker and his stunning blue eyes?" Theresa teased.

Millie regretted sharing too much with her friends. She never should have confessed her infatuation with blue-eyed men a few months ago during Movie Night, with *The Thomas Crown Affair* playing.

Kim blew out a sigh full of pity. "They do say the memory is the first thing to go . . ."

"The back, thanks to your aerobics class," Millie grumbled as she shifted on the stool where she sat, wincing and hoping fervently that her friends would drop the subject of Charles's eyes. "My memory is just fine. *I* remember we need to figure out how we're teaching this class."

Millie glanced down at the list again, the names swimming before her blurring vision. She hadn't counted on so many students. She pressed a hand against her fluttering heart, trying to settle her nerves.

She'd been anxious at the thought of standing up in front of her sons and friends and attempting to teach them, but they would understand and support her if she stammered and stuttered and made a complete fool of herself. Even Charles Moelker had seen her do that before.

But now there were strangers attending the class, more people who could watch her fall flat on her face.

What had she been thinking?

"You're teaching. We're going to just be there for support," Theresa reminded her. *Not helping at all.* "After all, *you* are the domestic goddess."

Maybe if she found a tiara to wear to class, she might get up the nerve to open her mouth to give instructions. As it was right now, she had no confidence that she'd be able to pull this off . . . even with her friends' help.

# Chapter Six

"The phrase '**domestic** cat' is an oxymoron."
—*George F. Will*

Kim tightly clutched her keys and the small canister of pepper spray attached to them, as she passed under the flickering street lamp and started up the sidewalk toward her condo. Not that she was afraid of walking alone at night. But she believed in being prepared . . . for anything. Thus the pepper spray. Unless she wanted to scare someone. That was when she brought out Harry.

She wasn't prepared for the shift of shadows near her door and the man stepping out of the darkness. She just barely smothered the squeak rising in her throat as her heart raced. With a shaking hand, she lifted the pepper spray, but then she recognized him and realized that she would probably never be prepared for George Fowler.

Even with her porch light shining on him, he was still in shadow, wearing a black T-shirt and jeans. His eyes, so dark, glittered in the faint light, as did the silver strands of his hair. Instead of settling with recognition, Kim's heart pounded harder.

George lifted his arms above his head. "Don't shoot."

"Cute," she said. And he was.

But she was so *beyond* interested in cute. When she was young and stupid, she had almost married cute. Twice. But she'd come to her senses in time to avoid making huge mistakes. Really handsome men were spoiled, expecting all of a woman's time and attention. Kim would *never* lose herself in a man like that. After two narrow escapes, she couldn't be tempted . . . not even by George.

"Out kind of late, aren't you?" he asked, his voice deep with concern.

The short hairs at the nape of her neck rose as irritation flickered. She wasn't used to anyone questioning her comings and goings. "Funny, you don't look like my father."

He chuckled. "Occupational hazard, I guess."

Perversely, a little disappointment settled her irritation. So his concern wasn't personal. "Is lurking around in the dark an occupational hazard, too?"

"No," he said, his teeth flashing white in a wide grin. "I thought I heard something earlier. I've been out here a while now, looking around, trying to figure out what it could have been."

"What did you hear?" Her ring of the doorbell? How could he not have recognized that sound?

"I don't know." He brushed a hand through his short hair. "Sounded like a sick dog. Some awful howling . . ."

She glanced the few yards from her door to his door

where, beneath the hip roof of his porch, his yard light illuminated his cement stoop. His empty cement stoop.

Where had the basket gone? Millie would probably not be happy if she didn't return that basket. More importantly, where was the cat? If George been out here all that time, why hadn't he found it? Was it scared of George? Had it run off? She could *so* identify with it.

"So did you find anything?" she asked, resisting the urge to sink to her knees and call out for the cat.

He shook his head. "Nope. Didn't see a thing."

Not the basket?

Not the pretty bow?

Not the welcome-to-the-neighborhood note?

Where had it all gone? And why did she care?

"Well, it's late," she said, brushing past him as she pulled open her storm door. "See you . . ."

"Around," he said. "After all, we are neighbors."

Even though he'd only lived there a day, she wasn't likely to forget it. The walls hadn't seemed so thin when Mrs. Milanowski had lived next door. Kim had never heard the sputter of water when the shower started and stopped for her. She'd never felt the vibration of the rhythm of music she had played. Of course Mrs. Milanowski had been more into Lawrence Welk than Lynyrd Skynyrd. How would she handle three hundred sixty-five days of George?

Kim shoved her key in the lock, turned it, then pushed open her door. As she did, something furry scurried from behind the bushes and brushed against her leg and . . . howled.

George laughed. "The basket's back there, too."

"Hey," she protested, "it was a gift. You're not supposed to return a gift."

"I had to return it. We don't know each other well enough to exchange gifts," George said, promise vibrating in his deep voice as he added, "yet."

Despite it being spring, the night air must have chilled because goose bumps rose on Kim's bare arms. He didn't mean anything by that, she was sure. And it didn't matter if he did because she wasn't interested.

She glanced down at the gray tiger cat. Its glowing eyes stared up at her, then one eye flickered shut as if it was winking at her.

The plastic bowl slipped in Millie's damp palms, so she had to adjust her hold on it. Why was she so nervous? It wasn't the walking alone at night. She'd insisted to both Kim and Theresa that she'd be fine getting herself home, except that she hadn't gone straight home.

She'd stopped here first, outside Charles' unit. There were only two in his building, each with a three-stall garage, arched windows, and cathedral ceilings. Even though it was only a street over from theirs, Kim called this area the swanky part of Hilltop. Remembering what she and Bruce had paid for their small unit, Millie had laughed off her comment. No part of Hilltop was exactly low-rent.

The wind rustled through the trees and shrubs, casting shadows between Millie and the glow of the streetlamp. But it wasn't the shadows outside making her nervous; it was the shadows she glimpsed behind the drapes in Charles's front window.

Two of them.

He wasn't alone.

And it wasn't his dog standing close to him in his living room. Or a man.

The silhouette behind the drapes, framed by the arched window, reminded Millie of the paper dolls she'd played with as a little girl. Part of the reason was its seeming two-dimensional; the other was that it had the curvy lines that mimicked Barbie doll's impossible figure.

Charles's visitor was definitely female, in as great physical shape as Kim. It might have been Millie's athletic friend but for the long hair flowing around the woman's shoulders. So who was it, and why did Millie need to know so badly?

Not badly enough, however, to walk up to the door and ring the bell. Instead she ducked behind the bushes separating the driveways of the two units, then peered between the holes in the foliage.

Now she considered what it meant that Charles lived in the "swanky" area. He had money. So not only was he a bachelor; he was a very eligible one. That meant nothing to Millie. But she knew it would matter to some women. Undoubtedly hers weren't the only casseroles he'd received. Was that what his visitor was doing, dropping off a casserole?

The pie container slipped again. Millie's fingers caught the lid—the only reason she didn't drop it behind the shrubs. She didn't care what those other women's motives were; hers were pure. She was only dropping off a pie.

Okay, maybe she'd been about to attempt a little more flirting. She wouldn't mind getting to know Charles better.

But if he already had somebody in his life . . .

She should walk up to the door, just knock and find out. So why was she hiding instead? This was so unlike her, skulking in the shadows, spying. It was more up Kim's alley; she was the one who had to know everything that happened in the complex. Not to spread rumors like Mrs. Ryers, but to make sure nothing "funny" was going on.

Millie had a five second warning that something funny was about to happen when water gurgled under her feet. Then the sprinklers started, shooting streams of water across the grass. And Millie's hair and shirt and pants. It even trickled down her ankles and pooled in her white canvas shoes.

Taken off guard by the impromptu cold shower, Millie's attention was drawn away from spying through the shrubs. She didn't notice that Charles had come outside until his dog was yapping around Millie's dripping ankles. She pressed a finger against her lips, hoping the animal would obey the universal silencing gesture before its master investigated what had it barking. "Shhh . . ."

It bounced around more, its little body shaking as it vigorously wagged its tail. A motor rumbled, louder than the water rushing through the spigots, as a car backed down Charles's drive. Millie caught a glimpse of his visitor through the driver's window. Blonde, beautiful, young.

Even though it was only a glimpse, Millie was pretty certain she'd never seen her before. The girl, and the car, disappeared from view as Charles stepped around the shrubs and blocked Millie's line of vision. But she'd already seen enough of her competition. Not that she was actually competing for Charles, at least not anymore. That was the problem with *men* Millie's age. They didn't want *women* Millie's age.

"How many times have I told you to stay out of the sprinklers?" Charles scolded his dog, his deep voice full of exasperation. And he hadn't even noticed Millie yet.

"This is the first time that I know of," she said, swallowing her sigh of disappointment as his gaze traveled from his dog, which was lapping the water off her ankles, up her drenched body, to meet hers. His amazing blue eyes widened with shock. He backed away, maybe out of fear, maybe just to give her room to get out from under the water spray.

Either way she took advantage, stepping around the shrubs to stand with him on his driveway. The dog, keeping close to her, shook itself, sending more water flying at her. Millie resisted the urge, barely, to follow the dog's example and shake off some water, too. Charles, speechless, still stared at her.

He undoubtedly thought her a psychotic stalker now. The tide of embarrassment that flooded her body wasn't entirely unwelcome as it warmed her chilled, damp skin.

Her brain scrambled for any half-baked explanation. "I was bringing this by," she said, extending the dripping plastic bowl toward him, "when I thought I noticed Kim's cat dart into the shrubs."

The nearly plausible story spilling from her lips surprised her; maybe cold showers did help clear the mind. At least it had hers. Or maybe the age and beauty of his visitor had.

He hesitated before reaching for the bowl. When he touched it, his fingers slid across the wet plastic and tangled with hers, warming them, before he took the bowl from her. It slipped in his grasp, and he fumbled it twice before getting a good grip on it. "More pie."

"I know you like it," she said. And now she knew what else he liked. Young blondes.

"You had some left?"

"No, it's fresh." Just like he liked 'em.

But he seemed less interested in the pie than her dripping clothes. She glanced down and noticed, highlighted in his porch light, how tightly her pale green knit shirt clung to her. A little pride joined her embarrassment now. She might actually stop complaining about all those tortuous exercises Kim made her do, since the results of all that hard work had brought about a flare of interest in a certain set of blue eyes.

"So was it?" he asked.

"Was what?"

"Kim's cat," he reminded her. "Isn't that why you were in the bushes?"

She wished it were. "Oh; yeah . . ."

"You didn't catch it."

She shook her head, and water flew from her curls like it had the dog's fur. She bit her tongue, holding in a dismayed gasp, as droplets darkened spots on his white oxford shirt. He wore it tucked into jeans faded by design not wear. Even in casual clothes, Charles Moelker looked like a movie star.

"That was probably Buddy's fault," he said, a bit apologetically.

"Buddy?"

"The dog," he said, "who adores you, by the way."

She glanced down at the little Schnauzer, who was leaning against her leg and staring up at her with its tongue hanging out.

For a moment there, she'd thought Charles had come close to looking at her that way. But it was clear to her that the dog was more interested in her than its owner. And she'd seen the reason why driving away. For now. Millie had no doubt that the young woman would be back.

But Millie wouldn't. Her attempts at flirting had embarrassed her enough for a lifetime.

"Well, I better go," she said, easing away from the dog who flopped on its back and gazed hopefully up at her. She couldn't deny it a quick pat to the belly, not after having almost run it over. How the dog could like her after that near miss she couldn't fathom.

"Well, thanks for the pie," Charles said, lifting the container in a little salute. "I hope you teach us how to do this."

"What?"

"In your class," he explained. "I hope you share your pie recipe."

The class. She might not come again to Charles's house, but she wouldn't be able to avoid him. Only now, knowing that he didn't spend his nights with only Buddy for company, she would not be flirting anymore.

Chapter Seven

"Making coffee has become the great compromise of the decade. It's the only thing 'real' men do that doesn't seem to threaten their masculinity. To women, it's on the same domestic entry level as putting the spring back into the toilet-tissue holder or taking a chicken out of the freezer to thaw." —*Erma Bombeck*

Class starts tonight," Theresa reminded Wally as she re-filled his coffee cup. She'd switched from decaf, skipped over the lite brands featuring half the caffeine, and gone right back to the leaded stuff she hadn't used in ten years in the hopes that it might give him more energy. Or at least keep him awake until noon.

Wally lifted his gaze from the newspaper, lowered his reading glasses, and blinked bleary green eyes at her. Although it was late morning, he still wore his robe, not the soft velour one she'd bought him for Christmas but the ratty plaid flannel one he refused to throw out. "It starts tonight?" he asked. "So did Millie talk her son into joining?"

Theresa nodded as she settled into the padded wicker

chair across from Wally in their sunbathed breakfast nook. This was her favorite part of the condo, with two-story windows that looked out over the treetops on the east side of the hill. Before he'd retired, Wally had never had time to appreciate the beauty of the view. She'd thought that would change once he wasn't rushing off to work early every morning. But still, he couldn't appreciate what he had.

"Yes," she confirmed, "she talked both of them into joining."

Wally turned the page of his paper and said, "Since they're going along with it, you don't need me."

She was tempted to agree with him. But they'd been together too many years. She reached for a piece of the paper and noticed that the business section was untouched. All he read now was the sports page, and she didn't think he had much interest in that, either, except to leave the wrinkled papers lying around the house.

"You *really* need to go," she insisted, staring him down over the rim of her coffee mug. Maybe the caffeine wasn't a good idea for her; it tended to shorten her usually long temper. "You promised that you would."

He sighed. "To help Millie's son. But his brother will be there—"

"He's only one other student. We need more than that, or Steven will catch on." And so might Wally, if she didn't control her frustration. She had to be careful not to tell him how many had actually signed up for their class, thanks to their Red Hat chapterettes. "He can't think this class is just for him, or he'll drop out."

"So what's it going to be?" he asked, in his usual

defeated tone. "Me and two guys young enough to be my sons? I won't be able to catch on as fast as they will. The only thing having me in that class will accomplish is my slowing them down." These were the most words he'd spoken in one conversation lately; it was no wonder that he had to stop to expel a ragged breath before adding, "and embarrassing you."

Theresa's heart softened, and she would have reached for one of his hands but he'd fisted them around the paper, crumpling it into illegibility. "You won't be the oldest," she assured him. "Mr. Lindstrom signed up. So did Charles Moelker."

"Moelker?" He blinked, eyes full of surprise. "He's married, too."

"Not anymore. His wife divorced him a while ago. She's already remarried."

Wally pushed the paper aside, sending the unread business section to the terra cotta floor. Of course he didn't lean over to retrieve it, just left it lying there. Then he took a sip of coffee, studying her silently as he swallowed. Could he taste the caffeine? She'd added some sugar, too, so maybe that masked the flavor.

To distract him from the coffee, Theresa said, "You should get to know Charles."

And not just because they might have something in common. She suspected Millie was interested in him, although she would hotly deny it if Theresa or Kim outright asked. Out of loyalty to Bruce? Or embarrassment? Was that why she'd dyed her hair, to attract his attention?

If so, Theresa had a feeling that the class was going to be really interesting. "I think you'll enjoy the course."

Hopefully he'd learn something, like how to pick up after himself. And maybe he'd find something, too, like the man he used to be before he sold his business, because Theresa missed him. She didn't know how much longer she could live with this depressed stranger.

She'd tried to get him help, but he wouldn't see a psychiatrist, wouldn't even admit to his primary care physician that he was struggling to deal with his early retirement. The class was her last hope to lift him out of his funk, and to save their marriage.

Millie clutched the lesson book to her chest as she leaned over the railing around the basement stairwell. Even from where she stood, she could see the mess on the family room floor. Along with a discarded dress shirt, a bag of chips lay on the carpet, crumbs spilling out and embedding themselves into the fibers. She had vacuumed just the day before. How had he made such a mess already?

"Steven?"

"I'm on the phone, Mom," he called up.

Hope lifted her heart. Maybe finally, after days of no communication between them, he was talking to Audrey. Millie would have crossed her fingers, but she had them clasped tightly around the thick binder.

She, Theresa, and Kim had spent a lot of time creating the lesson plans, a colored tab differentiating the cooking segments from the cleaning, shopping, and laundry. They had so much to teach their students.

Teach. Nerves kicked up in Millie's stomach, churning

the M&Ms she'd eaten to bolster her confidence. She'd never done anything like this. Even with Theresa and Kim's expert help, she had a feeling she'd wind up like she had the other night. All wet.

She closed her eyes, trying to squeeze out the image of those two silhouettes in Charles's front window, of the blonde as she'd backed down the drive. Young. Beautiful. Instead of stewing over it, she should have just asked Charles who his visitor was.

Maybe she would, if she could catch him alone during class. Her hands trembled with nerves—over teaching, not seeing Charles. She had no reason to be nervous over seeing him again, especially if he had someone in his life already.

But still, Millie had been careful when she'd dressed. She wore a bright orange, short-sleeved sweater and jean capris with colorful flowers embroidered down the seams. She hadn't chosen her favorite color for Charles, but to bolster her confidence, like the M&Ms.

Drawing in a deep breath, she turned toward the door. She'd wanted Steven's help carrying stuff out to the car—things, besides the lesson book, that were necessary for the first class. Coffeemakers, hers plus some she'd borrowed, were lined up along the hall, and even though the stove in the community center had six burners, she'd scrounged up some hot plates, too. Thank goodness she had dropped off the perishables at the community center.

She already picked up a coffeemaker and reached for the door just as it flung open, banging against the wall.

Startled, she juggled the maker, trying not to drop the glass carafe.

"Mom, what are you doing?" Mitchell asked as he tossed his briefcase onto the floor.

"I need to get this stuff to the community center," she explained.

"And you need help," he surmised. But he walked past her and leaned over the basement railing, yelling out, "Steven! Get your butt up here!"

"Shhhh," Millie cautioned. "He's on the phone. I think it might be Audrey."

Mitchell turned back, his brown eyes bright with hope. "Did he call her?"

"No, and no," Steven answered for himself, as he climbed the stairs. "That was a business call."

Not personal. He didn't have a personal life anymore, Millie realized. Disappointment soured her hopefulness. "Ah, Steven . . ."

"Call her," Mitchell urged.

Steven shook his head and expelled a ragged breath. "How many times do I have to tell you two that she wants nothing to do with me?"

"She doesn't know that you're taking the class yet," Millie pointed out. "You need to tell her that you're trying—"

"What's the name of the course?" Steven interrupted, pointing to where the lesson book precariously balanced on the top of the maker Millie still held. "A Bachelor's Survival course. That's why I'm taking it."

Millie's heart clenched with pain, but it was nothing

compared to what darkened Steven's eyes. "Oh, honey . . ."

"Face it, you two," he advised them, "I'm going to be a bachelor again."

"Technically I don't know if you can be one again," Mitchell said, perhaps hoping to lighten the mood with some humor. "A bachelor is someone who *never* got married."

Steven drew in a deep breath and quipped, "You should know. No woman alive would agree to marry you." Even though he teased, his mouth didn't lift into a smile, his eyes didn't brighten.

He *needed* this class. They both did.

Millie lifted her chin, squashing her nerves. She couldn't worry about herself, about a little potential embarrassment. She had a mission. "Okay, boys, help me load the car. We need to get this show on the road!"

"I'll hold the door," Mitchell offered, gesturing toward his suit and tie, as if carrying things might muss them up.

Millie took advantage of his open arms to load the coffeemaker into them, but she grabbed the binder. In addition to the lesson plans, it held many important recipes, ones she'd taken from what she lovingly referred to as her cooking bible, The Red Hat Society cookbook.

Her sons grumbled complaints under their breaths, but they helped her load the trunk, then unloaded it at the community center. But when they walked into the industrial-sized kitchen, with its stainless steel appliances and long, granite countertops and island, they re-

treated, claiming something had been left in the car.
They had probably not been overwhelmed by what they
were about to do, but by the argument between the two
women there, wrestling over a stool. Kim and Theresa
fought over the workstation setup.

Millie glanced from them to where Wally stood by the
sliding doors to the deck which encompassed two sides
of the brick building, and was suspended over the hill-
side. He lifted his hands to demonstrate his helplessness.

"We agreed on how we were setting up the class," Millie reminded her friends, moving between the pub tables
they'd brought in earlier that day from the rec room. With
them and some extra stools, they'd have ample work-
space. Although they kept bickering, Theresa and Kim
helped her set out the coffeemakers, hot plates, and other
materials required for this lesson.

"It's a beautiful evening," Kim said with a sigh. "We
should face the windows."

"It's a cooking class. We should face the stove,"
Theresa insisted.

"We're learning more than cooking," Kim argued.

"Ye—" Millie couldn't even agree before Theresa
snapped back.

"Yes, coffee making—"

"That's a bad idea," Kim said. "You definitely had too
much coffee today."

"The lessons are all planned out," Theresa reminded her.

"But you brought regular coffee. You know caffeine
isn't good for you. I taught that in my class."

"Well, this isn't *your* class," Theresa countered.

As strong women with strong opinions, Theresa and Kim often butted heads, but Millie couldn't afford to let things get out of control already. She raised her voice to shout above their bickering, "It's *my* class!"

Wally shot Millie a smile of approval. Her heart swelled with a little pride. If she could referee Kim and Theresa, and her boys, she'd have no problem teaching.

Then Charles walked in. And suddenly she felt as deflated as if she were standing wet and humiliated in his shrubs. Heat rushed to her face, and she busied herself behind the counter, putting away the extra ingredients until she heard Charles ask Kim, "So did you find your cat?"

Millie sucked in a deep breath, holding it, as she studied Kim's reaction.

Beneath her spiky bangs, Kim's forehead puckered with confusion. Then she nodded. "Yeah . . . I found it."

"Millie's some great friend. She got soaked in the sprinklers trying to catch it. Then Buddy rushed out to help her." Charles chuckled.

Before responding to Charles, Kim gave Millie a pointed stare across the counter. "Yeah, she's some great friend . . ."

Who was going to get grilled later, Millie suspected. Amusement twinkled in the blue depths of Charles's eyes as he met Millie's gaze across the counter. Uh-oh; he probably knew she'd made up the story about Kim's cat.

As a few more men filed into the room, Millie had to push that concern aside and deal with another: the nerves fluttering back into her stomach and chest. Compared to the class sizes Kim had undoubtedly taught, theirs was small. But to Millie, who had never done much public speaking, let alone teaching, the class felt huge, more than she could handle even with the help of her friends.

Then her sons returned, jostling each other with their shoulders like they were teenagers, and she remembered her mission. Nothing but their happiness mattered to her. Sure, she'd get something out of their success in this class, too. She'd get to retire her domestic goddess tiara and take some time for herself, some time where she didn't worry about anything but having fun for a while. Maybe she'd go on that annual cruise with the Red Hot Hatters of Hilltop.

"Welcome to our Bachelor's Survival course," she announced, in a voice she was surprised to find so clear and strong. Even the ensuing chuckles didn't detract from her determination. "Everyone take a seat and let's get started. We have a lot to pack into this six-week course." So much that she was glad they'd decided the class needed to meet twice a week. Her sons, however, weren't aware of that. Yet.

"I know not everyone is thrilled to be here," she remarked, smiling at her boys. "But we're going to have fun."

Someone groaned. She suspected it was Steven.

"Really, we are," she promised. "And more importantly, we're going to *eat*." She stepped back from behind the counter, gesturing for Kim to take over, but her friend just smiled and shook her head.

When Millie turned toward Theresa, she did the same, mouthing, "You're doing great."

"Okay," she said, "since this is our first class, we're

going to start with breakfast." She laughed at the expressions on the male faces, brows knitted as they looked from her to the eggs and pads of butter at their workstations.

Most of the men had doubled up into teams, Steven and Mitchell, Wally and Charles. One group had three, two sons and a dad. Only Mr. Lindstrom stood by himself, dapper in the dark, pinstriped suit he always wore, even when he attended Kim's exercise class.

"I know," she said, "it's seven at night, hardly the right time for breakfast, but this way you'll be prepared for the homework you'll have to do in the morning."

"Homework?" Mitchell scoffed. "I didn't sign up for that." Chuckles emanated from the students. Naturally her youngest would be the class clown.

She glared at him. "Of course there's going to be homework. Everything we teach you here, you have to do at home. That's the whole point of the class."

He grumbled some more, but she ignored him. She couldn't ignore Charles, however, and the fact that he and Wally were deep in conversation. About what?

She pushed the question from her mind as she read off the measurements for coffee and grounds and demonstrated how-to. Before moving among the students to supervise their attempts to make their first pots of coffee, Theresa and Kim squeezed her shoulders.

"You're doing great," Kim added her compliment to the one Theresa had earlier mouthed.

She mock-glared at them as she had Mitchell. "Thanks for the help, ladies."

"*You're* the domestic goddess," Theresa reminded her.

"Don't start that again," she warned Theresa and Kim.

"But it's so fitting," Kim insisted.

She ignored her friends' teasing, and walked over to check on her boys' efforts. Grounds swam in the nearly clear water streaming into the pot. "You guys need serious help," she said, sighing. "That's why we decided the class would meet twice a week."

"Mom, I never know when I'll get sent out of town," Mitchell began his argument, until she gave him her most beseeching look and a sideward glance toward his brother. "But I'll see what I can do."

"If he's not going, I'm not going," Steven said. Despite his deep voice, it was an echo of a thirty-year-old argument started when they were toddlers.

"I'll be here," Mitchell vowed, a muscle ticking in his jaw, as he ground out the words.

"So what happened with the coffee?" Millie asked, lifting the cover on the top of the maker. Her answer was a torn filter, undoubtedly a casualty of their wrestling. "Start over. And no fighting this time."

With a sigh she moved throughout the students, getting to know the men their Red Hat chapterettes had signed up for class. There were a couple of sons, not quite as inept as her own, a nephew, and two husbands whose wives had tired of waiting on them. Like Mitchell, Steven, and Wally, they had been coerced to join, but unlike them, they seemed willing to make the best of it.

Only two men had willingly signed up: Mr. Lindstrom and Charles. Kim was helping Mr. Lindstrom, who had yet to get the grounds into the filter, he was shaking so badly. She doubted it was due to his age or a medical condition; it was more likely Kim's fault for standing so close to the little old man. Instead of looking at the coffeepot, he was totally focused on the part of Kim that was directly at his eye level due to her height and his lack. Not only was he a little old man but a dirty one, too.

Charles caught the amused smile Millie tried to hide and returned it. His coffee brewed, he poured a cup. "Care to inspect it?"

She glanced around, looking for his workstation partner. But Wally stood near Theresa by the sink. Apparently she was already giving him a cleaning lesson.

So Millie took the cup from Charles's fingers, careful not to shake like Mr. Lindstrom and burn either of them. She inhaled the rich aroma, then admired the dark color. "You've done this before."

"I told you I was a bachelor a long time. I wouldn't have survived without coffee." His blue eyes held a trace of smugness.

"You could have bought it in the gas station like my son Mitchell does," she said, turning back to check on her boys, who were once again wrestling over the filter.

Maybe making them pair up had been a bad idea. As Steven poured coffee into the maker, Mitchell knocked his elbow, sending grounds flying across the counter and the white tiled floor.

"Those are your sons?"

She bit her lip and considered denying it . . . for a moment. "Yeah, they're mine."

"Wally said the oldest is why you wanted to start this class."

Now she knew what he and Wally had been discussing earlier. Her. Her heart did that giddy little flip.

"Yes. I hope his wife hears about it." If Steven would stop being so stubborn and call her. "And she'll realize that he's making an effort." But as she glanced back, the only effort Steven was making now was getting grounds into his younger brother's shirtfront. When she turned back to Charles, she caught his amused grin, and her mother's pride bristled. Sharing amusement over Mr. Lindstrom's crush on Kim was all right, but her sons' childish ineptitude was no laughing matter.

"If my brother were in this class, I might act the same way," Charles assured her with his soft eyes. The blue was even brighter tonight, probably due to the blue polo shirt he wore with his jeans.

"You have a brother?" It was nice to know that he had family. Millie had grown up an only child, so she'd been grateful her sons had a sibling. Until tonight.

He nodded, then said, "When you were over the other night, you just missed my—"

Whatever he'd been about to say was lost as Theresa launched into lesson two of the evening's class: kitchen cleanup. Her instructions were given, pointedly, to Wally, as they stood shoulder to shoulder at the sink.

Forever the referee, Millie rushed up next to her. "We'll hold off on a complete cleanup until after the cooking lesson." Out of the corner of her eye, she glimpsed the coffee scattered around her sons' work area. "But we do need to pick up any spilled grounds. They're not going to be very good flavoring if they get into the eggs. Dampen a paper towel."

She resisted the urge to personally address Steven and Mitchell. Barely. She sufficed with a mom-means-business glare directed their way instead. "That works best to get up all the grounds."

Her glare must have gotten her point across that the boys *best* clean up, because they didn't fight over who had to handle that detail; they both dampened paper towels and picked up their mess. She had a sorry feeling that it might have been the first time for both of them.

"What a neat trick," she heard one of the guys say. She shared a quick, commiserating glance with Theresa. Kim was still helping Mr. Lindstrom. What women considered common sense men considered a trick.

"I guess we really are from other planets," Theresa commented, a little bitterly.

Before she could get testy with Wally again, Millie started the cooking lesson. She quickly demonstrated how to scramble and fry eggs. Best to hold off on the Red Hat Society recipes until the students learned the basics. "All the stuff you need is at your workstation."

"For those of you watching your cholesterol, wisely," Kim spoke out, startling Mr. Lindstrom, "you can substitute egg beaters. I set those out, too."

Theresa grumbled out some smart retort, but Mr. Lindstrom's hearing aid screeched too loudly for Kim to hear the disparaging comment, and pick up where the two women had left off on their earlier argument. Millie silently thanked Mr. Lindstrom's hearing aid for running interference.

As she watched the students whisk broken eggshells in their eggs, Millie wished they would have used the egg beaters instead. Maybe she had gone too quickly with the instructions because she was disappointed with most of the students' efforts. Although his coffee had been good, Charles's eggs were burnt on the edges and raw in the middle. As for her sons, they'd cooked more of the shell than the yolks.

After all the students had filed out, she confessed her fears to her friends. Well, some of her fears. She didn't share the ones she harbored over her sons leaving in deep conversation with Charles.

She embarrassed herself enough on her own; she didn't need their help. But she needed her friends.

"That didn't go well," she said with an exhausted sigh, as she hoisted her weary body onto a stool at the cluttered counter.

Theresa shrugged, as she checked over the pans the students were supposed to have cleaned. Still operating at top speed, she vigorously scrubbed at a spot. "At least they showed up."

Kim nodded, as she reached for a towel and the pan Theresa held out. "That's the most important thing. You can't expect miracles with the first class, Millie. It's going to take time."

"Good thing we increased the number of classes a week." Every precious minute of class time was necessary to get their students to be self-sufficient in the kitchen. She doubted there was a domestic goddess in the bunch.

She really was an endangered species.

"You're right," she agreed with Kim, trying to summon

the energy to help her friends with cleanup. She slid off the stool. "It's just going to take time."

Time she hoped they had. "Audrey has to understand that Steven won't catch onto everything overnight. She has to at least appreciate that he's trying. This *is* going to work."

Because it had to . . . her son's marriage couldn't end in divorce. Not only would it leave him heartbroken, it might leave him living with Millie for the rest of her life.

Chapter Eight

"No matter how lovesick a woman is, she shouldn't take the first pill that comes along."
—Dr. Joyce Brothers

Kim eased into a Downward-Facing Dog pose, stretching the muscles in her arms and calves as she leaned forward. Her feet and palms pressed against the yoga mat lying on the carpeted floor of the family room in her walkout basement. In the darkened glass, her contorted body, clad in a black leotard, reflected back into the room.

Tension drained from her neck, as she hung her head and breathed deeply. She wished all her concerns would drain away, but she was too worried about Millie. Her friend was so hopeful that their new classes would cure all the problems in her son's marriage. Although Kim had never gone through with a wedding, she had a feeling that curing Steven's marital woes would take more than a pot of coffee and some scrambled eggs, especially if he didn't put forth any more effort than he and his brother had tonight. Like she'd told her friend, it would take time for them to learn, but they also had to *want* to learn.

But would learning some domestic skills be enough to get Steven moved back in with his wife? Kim worried that it wouldn't be and that Millie would be crushed.

Something soft and furry brushed against Kim's arm as a tiger-striped gray tail tickled her cheek. "Go away," she said, gritting her teeth so her lips wouldn't twitch.

The cat purred and rubbed against her arm again. Kim would have shoved it away, but she had to hold her pose for five minutes. So she endured the animal "petting" her. Then it suddenly tensed, its hair lifting along its back and neck, and let out one of those bloodcurdling howls as it stared into the darkened glass of the patio door.

The animal had seen Kim in her leotard and yoga poses too many times to be frightened of her reflection. She followed its stare to the door and noticed a movement in the darkness beyond the glass. Her heart shifted in her chest, pounding hard and fast against her ribs. Since she'd considered a night run earlier, she'd brought Harry out of the drawer next to her bed and left it sitting on the other side of the couch. She quickly reached for the pellet gun, then darted over to the sliding doors and flipped the switch to flood the patio with light.

The man who'd been peeking in her windows stumbled backward as he blinked against the bright light. He tripped over a steel chair and sprawled across the brick pavers. Before he could regain his feet, Kim darted through the sliders to stand over him with Harry pointing in his face. His very handsome face. His dark eyes glittered in the porch light, and his teeth flashed white as he grinned widely.

"So that's the infamous Harry," her new neighbor said, laughter rumbling from his throat and chest. "Your BB gun."

She would have been surprised if the toy had fooled a police officer. The gun was ugly enough to fool most criminals, who wouldn't be breaking laws in the first place if they had any sense. She was a cop's daughter through and through.

As such, by nature, she was too suspicious to lower her weapon even after identifying her intruder. Well, *almost* intruder . . .

He'd intruded on her evening, on her meditation. Even though he hadn't actually broken into her home, he'd broken into her thoughts . . . entirely too much. Her fingers tightened on her weapon.

His laughter died as he stared up at her from his incongruous position—half-sprawled, half-sitting on her patio bricks. "I think you could choose a better weapon if you're looking for protection. A stun gun—"

"I don't want to do any nerve damage." But she was beginning to think *she* had some. Seeing his long, lean body lying on her patio was doing all kinds of things to her nerves, like making her hands shake. She tightened her grip again.

"You'd rather shoot someone's eye out?"

She shrugged. "I'm not that great a shot—"

"A former police chief's daughter admitting that?" he teased, his dark eyes wide with feigned astonishment.

Pride stinging, she lifted her chin. "I can raise some serious welts, though."

"And give yourself enough time to get away," he surmised.

"Harry is really just for the fear factor," she confessed. "I have pepper spray for protection." And she had her attitude. Usually that was enough to scare men off, or that was what Theresa told her.

He grinned. "I guess I should be grateful you just wanted to scare me."

"I owed you for scaring . . ." She wouldn't admit to that little jump of fear in her heart over the movement outside her window. " . . . the cat."

"I scared the cat?" he asked with skepticism, as he lithely vaulted to his feet. *Did he do any yoga?*

She nodded. "Yes, the cat."

"Just the cat?" he asked, his shoes scraping against the bricks as he stepped closer to her. She had to look up to him; at five ten, Kim rarely had to look up to anyone. His head and shoulders blocked the porch light, surrounding Kim in shadows.

Her traitorous knees weakened. She locked them and stood firmly in place . . . too close to him. She could smell the fresh scent of soap clinging to his skin and see the dampness of his salt and pepper hair, straight from his shower. "*I* don't scare."

He tilted his head, studying her as if to judge the veracity of her words. Then he nodded.

"But what are you doing lurking around my patio," she glanced at her watch, "at this hour?"

In the bright glow of the yard light, his face flushed with color. "Not what you think—"

"What do I think?" she asked, trying hard to keep the amusement out of her voice. He was so darned cute, and his name was George. Now she struggled to hold in a sigh.

"Hopefully that I got home from work and noticed the light in the back. You didn't have any on upstairs. I got worried. Thought I should check it out."

"And you couldn't do that with a phone call?"

"You haven't given me your number."

He hadn't asked. But she wasn't about to point *that* out. "You're a smart cop." She'd asked her dad, or as everyone, herself included, called him—Chief—about George. From the sudden light flickering in his dark eyes, she guessed he'd figured that out. She ignored that little twinkle and said, "You should have been able to find it."

"You're unlisted."

She struggled to control the smile teasing her lips. "What does that tell you?"

"That you don't want to be bothered."

She touched the tip of her nose with her free hand.

"So I got it on the nose," he correctly interpreted her gesture. "You don't want to give me your number because I *bother* you."

He wasn't just cute like George Clooney; he was a flirt, too. Kim could recognize one because she frequently flirted herself, but only when she felt safe . . . like with Mr. Lindstrom. *He* couldn't catch her. George Fowler might.

"Don't take it personally," she assured him, ignoring

his innuendo . . . and trying to ignore his closeness. "Everyone bothers me."

"Is that why you're up so late?" he asked, switching gears so fast that she was a bit confused.

"Late?"

"Your lights are never on when I get home . . . except tonight." His voice deepened when he asked, "Were you waiting up for me?"

The man could turn the flirty charm on and off like a faucet.

"Don't flatter yourself," she said. "I had a little caffeine tonight."

"In the class." He nodded. "So how did it go?"

She released her sigh this time, unable to hold in her concern about Millie's hopeless optimism. Hopeless optimism? Now there was an oxymoron.

"Sounds like a story here," George surmised. "Come over and tell me about it. I was about to fix my after-shift snack. I'll feed you, too."

She was pretty sure he wouldn't burn anything . . . except maybe her if she got too close. "It's late."

"You just said you had too much caffeine. Come on. I have herbal tea." He reached for her hand but got Harry instead and tugged on it.

She had to follow him.

His own walkout basement was decorated as more of a rec room than a family room. A pool table took up half of the space, with a pub table and chairs pulled near it. On the other side, a big screen TV held center court in front of a sectional, leather couch. It was a man's fantasy room in which he could watch sports and play and scratch himself without having to worry about the disapproval of a wife or girlfriend. From his basement alone, Kim figured George was probably as commitment phobic as she.

Her nerves settled down a bit. She followed him upstairs. The kitchen was more homey and functional than hers. Rich red walls contrasted sharply with the white cabinets and gleaming countertops. Appliances, the built-ins as well as the smaller ones that lobbied for space on the counter, were state of the art.

"Nice," she said. "You actually use your kitchen?"

"You don't use yours?" he asked around the refrigerator door while he rummaged inside. Over his broad shoulder, she could see that it was full of food, not just the beer she would have thought prerequisite for a bachelor.

"No, I do. I just thought . . ."

"That because I'm single and a guy that I would need your bachelor survival course?" He lifted a brow as he set the tea kettle on the stove. Then he set about slicing and dicing the vegetables he'd pulled from the crisper.

Why had he teased her about private lessons if he already knew how to cook? She wasn't about to ask him that, though. She didn't want to remind him of the flirting.

"Don't worry. I won't poison you with my food," he promised. "I did all of the cooking while I was married."

"All of it?" she asked, coloring her voice with skepticism. "Why would any woman divorce a man who'd cooked every meal?"

"Why do you assume *she* divorced *me?*" he retorted.

Kim's lips curved into a begrudging smile. "You're right. I shouldn't assume."

He shrugged. "You were right. She did divorce me. Hated my shift. Hated my career," he said dismissively, as if it hadn't mattered. But Kim could hear the echo of old pain in his voice even though he hid it well under nonchalance.

"And you did all the cooking?" she asked, still unable to comprehend such a man. Her fiancés had been the type who'd expected to be waited on, not wait on anyone else. The former Mrs. Fowler must have *really* hated his job.

"Yes," he maintained. "I was the better cook. My mama taught me well."

"Don't let Millie hear you say that," she cautioned. "The whole reason the class started—"

"Was for her sons," he finished. "Theresa told me."

Theresa. He'd already gotten on a first name basis with the traitor, but then Theresa was Hilltop's welcome wagon. She hadn't invited Kim to participate, saying that she'd scare away the new residents rather than welcome them. Well, she hadn't scared George away . . . even after he met Harry.

He was quick as well as comfortable in the kitchen. In no time, she had a cup of tea and half a Western omelet in front of her where she sat at the breakfast bar. She lifted the fork he'd placed beside her plate and cautiously sank it into the eggs. No puff of smoke rose from them, as they had from Mr. Lindstrom's when she'd tested his. Her stomach churned at just the memory of that inedible mess. But then it rumbled as the aroma of red, green, and yellow peppers and onions wafted from her plate. She lifted a forkful to her mouth, and the flavors exploded on her tongue. "Mmmm . . ."

George hadn't taken a seat; he stood at the counter across from her. Instead of eating his after-shift snack, he watched her, his dark eyes unfathomable. "Good?"

She nodded, then swallowed, so she could speak. "Your mama did teach you well."

Later, after shoveling in the rest of the omelet, she asked, "Did she also teach you to decorate?" She gestured with the fork she'd licked clean, at the bright crimson kitchen walls.

He grimaced. "No, she did the decorating up here. Got the idea for red from the group she's in."

"What group is that?" she asked.

He lifted a picture from the wall between the kitchen and dining room and showed it to Kim. It was a group of women all garbed in purple with bright, red hats atop their heads.

"She's a member of the Red Hat Society?" Kim asked. No wonder she had such great taste.

He smiled as he looked at the picture, too. "Yeah, they're a fun bunch."

"I know. I belong to a chapter here at Hilltop with Millie and Theresa."

He shook his head. "You're too young."

"I just switched from a pink hat to a red one this year," she said proudly. In fact, Millie and Theresa had presented her with a wide-brimmed, be-feathered one for her fiftieth birthday, when one was able to become an official Red Hat Society member. The hat looked smashing with her little purple suit. Of course, on her birthday, she'd worn a purple hat, used only for birthdays, along with a hot red suit.

"You were only a few years older than me when you taught my gym class in high school," he said. "All the guys fantasized about Miss O'Malley."

Her face heated as she remembered overhearing a Miss O'Malley comment or two. Then she almost asked him if he'd had fantasies, but she resisted the temptation. Like she should have resisted joining him for his snack. She slid off the stool and stood. "I really need to head home . . ."

"And I bet they still do . . ." he said softly, just under his breath.

Although she chose to ignore his comment, she heard him. And a little thrill raced through her. "Thanks," she said, a bit breathlessly, as she headed toward his door. "For the omelet . . . and the tea."

Not the compliment. She was determined to ignore that. But she had to get away from him, from the temptation that was quickening her pulse and heating her skin. She excused her reaction because it was late. And she was tired.

All she had to do was open his side door, slip out of his garage, and walk a few short steps to her side door. Then she'd be safe. As she pulled open the door, his hand caught the top, holding it shut.

"You forgot something," he said, his deep voice rumbling close to her ear as his warm breath blew across the sensitive skin of her neck. She fought against the shiver teasing her nerve endings.

Was he going to kiss her? She hardly knew him; she'd have to hurt him if he tried anything. Then he pressed something cold and hard into her hand.

"You forgot Harry," he said, before opening the door for her.

She glanced at him over her shoulder as she stepped into the dimly lit garage. Amusement danced in his dark eyes, tempting her to pull the trigger. He deserved at least one welt for scaring her not once . . . but twice.

But she wasn't about to admit that he'd done that . . . to him . . . or herself.

"Goodnight," he called after her, as she fled to the safety of her condo. But it didn't feel safe . . . with only a wall between them. He was much too close.

*M*om, I hope you're happy," Mitchell grumbled as he staggered through the door. "I drove over here with my eyes closed."

She ignored the anxious little flip of her heart. "Well, the important thing is that you got here in one piece," she said, pulling him toward the kitchen.

"Too bad there's a squirrel that won't be able to say the same—"

"You hit a squirrel!" she exclaimed, slapping his arm. "Mitchell—"

"I'm kidding. It's too dark yet for squirrels. They're still sleeping, like I should be." Instead he was all dressed for work, well, but for his tie. That was undone, like half the buttons on his shirt. But he wore his suit jacket and pants. His hair, however, needed to be brushed and trimmed.

Millie shook her head even as a smile tugged at her lips. He was just so darned cute.

He closed his eyes again and sniffed the air. "Where's the coffee?"

"You're making it," she said, steeling herself to resist the temptation to help. "You're here to do your home-work."

She hadn't trusted him to do it alone in his apartment. If he bothered to try, he might have set off the sprinklers in the ceiling of the converted warehouse space.

"Mom, I have to go to work—"

"That's why you're here so early," she reminded him. "So you better get fixing that coffee—"

He whirled away from the kitchen and headed back down the hall.

"Mitchell!" She figured he was heading back for his car, then his bed. But instead he tromped down to the basement.

"I'm not suffering alone," he griped, stepping on the chip bag which popped and crunched as the chips exploded over the carpet. He slipped on the foil package, grinding the chips into crumbs.

Millie bit her bottom lip. She'd forgotten about that bag. After the class, she'd been too tired to come down-stairs and clean again. Obviously Steven had just stepped over it and continued to the bedroom, like Mitchell was now doing.

She chased after him. "Shhh . . . don't wake him up. He doesn't have to be at work—"

Over his shoulder, Mitchell threw her a look, his dark eyes narrowed with disgust. "Until nine. I know." But then he swung the bedroom door open with such force that it banged against the wall. He hit the switch, flooding the room with light. "Hey, sleepyhead. Time to rise and shine."

Steven, buried under a pile of blankets, shifted against the pillows, muttering a curse word and, "Go away . . ."

Chips clinging to the soles of his shoes, Mitchell grabbed one of the four posters and leapt onto the bed, jumping up and down. "Get up, get up, get up!"

Millie opened her mouth to protest Mitchell's childish antics, but all that emanated from her throat was a laugh.

"Mom!" Steven exclaimed, sounding more irritated with her than his brother, as he sat up and blinked bleary eyes. Puffy dark circles rimmed them.

Guilt nipped at Millie, making her wince. Her oldest wasn't sleeping well. This wasn't his bed, and he undoubtedly missed his wife. The guilt quickly evaporated. She was doing the right thing. "Get up," she echoed Mitchell's sentiment. "You two have homework to do."

Steven sank back into the bed and pulled his pillow over his face. But the feathered filling didn't muffle his curses.

"You're not too old for me to get out the soap," she warned him before heading for the stairs. If not for them both having to leave for work soon, she would have taken out the vacuum and sucked up the chip mess before it ground any deeper into the plush, tan carpeting.

But she didn't have time; she'd just have to push the mess out of her mind for now.

"Come on!" she yelled back at the boys. "I'm dying for coffee."

And a short while later, as she choked on the grounds Mitchell had brewed, she suspected it might kill her. Drinking his coffee had the same effect as licking a cat; she couldn't get the tickling out of the back of her throat.

Steven, in a ratty old T-shirt and loose, gray sweatpants, stood by the stove, blindly pushing a spatula around a pan.

"Honey, those should be done by now," Millie remarked, just as the smoke alarm emanated an ear-piercing screech.

"What do I do?" Steven asked, lifting his shoulders.

Millie picked up a dishtowel, swinging it around the air to dispel the thick smoke. Then she pushed Steven aside to flip on the fan above the stove as she carried the pan to the sink. Steam rose as she poured water over the blackened eggs.

She bit the inside of her cheek, quelling her sigh of disappointment. Even though they'd done poorly in the class, she'd chalked that up to inexperience. And she'd set up the early meeting with Mitchell so that she could give them another chance to prove they had the aptitude to learn.

"See, Mom," Steven said, "it's hopeless."

She shook her head. "Honey, you're half asleep, and this is only your second try. You'll get it," she promised him and herself.

"Sure," Mitchell said, his handsome face earnest as

he tried to be supportive. "You'll get better. You'll be making eggs for Audrey and Brigitte in no time."

Steven sighed. "Give it up. How many times do I have to tell you guys—"

Millie left the pan in the sink to turn around and take Steven's hand. She squeezed it, reassuring him, "You'll patch this up. Just give her a call."

He lifted his chin, which was starting to double. "If she wants me back, she'll call me."

Darn it, he had his father's stubborn pride. Okay, maybe it was a bit hers, too. "Steven—"

He pulled his hand from hers. "I'm going to take a shower now. Since I'm up, I'll go in to work early."

Mitchell widened his eyes. "Really? Eight-thirty?"

Steven didn't take the bait, just shoved past him to head downstairs. Finally Millie released her pent-up sigh. "This is so hard . . ."

Mitchell wrapped an arm around her shoulders. "Don't worry, Mom. He'll come around."

Thankfully Mitchell had inherited her hopeless optimism. She nodded. "Right. We're not giving up."

Mitchell lowered his voice. "No, but he has."

That was what she was afraid of, that and the mess the boys had left in the kitchen. She glanced around at the coffee grounds and eggshells and egg white strewn around the countertop. Mitchell squeezed her shoulders again. "Wish I could stay to help clean up," he said, insincerely, "but I have that early meeting. Can't miss it—" He was already halfway to the door.

"Mitchell!"

"Really, Steven needs the homework more than me. Let him clean up."

But Millie had already left the crumbs downstairs. She couldn't leave the mess in the kitchen, too, and not be able to concentrate on Kim's class. She glanced at her watch. Kim's class was due to start in thirty minutes.

She sighed and reached for the faucet and wondered where she could sign up for that how-not-to-mother-your-children-for-the-rest-of-your-life class.

# Chapter Nine

"Marrying a man is like buying something you've been admiring for a long time in a shop window. You may love it when you get it home, but it doesn't always go with everything else in the house."   —*Jean Kerr*

Theresa walked into the kitchen and dropped her house keys on the counter. For once her muscles weren't aching and protesting her every movement as they usually did following one of Kim's aerobics classes. Kim had been off her game today.

She'd been late . . . and sleepy. And Millie, who usually vigorously followed every routine with her innate passion and dedication, had been distracted and out of sync. The bachelor survival course hadn't gone that late the night before, not late enough for them to be so tired.

Then there'd been the gossip that Theresa had overheard from the back of the class. Between pants for breath, probably more from excitement than exertion, Mrs. Ryers had spread rumors about Millie walking all wet out of Charles's bushes and Kim having clandestine rendezvous, while skimpily dressed, with strange men on her patio in the wee hours.

Usually only half of what the old busybody said was ever true, but it was still more than Theresa knew. She sniffed back a little disappointment. These were her closest friends. She wanted to know what was going on with them, but they'd left the community center before Theresa could head them off at the pass. Oh, no, she'd been inadvertently absorbing the jargon from Wally's western marathons. She'd have to make sure he turned the volume down, or got one of those earplug things so she couldn't hear them at all. Because it looked like all she would have for company for the rest of the day was Wally and his ever-running TV.

After the class, Kim had dashed off as if training for a marathon, which she very well could be. And Millie had been on her usual mission of marriage repair for her son. They had both passed on their standing after-class coffee/herbal tea date, ditching Theresa, leaving her alone. She sniffed again.

The paper rustled and Wally peered blearily over the top of the crumpled page. "You're home early."

"You're up," she said, letting him hear her surprise.

"Barely," he admitted. "You didn't leave a pot of coffee going."

Like she usually did. Since she'd switched back to caffeinated, it was no wonder he looked like an alcoholic suffering withdrawal. His hair was standing on end and pillow creases had left haggard lines in his face. Nothing was left of the vital, young man she'd married so long ago.

She turned away from him and glanced over to the

counter where the black and stainless steel coffeemaker sat empty. "Why didn't *you* make some?"

His face flushed red, and he sputtered, "But . . ."

"Homework," she reminded him. "You were supposed to make coffee and eggs this morning." But he hadn't even been up when she'd left. "Like you learned last night. You didn't forget already?"

"I'm just taking that class to help Millie with the situation with her son." His tone was doubtful, as if he was beginning to realize she'd had another motive for getting him to join.

"So? It wouldn't hurt you to learn something new." She'd thought her irritability was courtesy of the caffeine. But she doubted that now. It was courtesy of this man to whom she was married. This stranger.

She needed her friends. Until Wally's retirement, Theresa would have never guessed that a woman could be married and still be lonely.

Hand shaking, she reached for the carafe and held it under the faucet to fill with water. But strong fingers closed over hers.

"Let me," Wally said, taking the pot from her hand.

She looked up at him, and his green eyes, once so bright with intelligence and energy, held a faint glimmer of that former brightness instead of the bleary fog that had filled them since his retirement. She sputtered, "But . . ."

"I remember how," he insisted, but he stared at her instead of the pot, which overflowed with water.

She wasn't sure if he was talking only about making coffee . . . or something else.

Millie fidgeted as she waited on the front porch of her son's house. She knew there was a spare key hidden in the hollowed-out newel post at the bottom of the steps. If she tipped it, the post would open on a hidden hinge and reveal the key and she could let herself in.

If Steven were still living in the house, she might have. But things were different now. Steven was as much a guest in his home as Millie was.

She had "dropped by," hoping to help both her son and daughter-in-law. Except that no one was home, so she waited outside with a casserole bowl in her hands. She should have called first, and she would have except that every time she had, Audrey had found an excuse for her not to visit. Millie had thought that was all they were, excuses, because Audrey didn't want to hear Millie pressuring her to take Steven back. Undoubtedly she got enough of that from Brigitte.

But now Millie realized her daughter-in-law had probably been telling the truth; she was too busy for visitors. So busy that she wasn't even home. Millie considered leaving the casserole on her doorstep like she'd done for Charles in those months that she'd thought his wife had died.

"Mom?" Audrey yelled with the exasperation of someone who'd called her more than once.

Millie turned toward where her daughter-in-law stood next to her car in the driveway. She hadn't even heard her drive up. Kim claimed the memory was the first thing to go, but maybe it was the hearing. However, at her last check-up her doctor had declared Millie's hearing perfect.

Audrey wore scrubs, in that universal green that was a mix between sage and pastel aqua. Her hair struggled free of the elastic band holding it in a haphazard ponytail. Wisps of blond framed her face, highlighting the dark circles beneath her eyes. She didn't look any less miserable than Steven. Despite what he believed, Millie thought there was hope for a reconciliation.

"Mom?" Audrey said again, in a questioning manner . . . either of her presence or her distracted state of mind.

"I knew you were starting your internship, so I brought something by that you or Brigitte can heat up for your dinner."

"Why are you standing outside with it?" Audrey asked. "You know where the key is."

Millie shrugged, unwilling to admit how uncomfortable she was now in her son's house. "I just got here," she maintained. It wasn't exactly a lie; she had no idea how long she'd stood on the porch.

"You looked like you were a million miles away," Audrey said, as she stepped around Millie to unlock the front door, then pushed it open. "Come in," she said, stepping into the living room.

Millie had rarely been in this room; it was the place for receiving strangers, through the front door. Family walked through the garage and down the hall to the kitchen. This room, with its sterile white walls and light beige carpeting, didn't even look lived in. While Millie respected the cleanliness of white walls and the floral couches, she wanted to feel at home in her son's house . . . for however much longer it might be his house.

"So how is everything going?" Millie asked.

Audrey turned and studied her through narrowed eyes, undoubtedly gauging her sincerity. "Good. I'm interning at St. Mary's, in the ER, so it's busy. It's interesting." She dropped the forced cheerfulness with a sigh and admitted, "Exhausting."

Millie hadn't needed Audrey's confession to figure that out. She put her free arm around her daughter-in-law's shoulders. "Ah, honey . . ."

"It's not that I don't love it," Audrey hastened to explain. "Because I do. I know this is what I want to do . . ."

"But?"

"It's harder than I thought it would be."

"I'm sure it is. But you're a smart, strong woman. You'll handle it just fine, Audrey."

"That's what I keep telling myself," Audrey said, followed by a little self-deprecating chuckle. "I don't think I'm listening, though."

"You and Steven have that in common. He didn't listen when you said you needed help."

"Mom," Audrey's tone cautioned Millie to back off.

Millie had made that mistake before, when she sensed there were problems in their marriage and didn't want to interfere. "Audrey, you don't have to do this alone."

"I told you already that I appreciate it, but I don't want *your* help." But even as she said it, she took the casserole bowl from Millie's hands.

Millie followed her into the kitchen that she'd helped decorate with granny apple green walls and an apple border. Unlike the plain living room, this room was bright and cheerful. "I wasn't talking about *me.*"

Although she did intend to help.

"Steven?" Audrey snorted. "Like that's going to happen."

Millie hoped it would.

"He didn't help me when I asked," Audrey reminded her, "why would he now?"

"Because he can."

Audrey turned away from the butcher-block counter where she had set the casserole and lifted a dark blond eyebrow. "What?"

Honesty forced Millie to admit, "Well, he can make coffee and eggs. But it's a start. He's taking a class on cooking and housekeeping."

Audrey's green eyes widened and her mouth fell open. "He is?"

Millie wasn't about to share the name of the class with her daughter-in-law. She didn't want to give her any ideas.

"Where is he taking this class?" Audrey asked, skepticism heavy in her voice.

"At Hilltop's community center."

"So this is your idea?" Audrey answered her own question with a nod, then added another, "You're teaching it?"

"With Kim and Theresa's help."

Audrey shook her head. "Mom, you're so sweet to try. But you're putting in all the effort, not him."

"He's taking the class, Audrey."

"Why?"

She'd rather not answer than respond honestly to that question, that his brother had goaded him.

Audrey pounced on her hesitation. "So he's not taking it for me? For our marriage?"

"He hasn't admitted it," Millie confessed, "but I'm sure he is." Or at least the hopeless romantic in her was certain.

"It's going to take more than coffee and eggs for me to ask him to move back home, Mom."

And Audrey hadn't even tasted his ground-laden coffee and eggshell omelet. "We're going to teach them more than that," Millie promised, and she was determined to make sure that they actually learned.

"Them?"

"We have a whole class of . . ." She caught herself from saying bachelors, which wasn't accurate anyway. Not all of them were. Yet. Millie had an uneasy feeling that Wally might be in the same situation as Steven soon, about to be kicked out of his home.

Guilt nagged at Millie for having skipped the after-aerobics gabfest with Theresa and Kim. Kim hadn't planned on going, either. But Theresa had. She'd seemed anxious to talk, as if she really needed to. Despite his attendance in their class, her impatience with Wally was growing.

"Class of what?" Brigitte asked, as she joined her mother and grandmother in the kitchen. She tossed her backpack on the floor, where it toppled over.

"Guys," Millie said. "We're teaching them to cook and clean and do other household chores."

Brigitte's dark eyes brightened with hope. "And Dad's in it?"

"Yes," Millie said, giving her granddaughter a quick, greeting hug, "he's taking the course."

"That's great!" the teenager exclaimed, excitement bubbling out of her. "Then he can come home—"

Audrey shook her head. "That's not for you to decide. That's between me and your—"

"Father," Brigitte interrupted, her pretty face pulled into a sulky pout. "I know. You keep saying that."

"Your grandma brought us dinner," Audrey said, pointing to the casserole bowl, probably hoping to distract her daughter from an argument. "We won't be able to eat it until we get home again. We have to go, Mom. I have to drop Brigitte at practice, then do some studying."

From the clothes piled on the dining table, either dirty ones that had really overflowed the hamper, or clean ones that hadn't been folded and put away yet, Millie surmised that Audrey had more than studying that needed to be done. "I can stay here and take care of some things for you . . ."

"That's nice of you to offer," Audrey said, seeming to choose her words carefully, "but . . ."

She didn't have to say it again. She didn't want Millie's help. Millie nodded. "Okay, then. But let's plan on getting together another day, a girls' night out. We can go shopping or to a movie."

Brigitte nodded and sniffled, on the verge of tears again. The teenage years were emotional enough without her parents having problems.

Problems. That was all Millie would consider it. She

wouldn't even think about how this could end. She wouldn't let it end, not even if she had to teach the class seven nights a week.

But would it be enough? As she hugged her granddaughter and daughter-in-law goodbye, she thought about what Audrey had said. Maybe it wasn't that the eggs and coffee weren't enough to get Steven moved back home. Maybe she meant that the classes wouldn't help what was wrong between them.

But Millie couldn't consider that a possibility. The classes *had* to help. She wouldn't give up until they did. When Millie was done with him, Steven would give Martha Stewart a run for her money.

And Audrey a run for her heart.

Chapter Ten

"Positive reinforcement is hugging your husband when he does a load of laundry. Negative reinforcement is telling him he used too much detergent."   —*Dr. Joyce Brothers*

*M*artha Stewart probably didn't do laundry. No doubt she sent that out. Maybe that's what Millie should have advised her class to do.

The thuds and pounding of an uneven load in the washer echoed off the walls of the utility room in the community center basement. Water rushed and suds foamed, bubbling up beneath the top cover of the rattling and shaking machine. It knocked against the dryer next to it, which rubbed against the machine on its other side. Four sets of washers and dryers were lined up along one wall of the big, square room with its white laminate walls and fluorescent lights. Only one washer thrashed around, the one her sons were using.

"Which one of you loaded it?" she demanded. They stood behind her in the doorway.

"Mitchell put the stuff in," Steven, always the first to confess, said. "I put in the detergent."

"I think you used more than I directed," Millie said, pointing to the foam sliding down the sides of the machine. She rushed forward, bobbing and weaving with the machine as it thrashed around. Unable to reach the controls, she leaned against the foamy front and fumbled with the dial, pushing it in to shut down the cycle. The washer shuddered once, then again, before subsiding onto the cement floor like roadkill in its death throes.

The suds soaked through her knit shirt and pants, reminding her of the night she wound up in Charles's sprinklers. "Why didn't you shut it off?" she asked, patience wearing thin.

Now she knew why she hadn't bothered teaching them household chores before; it wasn't that she was too old-fashioned or preferred doing it herself. She just didn't possess the necessary patience to be a teacher.

"You didn't teach us how," Mitchell said, his brown eyes sparkling with amusement as his mouth twitched into a wide grin, totally unrepentant.

He had her there. She hadn't covered what to do if they overloaded the machine with clothes and soap. Exasperated, she reached through the foam to lift the cover. Bubbles floated up, drifting around the room, while others popped between her fingers, leaving her skin wet and sticky.

"What did you guys put in here?"

At the last class, she'd given each student a laundry bag to fill and bring next time. Before she'd sent the students to the basement to do their washing, she'd given them instructions on how to sort their clothes. She hadn't actually checked to see what they'd brought. So she plunged her hand inside the machine, pulling up jeans and more jeans, which she transferred from the battered washer to the deep utility sink next to it. A shoe dropped free of the soaked clothes, tumbling to the floor where the cleats scratched the wet cement.

"Golf cleats?"

Mitchell shrugged. "The shoes were stinking pretty bad."

She didn't want to think about what the cleats had done to the inside of the washing machine, not to mention the motor. She really shouldn't have included her boys in the group that had gone first. But then she'd thought they would be more likely to remember the instructions if they went immediately after she gave them. Of course, to remember them, they would have had to *listen* to them.

Mr. Lindstrom, with his screeching hearing aid, already had his small load in the dryer, which hummed quietly in the row of machines. And two other groups of men had finished with the washers as well. They'd all gone upstairs for the lessons Kim and Theresa were giving.

This was the third class, on Tuesday of the second week. Some of the students were starting to come along pretty well. Last class, they'd learned how to heat cans of soup and make sandwiches, both cold and hot. And of course they'd covered dusting, one of Millie's favorite chores. The students still struggling were, of course, Mitchell and Steven. They'd even messed up the cold sandwiches, overloading the bread with mayo and pickle juice until it had dissolved into mush.

"You put all this in one load?" she asked, as she unwound a few more dripping pairs of jeans from the washer drum.

"Yeah." Steven sighed. "He's a slob. He dirtied that much stuff in just a couple of days."

"Hey, a few of those jeans are yours," Mitchell protested.

"A few?" Millie asked. "There must be at least ten pair in here."

"Told you he's a slob."

"What'd you do? Put them in with a shoe horn?" Millie asked. Even her damp clothes couldn't cool off her simmering temper. *What am I going to do with you boys?*

The question reverberated inside her head; she didn't dare ask it aloud. She knew what they'd advise her to do, fail them out of the class. Were their little mishaps accidents, or attempts to manipulate her the way she had them?

She wouldn't put anything past them. They were too clever. "Go upstairs," she said. "I'll take care of this."

She could have had them clean up, but they'd take so long that they'd miss Theresa and Kim's lessons on starching and ironing and loading a dishwasher. She hoped her friends were more successful teachers today than she'd been. Laundry lessons had been a mistake. Maybe the whole class was.

Not only wasn't she teaching her sons anything, she wasn't learning what she'd wanted to. She still found it easier to just do things herself. Frustration pounded at her temples. She slammed the lid on the washer, with half the pairs of jeans her sons had packed into it, and tried to push it back into place beside the dryer. Her shoes slipped on the sudsy floor, and her hands slid off the wet front.

If not for strong hands catching her around the waist, she would have fallen onto the cement. As it was she could barely regain her feet; they dangled above the floor as the hands held her up. Her heart pounded as hard as the cleats had against the sides of the washer, knocking her as off balance as the oversized load had the machine.

"Whoa," Charles's deep voice rumbled close to her ear. His hands tightened around her waist for just a moment, until she regained her footing and pulled away. "You're all wet again . . ."

"At least it wasn't my fault this time," she said, her voice shaking almost as much as her body. She had to be cold. Although it was warm outside, the basement was cool, and her clothes were damp.

"It wasn't your fault the *first* time," he reminded her.

Her mind remained as blank as it had since he touched her. "What?"

"It was the cat's."

The cat. That was why she never lied. She couldn't remember fact from fiction. "Yes," she agreed, barely resisting the urge to squirm.

She really should tell him the truth; it wasn't as if she could embarrass herself any more. But then how did she admit to being jealous of a shadow in his living room window?

Jealous? Until this moment, she hadn't even admitted that to herself.

"Are you all right?" he asked, reaching out to touch her cheek. Against her skin, his fingertips were cool and damp from contact with her wet clothes.

She glanced down at herself, at the dark spots of water and the graying foam from the suds liberally dotting her navy blue shirt and khaki pants. "I'm fine," she lied, again. So much for honesty.

A grin creased his handsome face as his gaze traveled down the short length of her. He didn't call her on the lie, but his blue eyes twinkled.

Heat rushed to her face, so she turned away, busying herself with squeezing the excess water and soap from the jeans sitting in the washtub sink. "So what brought you to my rescue?" she asked, trying for humor even though she felt more like crying than laughing.

"Steve and Mitch told me it was my turn and sent me down," he said.

Steve and Mitch? He was already close enough to her sons to shorten their names? How had that happened? More importantly, what had her boys been telling him about her?

"Well, they weren't exactly telling the truth." *Must get that from their mother.* "They should have known it would take me a little while to clean up their mess and for the load to finish. I'm afraid these lessons aren't going as well as I'd planned."

One of those strong hands that had saved her from flattening her face squeezed her shoulder. "Give yourself a break. You're doing great."

She turned back toward him, to narrow her eyes skeptically. "Great? I don't think so."

"I made breakfast the other morning," he bragged, lifting his chin with pride.

"You already knew how to make coffee."

"But I made the eggs without burning them."

"That is great," she said, wishing Steven had had as much success. "I'm glad someone's learning something."

"Your sons will catch on," he encouraged her, then added, "when they start taking it seriously."

And that was the problem in a nutshell. One she hadn't a clue how to solve. Yet.

"I'll be a while here," she sighed. "You can go back up to the kitchen. You don't want to miss Theresa and Kim's instructions."

"I just finished with Theresa's starching and ironing lesson," he said, then referred to Kim's lesson, "I already know how to load a dishwasher."

"Another skill, like your coffeemaking one." Did he really need this class? And if not, why had he signed up?

"Yes," he agreed, "one born of necessity. There are some things you have to learn for yourself. I wish I'd had your class back then, in my single days." He sighed. "Would have saved a set of dishes and more glasses than I can count."

A smile teased her lips. "So your self-taught method was trial and error," she surmised.

"A lot of error," he admitted, with that adorable self-deprecating grin that creased his bearded face.

"Too bad that's also how I'm teaching this class," she said, sighing. "With a lot of error."

"Stop being so hard on yourself," he said, touching her cheek again. This time his fingers lingered, softly stroking her skin. "Like I said, you're doing great."

Millie's breath caught in her lungs, which her heart battered with its frantic beating. Charles's gaze slid away from hers and focused on her mouth. Then his head started to dip.

Someone called her name down the stairwell. "Millie!"

A growl burned in her throat, an emphatic, frustrated *No.* But she held it in, with her trapped breath. Her *no* wasn't for Charles but for whoever had stopped him from what he'd been about to do.

Kiss her?

She'd never know now. He stepped back, standing a few feet from her by the time Theresa rushed into the room. "Millie, you better come quick. Kim's about to take Harry to your boys."

Millie considered letting her. Mitchell and Steven deserved a few welts. "I'll be up in a little while. I have to clean up this first."

"They left a mess here, too?" Theresa asked, blowing out an exasperated breath as her gaze scanned the wet room.

"I'll take care of this," Charles offered, reaching for the mop sitting in a bucket near the floor drain.

"No, you don't need to do that," Millie protested, but Theresa had her arm, tugging her toward the door.

"It's a mopping lesson," Theresa said, justifying Charles's help.

But Charles handled the mop efficiently, pushing the water and fizzing soapsuds toward the drain. It was another skill he already had. What skill had she just missed out on experiencing because her sons were causing more trouble?

Maybe it was time to let them manipulate her into what they wanted. "Is it worth it?" she asked Theresa as they climbed the stairs to the kitchen.

Theresa shook her head. "Men? No."

"I'm talking about my sons."

"We haven't talked, really talked for a while," Theresa said.

"We will," Millie assured her. "But about Steven and Mitchell, I'm beginning to think I'm wasting my time."

"Do you want Steven to get a divorce?"

"Of course not."

"Do you want him to continue living with you?"

"No."

"And what about Mitchell? Want him to stay a bachelor the rest of his life?"

"No."

"Then this class is worth it."

$\mathcal{J}$f she kept on feeding everyone, Millie would run out of storage containers. Soon. But since Charles had cleaned up after her boys, he deserved a treat. She grasped the plastic bowl tightly as she walked purposefully up the drive to his condo, past the car the unknown woman had used last week to drive away from Charles's place.

She was back.

But Millie wasn't hiding in the bushes this time. *She*

was the woman Charles had almost kissed just a little earlier that night. Even though it had been a while since she'd been kissed, she remembered how a man looked when he was about to do it, the flare of interest and passion in his eyes.

That wasn't why she'd walked the short distance between her condo and his; she didn't want to realize the promise of that kiss. Or that was what she kept telling herself. *Liar.*

But she did want to thank him . . . for cleaning up and putting up with her sons' nonsense. What had they talked about with him? How had they gotten so friendly that he'd shortened their names? Had they talked about *her?*

Her concern wasn't due to embarrassment. Not anymore. She'd moved far beyond that. But if someone were to talk to Charles about her, she preferred it was someone who actually *knew* her, like Theresa or Kim. Or any of the other Red Hot Hatters of Hilltop. Her sons knew her only as a mother; her friends knew her as Millie, the woman. The complete person.

She climbed the wide brick steps up his porch to the arched front door. As she reached for the doorbell her hand trembled. Should she do this? Should she interrupt his visit with the blonde? If she wanted to learn more about Charles, for instance who the woman was, she had to. So she quickly pressed the button.

Barely a second passed before the door opened, not nearly enough time for Millie to run away and dodge behind the bushes. Just enough time for her to entertain the notion.

"I thought I saw you walking up," Charles said, his handsome face creased with that now-familiar grin.

"I was just bringing you this," she said, holding out the storage container.

"More pie?" he asked, his blue eyes alight with hopefulness as he took the plastic bowl from her hands, his fingers brushing hers.

That little electric current flowed from the tips of her fingers up her arm . . . almost to her heart, if she wasn't careful. She shook her head. "Sorry, just oatmeal raisin cookies."

"I'm sure they're just as good, since you made them," he complimented her.

"Since you and my sons are so enamored of that pie, I'm going to have to teach you how to make it."

If she continued teaching. After tonight, she wasn't so sure. Not only had the boys flooded the utility room, they'd done the same to the kitchen and each other with the sprayer from the sink. Millie had cut the class short, giving laundry as homework and a stern lecture to her sons.

Okay, it hadn't been that stern. She didn't want them to quit; they were her only reason for teaching it.

Or were they?

Charles flashed that grin again, and she accepted that her sons weren't her only reason. "So we'll be making apple pie next class?"

She shook her head again, tumbling her curls around her face. She resisted the urge to brush them back; she didn't want to fuss with her hair in front of Charles.

"Oh, I don't think anyone's ready for baking yet," she

said. "Maybe after a few more classes." If she made it that long. It was ironic that she was the one struggling to survive the bachelor's survival course.

"Come in," he said, stepping back from the doorway and gesturing his arm wide for her to enter. The two-story foyer was aglow with light streaming through the tall, arched windows, even though the sun would set soon. Beneath their feet the polished oak floor gleamed. He added, "Maybe I can persuade you to change your mind."

About what?

She reminded herself, as well as him, when she said, "You have company. I don't want to intrude. I only wanted to drop off the cookies to thank you for helping clean up. And to apologize."

"Apologize?" he asked, his tone echoing the shock widening his eyes. "For what?"

"I'm sure you expected more from this class." She couldn't truly be sure of that, though. She had no idea what he'd expected from the class, but she felt safe assuming that it wasn't clean-up duty. "But my sons are so disruptive—"

"Millie," he said, reaching out with his free hand to grasp her shoulder. "You have nothing to apologize for."

"That's sweet of you," she said, warmth spreading through her chest, "but—"

He squeezed her shoulder, then drew her closer, against him and just inside his front door. His eyes flared with that certain look again as he said, "I find I'm getting *more* out of the class than I expected."

Millie's breath caught and held, burning in her lungs

as Charles lowered his head. His breath touched her lips, then . . .

Someone cleared her throat. Millie's first thought was that it was Kim, in her role as neighborhood watch captain. But then she remembered his company.

How had *he* forgotten?

Millie blinked her eyes open, embarrassed she'd closed them in anticipation of a kiss she'd likely never receive. Heat rushed to her face as she turned toward where the young, blond woman stood in the foyer behind Charles.

Amusement, not jealousy, sparkled in the woman's blue eyes, and a smile lit her beautiful face. "Sorry," she said, "I didn't mean to interrupt. I was just leaving . . ."

"Wait," Charles said.

Confusion furrowed Millie's brow. "No," Millie said, "I'm the one who should be leaving—"

"No, really, I should," the young woman insisted.

Charles's deep chuckle echoed off the walls of the foyer. "Nobody's leaving until I introduce you two. I've been looking forward to doing that. Millie, this is my niece, Victoria Moelker, esquire. And Vic, this is Millie, my neighbor and the instructor for the bachelor's survival course."

Victoria chuckled, the rumble of her voice amazingly deep for such a slim, feminine-looking woman. She wore a suit, but it was a skirt/jacket combination in a deep blue that complimented her stunning eyes, which were no doubt a Moelker legacy. "Too bad you didn't take a class like that when I was growing up," she said, but there was no criticism in her smile. "We might have eaten better."

He popped the lid open on the container and extended an oatmeal cookie toward her. "Try this. You'll see we definitely would have."

She obliged and took a bite, then murmured around the mouthful, "Mmmm . . ."

"She approves," Charles translated for Millie.

"She loves," Victoria corrected him. "You see, Uncle Charles took over raising me when I was ten. We struggled a bit domestically." She looped her arm around his shoulders. "But he was great about everything else. And still advises me when it comes to our practice."

"It's your practice now," he chided her.

"Because Ellen made you retire," she said, her pretty mouth twisting with obvious disapproval of his ex-wife. "But seriously, I have to go. I have a mountain of paperwork waiting at home." She extended her hand to Millie, her shake firm and purposeful. "It was nice meeting you, Millie. Goodbye, Uncle Charles," she said, and as she hugged him she sneaked a couple more cookies from the open container. "I'll see you later. Maybe you, too," she said to Millie with a wink.

Charles sighed as she slipped out the door and rushed to her car. "That girl only has one speed. Fast."

"She must have been a handful as a child," Millie said.

Sadness dimmed Charles's usually bright eyes. "She went through so much. Her parents died in a car accident."

"That's why you raised her."

"My brother made me her guardian. I was supposed to raise her. But I think she was the one who made me grow up," he ruefully admitted, flashing his wide grin again. "She was a great kid."

"And a beautiful, charming young woman," Millie said, praising him for his good parenting. Obviously he hadn't needed domestic talents to raise a happy, well-adjusted child.

"She takes after her mother," he said. "My brother was a rascal. He and I treated each other the way Mitchell and Steven do; everything was a competition."

Millie nodded. "I used that to get them both in the class. Now I wish they'd cut it out."

"You'll get through to them."

At the moment, she wasn't as worried about that as she was about Charles getting through to her, straight to her heart. The more she learned about him, the more she liked him. And that was dangerous; she was losing her focus. She wanted her life to be *less* complicated, with more free time, not *more* complicated.

"Come inside," he invited her, gesturing beyond the foyer to the great room aglow with light from the tall, arched windows. Deep, brown leather couches with plump cushions invited her to sit down.

But she shook her head, losing her nerve, too. "It's getting late," she reminded him.

"Do you have a curfew?" he teased.

She laughed, but it sounded disturbingly like a giggle. "I don't, but sometimes Steven thinks I do." He had taken to commenting on her comings and goings, that she was so busy. She doubted that he was as concerned about her overdoing it as he was about her not being available to wait on him.

"Is it nice to have someone living with you again?" he asked.

Striving for nonchalance, she shrugged. "I'd rather he were back home, living with his wife and daughter. And I haven't actually lived alone that long. My dad just moved out last year, when he got married again."

He nodded. "That's about how long I've been alone. Well, except for Buddy."

"Where is Buddy?" she asked, curiously getting attached to the little yippy dog.

"I have to shut him in a bedroom when Victoria's here."

"They don't get along?"

He grinned. "It's probably because they're too much alike, both too hyper."

"How is it that you were alone so long? I thought that Ellen left you while you were in Arizona." Realizing how personal she'd gotten, Millie pressed a hand against her mouth. "I'm sorry. I don't mean to pry."

His blue eyes twinkled. "You're not prying. She moved out before I went to Arizona, right after she went to a class reunion and ran into her old flame."

"She must have really loved him." But Millie couldn't imagine a woman leaving Charles for anyone.

He shrugged. "Probably. After all, she didn't just leave me, but Buddy too." His self-deprecating grin flashed again. "I suspect it was harder for her to leave Buddy."

Millie couldn't miss the bitterness in his tone. Charles

carried scars from his divorce, and even though a year had passed since Ellen had left, Millie wondered if he was ready to move on with anyone yet.

"I have to let Buddy out," he said, "so come inside."

Millie heard the rhythmic pounding from the interior of the condo. Somewhere Buddy was hurling his little furry body against a door. She winced, hoping he wasn't hurting himself.

"I have to go," she said, shaking her head with regret. But her regret wasn't over leaving; it was over Charles not being ready for more than neighborly friendliness.

But then she wasn't ready either, not until the bachelor survival course was over and Steven had returned home to his family and Mitchell didn't need her. Then she could concentrate on what she wanted, once she figured it out . . . because suddenly she wasn't so sure anymore.

# Chapter Eleven

"They shared the chores of living as some couples do—she did most of the work and he appreciated it."
—Paula Gosling

*H*ow can he live like this?" Steven asked, as he and Millie stepped inside Mitchell's loft apartment.

The hardwood floor, what was visible under clothing and discarded pizza boxes, was dull with stains. In the light streaming through the tall windows, dust particles danced. At the other end of the expansive living area, the galley kitchen was cluttered with empty milk cartons and pop cans, the milk glass cupboard doors standing open.

Just a week ago Millie had cleaned the apartment so that the oak floors had gleamed, the windows sparkled, and the kitchen had been neat, inviting guests to sit at the leather stools at the concrete countertop. When it was clean the space, with its exterior brick walls and open ceiling, befit a young professional like Mitchell. Now it once again befit a fraternity house.

A grimace of disgust twisted Steven's mouth. But he really had no room to criticize. Despite the classes, he had yet to pick up the basement himself. The chips would probably still be there if Millie hadn't vacuumed.

"He's a slob," Millie said, surprised at how easy it was to admit now when the words had nearly stuck in her throat the first time. Steven laughed, but she lightly tapped his arm and reminded him, "You are too."

"Mom—"

"You two are not using anything you've learned." But that was the problem; they hadn't learned.

Mitchell's steel door rattled as he fumbled with the lock. Apparently he hadn't worked much later than his brother today. When Steven pulled open the door he nearly fell inside, with the keys stuck in the lock and his briefcase wedged between his knees. "What's this?" he asked, brown eyes widening with surprise.

"An ambush," Steven warned him. "Save yourself. Mom's giving a private lesson."

"Homework." She gestured around the trashed room, then toward the container of cleaning supplies sitting just inside the door. "Get busy."

Her plan had been to sit on the couch and supervise, without lifting a finger, to be a true goddess. She'd even thought about having one of them cook dinner. But her stomach churned when she lifted pizza boxes from the couch, or tried to, as the cheese stuck to the leather.

She wouldn't be able to sit or eat. Not until she cleaned. "Get me the bucket," she told Steven.

"Yeah, I feel like throwing up, too," he remarked.

*M*illie set her hat on the island in the community center kitchen and fluffed her curls out. She loved her red hat, but no matter how wide the brim, her curls poofed out beyond it, and she wound up looking like Annie Hall.

"Why'd you volunteer us for clean-up?" Kim asked Theresa, as the friends each carried a load of dishes into the kitchen. "We do enough of that after class these days."

"I've got this," Millie told them, as she turned on the faucet. "You two don't have to stay."

"We're staying," Theresa insisted, "and we're finally going to talk. That's why I volunteered us."

Guilt flashed through Millie. They were so busy these days that they didn't have as much time to talk as they used to. That was her fault, too. She'd counted on the classes giving her back more of her time, not stealing it all away. "Things have been crazy," she agreed. "So let's talk."

"Like we haven't just done enough of that," Kim said with a smirk.

It was true. They'd talked a lot during the get-together of the Red Hot Hatters of Hilltop. The room echoed with the buzz of all the lively conversation. Several of the women had thanked them for teaching their husbands, sons, or nephews how to make coffee and do laundry and dishes. At least some people considered the class a success.

"It was a great get-together," Millie commented, still basking in the praise of her chapterettes.

"But I didn't get the chance to talk to the two of you,"

Theresa pointed out. A bit of desperation strained her voice as she added, "And I've been trying to do that for days."

"Uh-oh," Kim said with an exaggerated sigh. "We're in trouble now, Millie."

Millie shut off the water and turned from the sink to reach for Theresa's hand. "Oh, honey, what's wrong?"

Theresa shrugged. "I've just . . . missed you guys."

"We've been around," Kim said.

Theresa laughed. "Yeah, I've been hearing rumors. In your aerobics class and again today. Kim, you've been seen with your neighbor in compromising circumstances."

Her cheeks grew a bit pink. "That was one time! So what?"

"I still haven't met him," Millie realized, but from the defensive way Kim acted, she suspected she would, maybe sooner than later.

"You're missing out," Theresa told Millie, with a little sigh. "He's really cute." Then she turned toward Kim. "So you're seeing him now?"

Kim's brown eyes sparkled with mischief as she replied, "Through my window one night. Not since then."

"What?" Millie asked, drawing her brows together in confusion.

"He saw my lights on and wanted to make sure I was okay. There was nothing more to it," she insisted.

Theresa skeptically arched a blond brow.

"Really," Kim maintained. "I haven't even seen him since. We're on different shifts. I haven't been up that late since the night he was on my patio."

"Hmmm, I don't know. You've looked a little tired

lately. I think you've tried to stay up. It's just that as you get older, you need more sleep," Theresa teased.

Kim shot her a mock glare. "Remember which one of us is older."

"I'm trying to remember who it was that always claimed men are too much trouble?"

"You're preaching to the choir here," Kim said. "I don't intend to get anywhere near an altar *ever.* I'm too set in my ways, too independent."

"I wasn't preaching," Theresa insisted. "Just trying to find out what's going on with my friends. It's sad when Mrs. Ryers knows more than I do."

Kim shook her head, but she didn't dislodge her red hat; it perched regally on her head. "She *thinks* she knows more than everyone else."

Theresa's blue eyes twinkled with amusement. "True, but in this case, I think she may be right, because then there's Millie."

Uh-oh, she silently echoed Kim's earlier remark. Both her friends turned on her now. "I've been busy," she reminded them. "With the class."

"With Charles Moelker," Theresa said. "Are you forgetting what your plans are? To be independent?"

"I am independent," she said. "Bruce has been gone five years." Sometimes it felt like more, when she struggled to remember his face. Sometimes it felt like less, when she turned to him in the night, seeking the heat of his body and the security of his arms, but she found only emptiness.

Theresa shook her head. "But your dad just got married last year."

To one of the Red Hot Hatters. Lady Lucky was the

Red Hat name of Millie's stepmother because Barbara always did so well at the slots. She'd done well in love, too, when she'd fallen for Pop.

"So?" Millie knew the point Theresa was trying to make, but she wasn't about to admit it.

"You're used to taking care of a man. That's the *way* you're set in," Theresa pointed out.

"Still not seeing the danger there," Millie said. And now she was lying to her friends. She'd seen the danger the other night, when Charles had almost kissed her then invited her in. "Dad's married off. And I'm hoping to train my boys to take care of themselves."

"And that's why you're looking for someone else," Theresa said, almost as if saying "ah ha" upon finding a suspect in a crime.

Was it a crime to look for someone? To want to spend some time with someone else? Millie doubted it. But Theresa wasn't in the mood to listen. She was in the mood to lecture. Millie suspected her fear wasn't for Millie but that she might lose her friends.

"You *need* someone to take care of, to do everything for," Theresa said, obviously finding Millie's need incomprehensible. She shook her head. "What do you think, Kim?"

Millie turned toward her tall, blond friend, curious to hear her opinion. Kim was usually an uncanny judge of character, if sometimes a bit harsh with that judgment.

Kim, clad in a sleeveless purple suit, shrugged her bare shoulders. "She can't help it. She's been taking care of all the men in her life since her mom died. She was just a kid then; that's all she knows."

"*She*'s also standing right here," Millie reminded them. These were her friends, Millie thought, as irritation gnawed at her nerve endings. "And I'm not a kid anymore. I know what I want."

"So what do you want?" Kim asked her.

"Charles Moelker?" Just his name was Theresa's question.

"What if I do?" Millie turned the inquisition on them. "What if I want to be with someone? Yeah, I'm not a kid anymore. But I know you're never too old to find love. My dad and Barbara are so happy."

"Do you love Charles?" Kim asked, her voice, usually so brash and sassy, soft with concern.

"I don't really know Charles," she admitted to her friends and to herself. Then she added another confession, "But I think I'd like to get to know him better."

Theresa sighed. "Ah, Millie . . ."

"What?"

"You said you wanted to retire your tiara, that you wanted to travel. To have fun."

Millie nodded. "Yes, that's what I said. I haven't changed my mind about that." With each class of the bachelor's survival course it became that much more important to her. "But I never said that I wanted to do that alone."

Theresa squeezed Millie's arm. "Just be careful that you're not looking for someone to take care of again and that you forget what you want."

Millie smiled, feigning confidence for her friends. "Of course I won't. You're worrying for nothing. Like I said, I don't even really know Charles. He and I may want completely different things out of life."

Theresa snorted. "Yeah, he may want a maid."

"If he did, he wouldn't be in the class," Millie defended him.

Kim chuckled. "Oh, I don't know. It might be the perfect place to find one."

"Come on, you two," she said, waving off their concern as she turned back toward the sink. "You're starting to nag."

"Is it working? Are we getting through to you?" Theresa persisted.

"Don't worry. I'm going to whip the class into shape. I'll get my sons trained. Steven reconciled. Mitchell married off. I will retire my tiara. I will travel the world far and wide," she promised them and herself.

"I will never wait on another man," Theresa added, but was she saying it for Millie to repeat or for herself?

Kim must have wondered, too, for she ignored her friend's comment to add a cryptic one of her own. "Just remember this, Millie. It's what I realized as I was nearing the altar. It's easier to do what you want when you're alone."

"Well, I wouldn't know that. I won't be alone until I get Steven moved out."

Maybe she would increase the number of days the class met a week. Not only would it increase the likelihood of the instructions sticking, it would give her an opportunity to get to know Charles better. To see if they did indeed want the same or different things out of life, and if they were ready for more than friendship.

Chapter Twelve

"Man can be chained, but he cannot be domesticated."

—*Robert Heinlein*

*W*hen her kids were in school, Millie had always volunteered to chaperone the field trips. Apparently, she'd forgotten the headaches they'd caused because she'd suggested another one for the class. This was the fifth time the bachelor survival course had met. She'd hoped her sons would have gotten the hang of things by now.

Her temples throbbed as she raised her voice so all the students, gathered just inside the entrance to the grocery store, were able to hear her. Not that they were listening, as Mitchell and Steven's voices rumbled disruptively in the back of the group.

"This is an important lesson," she called out. "You all need to know that when you're cooking, the food isn't automatically set out for you. You have to get the ingredients yourself. And if they're not in the refrigerator, you need to head to the store. So pull out your recipes, grab a cart and make sure you buy all the things necessary to make dinner. Here are a few suggestions to keep in mind. Pick up canned food and wine first, then fresh and frozen last."

The students appeared to listen, as most of them grabbed a cart and headed toward the aisles, of which there weren't many. She'd chosen the local grocery closest to Hilltop for proximity, since they'd all had to drive, and convenience, since its smaller size made it less overwhelming than a supermarket.

Millie did most of her shopping here. She liked the cleanliness of its white and green tiled floors and walls, and although the lighting was soft instead of harsh fluorescent, the store was bright. The meat and produce were fresh, the gourmet selection was extensive, and there was nothing in bulk. Millie resented how so much was sold in bulk nowadays. What was a single person to do with all the excess? Her freezer and cupboards were already too full. For its single-sized portions, Millie preferred this grocery.

"Where's your recipe from?" Kim asked, as she leaned over Millie's shoulder to read the copy from the binder, under its orange tab.

"Where do you think?" Millie teased, turning to smile at her friend.

"Your cooking bible," Kim surmised with a smile.

"*The Red Hat Society Cookbook,*" Millie said with pride. She'd tried every recipe in the book, finding most of them better than the recipes she'd used for years. Like the apple pie. Wouldn't the guys be surprised when she told them the trick to making that . . .

But she wasn't about to start these bachelors-in-training off with dessert. They had to work up to that, by learning to make an entrée first.

"Oh . . . Chicken Thighs in Wine. I love that one," Kim said, smacking her lips together as if ready to eat.

Millie wasn't so certain the students' efforts would be any more edible than their eggs had been. But they had managed the soup and sandwiches at the second class, or most of them had. And last class they'd tackled pasta. Except for Mitchell and Steven, who'd had a stuck-together mess, the rest of the students had done well, so it was time for a greater challenge. She said, "Should be simple."

"And delicious if they do it right," Theresa agreed. Her gaze landed on Wally, who was struggling to free a cart from the clutch of them at the store's entrance. His shirt, a cotton plaid, came untucked from his khakis. "Look at him. He has turned struggling businesses into Fortune 500 companies, but he can't even get a cart loose." She shook her head instead of going over to help him.

Charles did, holding the rest of the carts while Wally pulled the one on the end free. No doubt grocery shopping was another skill Charles already had. Now that Millie knew he'd raised his niece, she understood why he had so many domestic skills, but she didn't understand why he'd enrolled in the class.

He glanced up from his perusal of the recipe, then winked one of those bright blue eyes at her. Millie swallowed the besotted sigh at the back of her throat, reminding herself that they were just neighbors and maybe friends.

Kim bumped her shoulder. "Okay, I get it."

"What?" she asked. She probably wouldn't have understood Kim's comment even if she hadn't been distracted.

"I know," Kim said, "why you're tempted to forget your plans." She nodded her head toward where Charles stood, dressed in his casual gear of faded jeans and white Oxford and still looking as elegant as a movie star. Or a lawyer.

She wouldn't have suspected that as his profession. He didn't come across as aggressive. After all, he hadn't even managed to kiss her yet although he'd tried. Nor did he interrogate; he listened more than he spoke. Obviously he'd not been a trial lawyer.

"I'm not tempted to forget my plans," Millie insisted, then checked to make sure Theresa had wandered out of earshot before adding, "But maybe I could alter them." To include someone.

If he were interested . . . and sometimes she had a feeling he might be. Charles pushed his cart up close to her. "So who's Dame Judy?" he asked, raising his copy of the recipe in the air.

She smiled, not surprised the name would interest him. "Obviously the author of this recipe and a great cook and fellow Red Hat Society member."

"You're the great cook," he praised. "I thought all the recipes we used would be yours."

Her smile widened with pleasure from the compliment. "I'm a great cook because I use these recipes and don't try to concoct my own."

Kim looped her arm around Millie's shoulders. "But she makes them taste ten times better than my best efforts. She's our domestic goddess."

"Domestic goddess?" Charles studied her silently for a moment. Then he nodded in agreement. "That fits perfectly."

"That's her Red Hat name," Kim shared.

"Because you all made me change it when we started the class," Millie reminded her.

"What was it before?" Charles asked.

Heat spread from Millie's heart up to her face, probably turning it as red as the blouse she wore. "It wasn't very interesting . . ." she hedged, flashing Kim a quick warning look.

Kim, in a yellow tracksuit, shrugged and backed away. "I better see where Mr. Lindstrom is."

Charles wasn't leaving. His cart was parked directly in front of Millie. He leaned close. "Come on. Tell me."

She laughed and shook her head. "I couldn't think of anything then. Theresa and Kim came up with the name—Princess Sweet."

"Mmmm . . . because you like sweets or because you're sweet?" His gaze was focused on her mouth now, as if he were thinking about answering his own question.

Millie shivered, and she was nowhere near the freezer section. "Y—you haven't started shopping yet," she said, pointing to his empty cart.

"I shop here all the time," he said, confirming another domestic skill. "I'll find everything. I'm in no hurry. It's not a competition." He stopped to flash a grin, before adding, "Despite what your sons think."

Her sons. She needed to check on them more than Kim did Mr. Lindstrom. The thought had no sooner occurred to her than a crash of tin against ceramic tile reverberated throughout the store. She winced, hoping it was Mr. Lindstrom who'd caused the commotion, but her sons' voices rumbled from the direction of the crash.

She headed toward the canned vegetable aisle, her footsteps slow and hesitant. The situation was as bad as she'd thought. In the middle of aisle seven, her sons stood amid a mess of spilled tin cans. Well, actually, only one of them stood. The other, Mitchell, lay sprawled next to his overturned cart. Chickens, two whole ones instead of the thighs indicated in the recipe, lay beside him.

A bottle of wine was still spinning from the force of the collision, thankfully unbroken. It wound down to a stop, the cork pointing toward Millie. She nearly laughed. Spin the bottle? She wasn't likely to ever get kissed, not with her sons demanding so much of her time and attention.

It was past time to retire her tiara. They had to take the class seriously.

Now.

$\mathcal{J}$'ve had it!" Millie said, resisting the urge to utter the swear words echoing in her mind. Instead of cussing, she had her fingers tight around an ear of each of her sons, dragging them into the condo like she used to when they were younger.

She hadn't had to drag them out of the store; thankfully they had come of their own accord, after picking up the mess they'd made. She'd ranted and raved at them in the store, her cool totally lost. Her face heated again, just remembering her shrill outbursts. But she was through tidying up after them. Hopefully the store owner wasn't too upset, since the grocery was Millie's favorite place to shop.

She stopped in the kitchen, backing Mitchell and Steven against the hickory cabinets so that they couldn't get away from her. She wasn't done yelling yet.

"It was an accident," Mitchell repeated the defense he'd been uttering since she'd come upon him lying on the tile floor amid cans and chickens. "The aisle was narrow, and they had that pyramid of cans right in the middle of it. There was no way to get around it without knocking them over."

"I did," Steven pointed out as he wriggled free of Millie's grasp. "He's the one who made the mess—"

Millie let Mitchell loose, too, then she did the same with her temper. "He's not the one Audrey threw out. You made the mess there, Steven."

Steven gasped in shock at her tone.

But she continued, her anger driving her, as she accused him, "You never helped her around the house. You never even picked up after yourself. The poor girl has enough going on; she doesn't need to take care of you, too. You should be able to take care of yourself. You're almost thirty-six years old, for crying out loud."

"Mom?" Mitchell was the one to ask the question, his tone cautious as he glanced between her and his brother.

Steven was silent, all color drained from his face, leaving him looking pale and old. He leaned heavily against the counter. When he finally spoke, his voice rasped, "So you did start the class for me. You manipulated me. Both of you."

Millie snorted. "I manipulated Mitchell, too. You don't think he needs the class? He can't keep a girlfriend because he's such a slob."

"Mom!" This time Mitchell was indignant, his face flushed with bright color and his dimples nowhere to be seen.

"Come on," she said, no longer charmed by her youngest's boyishness. "Do you really think every one of them—Heather, Tammy, Amy, and the other ones who weren't even around long enough for us to meet—had a problem with your *hours?* They had a problem with *you.* They didn't want to take over for your mother, cleaning up after you like you're a toddler."

A chuckle gurgled out of Steven's throat until she whirled back toward him, then it became a strangled cough.

"And you, yeah, I started this class for you. I had to do something to save your marriage. I promised Brigitte I would try. You're sure as heck not. You haven't done a darn thing to reconcile with Audrey, to make an effort to win back your wife."

"You think a few cooking and cleaning classes will make Audrey take me back?" he asked, clearly disbelieving.

After her conversation with her daughter-in-law, Millie had her doubts that anything would be enough. Steven epitomized the too little, too late scenario.

"I don't know," she honestly admitted. "But if she doesn't, at least you'll be able to take care of yourself."

Before her anger ran out of steam, she forged ahead with another confession. "I don't want to take care of you two anymore. I'm tired of cleaning up after you. You're grown men. It's time you both start acting like it. Take this class seriously, or don't take it at all."

"Mom." Steven was the one to utter her name in shock this time. "This is how you really feel?"

Embarrassed. Aggravated. Those were the emotions she was feeling now. But she sensed they knew that already. She nodded. "If you two weren't going to at least try, why'd you agree to take the class?"

If it were to help each other, as she suspected, they wouldn't admit it, at least not in front of the other. Mitchell confirmed this when he said, "I convinced Steven that we needed to check out Charles since you were interested in him."

"So that's what you've been talking to him about," she realized, as she stepped back, coming up hard against the white side-by-side refrigerator. She leaned against it as her knees weakened. "You've been grilling him." And because of that, they probably knew more about him than she did.

"We have asked him some questions," Steven admitted. "Dad left you with some good investments—"

"So you think Charles is an opportunist?" she asked,

insulted for him. Charles shouldn't have had to endure an interrogation.

"We know better," Mitchell freely conceded, "now that we've talked to him. He's not after your money."

"So what if he was? Do you think I'm so stupid that I'd give it to him?" she asked, insulted for herself.

"No, Mom," Mitchell protested, "you're not gullible. But you seem to like this guy. You dyed your hair."

She hadn't thought they'd even noticed. "I didn't do this for Charles," she told them, patting her cinnamon-colored curls. "I did it for me."

Steven expelled a ragged sigh. "We just wanted to look out for you, Mom."

"So you don't think I can look out for myself?" No matter how many times she'd told them she could. "Or maybe you're going to say the same thing Theresa and Kim have, that I shouldn't get involved with someone that I might need to take care of."

Steven shook his head. "No, Mom. We weren't worried about you taking care of Charles. We were making sure he could take care of you."

Mitchell nodded. "And he can. He was a fairly successful lawyer."

Millie wasn't sure if Charles had told them that, or if they'd found out another way. But she didn't care what they'd learned about Charles. She was the one they didn't know.

They didn't understand that she wasn't the fragile little woman they thought her. She didn't need a man to pay her bills or investigate any noises in the night. She could do that herself. She already did everything else.

It was the *everything else* she was worried about. She didn't want to keep doing all the cleaning and cooking for the men in her life. But with the way she'd just told off her boys, she doubted they would be interested in learning to take care of themselves.

Neither they, nor she, had survived the bachelor survival course.

Chapter Thirteen

"It takes patience to appreciate domestic bliss; volatile spirits prefer unhappiness."

—*George Santayana*

*P*hew," Wally commented, as he set his grocery bag on the granite kitchen counter. "I've never seen Millie mad before."

"It's about time," Theresa said, as she settled into a wicker chair in the breakfast nook. She didn't suffer from Millie's hangup. She had no problem letting Wally do for himself.

The bag rustled as he pulled a bottle of wine from it. "I didn't know she could get that mad," Wally said, awed. "She didn't even have to say anything . . . just the look on her face . . ."

But she had said plenty, too. Theresa's lips curved at the memory of the angry words spilling unchecked from Millie. Then she glanced up and found Wally's gaze intent on her. She hadn't seen him look so thoughtful in a long time.

"You don't have to say anything either," he told her. "I know when you're unhappy."

"So am I?" she asked, calling him on his claim. Since she wasn't a western or the sports page, she doubted he paid enough attention to know anything about her, but because of the class he'd been spending less time watching TV and reading the paper.

He didn't hesitate before nodding. "I think so."

She didn't fight the amused smile from lifting her lips. "It's ironic that you think I'm unhappy. You're the one who's been depressed."

"It's been a struggle to adjust to retirement," Wally admitted with a ragged sigh. "Selling the business totally changed my life."

"Mine, too," Theresa replied vehemently.

"Does my being home all the time cramp your style?" he asked with a teasing lilt to his voice. But his gray eyes were serious, watchful.

Theresa wasn't sure how honest she was prepared to be. He didn't seem as depressed as he'd been. But if he was getting better, she didn't want to cause a setback. "I wouldn't call it that . . ."

"What would you call it, Theresa?"

"Like I said, you've been depressed." She swallowed, then added, "You're no longer the man I married."

He nodded. "Of course not. That was a long time ago. I've grown up."

"Grown up or grown old?" she asked quietly.

"Older," Wally conceded. "Maybe wiser. We all grow older, Theresa, even you."

She nodded in ready agreement. "Yes, we all grow

older." She wasn't fighting age. She was accepting it gracefully and wearing it the same way: today with a blue silk, sleeveless blouse and linen capris.

"But you're still as beautiful as the day I met you," he said, walking over to join her at the table in the breakfast nook. He settled into the chair across from her and reached across the glass top, brushing her hand with his, as if he wanted to take it into his but didn't dare. He added, "Maybe even more beautiful."

She tipped her lips up into a smile, touched by the brief resurgence of the old charm that gave her a glimpse of the man he used to be. "I can't argue with you about that," she said, patting her hair in mock arrogance.

He chuckled. "But you want to argue with me about something else?"

"We don't *all* grow wiser," she maintained.

"So now I haven't just been depressed but stupid, too?" he asked, no trace of humor in his deep voice now, as his gray eyes darkened with anger. He drew his hand away and leaned back in his chair.

She was as touched by his anger as his charm. Lately he hadn't cared enough about anything to get angry. But then she'd struck him where his retirement had done the most damage, his pride. Shame washed over her; she hadn't meant to hurt him. "You're not stupid, Wally. You're such a smart man. That's why it's so sad . . ."

"What's so sad?" he asked, crossing his arms over his chest defensively.

She didn't want to hurt him, but he was listening to her for the first time in a long time, so she had to take advantage of the opportunity to reach him. After clearing the thickness of emotion from her throat, she answered him softly, "What's so sad is what you've become."

He sighed raggedly. "I don't like it either, Theresa. I can't look in the mirror because I don't know the old man staring back at me. Defeated."

Tears burned Theresa's eyes. He saw it, too. "Defeated? So you've given up?"

"I don't know . . ."

"The old Wally would know. You fixed all those dying businesses. You can fix yourself."

"Is that why you really want me in the class?" Wally asked. "To fix me?"

She borrowed his phrase. "I don't know." Then she added, "I don't know how to *fix* you." She wasn't sure that what was broken could be fixed. Could a man repair his pride once it had been shattered?

"Then what's the point of my learning all this stuff?" he asked, his voice unsteady with emotion. "Am I going to be a bachelor again? Are you so unhappy that you want to leave me, Theresa?"

"I don't want to leave the man I used to know, that I used to love," she said, swiping at the tears that ran unchecked down her face.

"You don't love me?" he asked, tears welling in his gray eyes.

"I don't know you."

Footfalls pounded hard on the asphalt behind Kim. She quickened her pace, her lungs burning as she struggled for breath. Pain traveled up the arches of her feet, radiating in her shins as she exerted more speed, desperate to outdistance her pursuer.

Excitement, not fear, had her heart pumping hard and fast. If she were afraid, she'd stop and confront the man following her, whirling on him with the canister of pepper spray clipped at the waist of her blue running shorts. But she wasn't afraid, not as much as she should be.

If she had any sense . . .

Where had it gone?

She'd been so careful to avoid temptation, shutting off her lights long before his shift ended, stumbling over the cat in the dark so that he didn't have an excuse to come to her door . . . or window again.

But now temptation was chasing her down. And as she'd suspected before, she might not be able to outrun him. Yes, she was far safer flirting with Mr. Lindstrom!

Kim had a bruise on her upper thigh from the old man. Since he didn't drive, she'd played his chauffeur for the trip to and from the grocery store. Despite his age, he'd managed to reach across the console between them and squeeze her leg a few times, nearly making her veer into a ditch. He might be old, but the man was still strong. Too strong.

A giggle tickled her throat from the memory of fending off Mr. Lindstrom's clumsy advances as well as this ongoing chase. She could hear him breathing in loud pants. Then she could feel him, as his breath blew across the back of her neck.

"Gotcha," he gasped, as his fingers closed around her arm, drawing her up short.

Off balance from the momentum of her run, she spun

around and fell into his arms. Hating the weak gesture and how strong and hard his chest felt against hers, she mock-threatened, "I'm a cop's daughter. He taught me self-defense moves that could put you in the hospital."

His face so close to hers, George chuckled. "I believe you. But since you haven't pepper sprayed me already or used Harry to shoot me, I think I'm safe."

She could argue with that. He was everything but safe. Just being close to him made her feel reckless and out of control. She hated that feeling. "Never underestimate me," she warned him as she pulled away.

"After how hard I had to run to catch you, I would never make that mistake," he promised, his breath still coming fast and hard.

A smile teased her lips, and she found herself flirting with him. "You only caught me because I slowed down."

He laughed; it rumbled deep in his chest. He wore a dark blue tank top that showed off his muscular arms, while sweatpants cut off just above the knee showed off his strong calves. "I'm not going to disagree with you," he said.

"You're not?"

He shook his head, sending sweat trickling from his graying temples down his chiseled cheekbones. The man was hot. "Nope," he said, "you might challenge me to a race."

"Scared of me?" she teased.

"Oh, yeah," he admitted, his grin fading and his dark eyes burning in intensity as he stared at her.

She didn't think he was afraid of her athleticism but something else. Maybe how she made him feel? If it was half as confused as he made her, she could understand his fear. And she could almost admit to feeling some herself.

Almost.

"Don't be," she told him. "I might let you win."

"You would do that?" he asked, dark eyes widening in surprise.

She solemnly nodded. "I understand how fragile the male ego is."

"Is that why you let me catch you?"

She wasn't sure why she'd done that. But she knew that she had. She could run faster. She shrugged, unable to answer either of them.

"You must have some peripheral vision," he commented, "to have known it was me. You never looked back."

She hadn't had to look back and not because she'd seen him out of the corner of her eyes. She'd known it was him just by the way her pulse quickened. Yeah, she'd been smart to avoid him. He was trouble.

"I didn't know it was you," she lied. "I thought it was Mr. Lindstrom."

"Mr. Lindstrom? Is that the old guy that walks past your condo a couple times a day?"

She hadn't known he did that. "A short guy, usually wears a dark, pinstriped suit?"

He nodded.

"Then, yes, I guess that is him." No wonder he stayed in such great shape for his age; he participated in her exercise class and walked.

"You have a stalker," George surmised.

"Some cop you are," she scoffed. "You haven't run him off yet."

"He seems harmless enough."

"Oh, I don't know," she mused, stroking her hip. "He bruised me today."

"He hurt you?" The brown eyes darkened with concern and something far more primitive, something possessive.

Despite the excitement quickening her pulse again, she managed a dismissive shrug. "It was an accident." Except for the grab in the car. "He got me with a shopping cart during a field trip for the class today."

"How's that going?" he asked, seeming to be genuinely interested, unlike her ex-fiancés who'd only been interested in talking about themselves.

She didn't like remembering how young and stupid she'd been during those engagements. At least she'd come to her senses in time. She only hoped she could do the same with George.

"Are you having problems with the class?" he asked when she didn't immediately answer.

She groaned. "Next subject."

"That bad?" he asked, voice deep with sympathy. Not only was he interested in someone's life besides his own, he cared.

She answered with a nod.

"So you've been busy with the class?" he asked as he settled his hands onto her shoulders.

She nodded again, only half listening as she considered pulling away from his loose embrace. But it felt too good to have someone hold her, even if just her shoulders, after the day she'd had.

Poor Millie, hers had been infinitely worse.

"So you haven't been avoiding me?"

She shook her head. "Why would I do that?" she asked, not to stall but because she needed time to remember her reason for avoiding him.

He helped her by admitting, "Maybe I come on a little strong." Suddenly his loose embrace wasn't quite so loose. His hands slid from her shoulders to her back, pulling her closer.

"You?" she scoffed.

"And maybe I freaked you out a little when you found me on your patio."

"I already have one stalker," she said, as if she had a quota that had already been filled.

"Yeah, I don't want to have to write up a report on myself."

"Might be kind of hard to have a restraining order against you when we live just a wall apart." She'd thought that was close . . . until now . . . when he had her wrapped up tight in his arms.

"Yeah, that whole stay-so-many-yards-away rule would be a little difficult."

Kim tried to summon her strength, which was usually considerable, and pull away from him again. But he was staring at her, his eyes so intense. Her knees weakened, making her legs shaky. She'd like to blame it on the intensity of the run. But she knew it was his fault.

A car slowly passed them where they stood on the side of one of Hilltop's streets and a horn beeped, reminding Kim of where they were. She glanced toward the retreating car, where it moved uphill at a snail's pace. "Mrs. Ryers," she groaned, recognizing the red Cadillac.

"Not a friend of yours?"

"Hilltop's grapevine," she informed him, finally dragging herself out of his arms. She should have done that earlier, before Mrs. Ryers got an eyeful and more ammunition, as if the patio story hadn't been juicy enough for the old gossip to spread.

"So she'll be talking about us," George said, his voice deepening on the last word.

Us?

"Yes," Kim said with a sigh. "She'll be scorching the phone lines tonight."

Kim didn't want to think about her morning aerobics class. Mrs. Ryers didn't come for the exercise as much as the opportunity to gossip. Her mouth would definitely get a better workout than her body tomorrow.

"You care what people say about you?" George's graying brows arched above his eyes in surprise.

She shrugged. "I don't care about gossip. I'd rather have her talking about me than my friends."

"I know you don't want to talk about it, but the new class isn't going well?"

Kim sighed again. "That's an understatement. We cut today's class short." That was why she'd found time for a run. How had he? Probably a day off after another long shift. "Tomorrow we're supposed to have another cooking lesson."

"But?"

"I'm not sure if we're even going to keep the course going." Not after Millie had all but dragged Mitchell and

Steven from the grocery store, as if she'd been dragging misbehaving boys home from a field trip.

"So it is going bad," George said.

"Really bad."

"Let me make you dinner, and you can tell me all about it," he offered.

She glanced at the sun, setting behind the hill for which the complex was named. "It's kind of late for dinner."

"How about dessert then?" he offered, stepping close again.

She had a feeling he wasn't talking about food. What he was hinting at, with the sparkle in his dark eyes and his wicked grin, was far more dangerous than empty calories. Unlike her friend Millie, Kim wasn't addicted to sweets, but she could get addicted to George.

She summoned her strength as she fought temptation again, shaking her head. "I don't eat dessert."

Chapter Fourteen

"I'm not interested in being a wife. I'm interested in being an empress."   —*Fran Lebowitz*

Millie tried to convince herself that it didn't matter whether or not her sons showed up for class. She had an obligation to the rest of the students, even though none of them needed domestic skills as desperately as Mitchell and Steven did.

She shouldn't have lost her temper. Despite the provocation they'd given her, she hadn't often gotten mad at them while they were growing up. But then they'd been kids, so she'd been able to overlook their stupidity. Now they were men; it had been time to call them on it. They needed to shape up or ship out. Unfortunately, they'd probably choose to ship out.

She hadn't seen Mitchell all day; he'd left the night before after her lecture and hadn't come back. Steven had only come up from the basement once, to make himself a sandwich. Then he'd left early for work this morning and she hadn't seen him yet today.

Despite the dismal field trip, the rest of the students had shown up, even the ones who really didn't need the skills like Charles. And he had not come alone. Victoria tagged behind as he carried his grocery bag into the kitchen, which was awash with sunlight streaming through the sliders.

"Oh, Millie, check out your competition," Kim teased, leaning over to nudge Millie's shoulder with hers as they stood side by side at the granite island in the kitchen.

"I swear, men get more foolish as they get older," Theresa grumbled from the other side of Millie. "Wiser, my—"

"She's his niece," Millie said, cutting off Theresa before they could be overheard. "Hi, Victoria," she said, as she stepped around the island and joined her and Charles at his cooking station. "It's great to see you."

All the male students who were staring at the beautiful young woman undoubtedly agreed. Millie found it easier to focus on Victoria, too.

She could barely glance at Charles, her face heating with embarrassment over the disastrous field trip. He'd seen her lose her temper, too, so he knew there was nothing sweet about her now. Maybe that was why he'd brought his niece along, for protection.

"Is it okay that I'm here?" Victoria asked. "Uncle Charles dared me to come." From the cream colored linen suit she wore, she obviously hadn't planned on cooking and cleaning today.

"She needs help in the kitchen," Charles maintained. He was more appropriately dressed for class in jeans and a gray polo shirt.

"That isn't where I need help," Victoria protested.

Millie wasn't about to ask where. "It's definitely okay that you're here."

"See?" Charles said triumphantly. "The bachelor's survival course can include bachelorettes, too."

Millie nodded. "Yes, it most certainly can." Especially since she was down a couple of bachelors. Or maybe not. She noticed a couple of big guys slinking into the back of the room. "They're here," she murmured, almost to herself.

"Who?" Victoria asked, no doubt curious about the relief in Millie's voice.

"Her sons," Charles explained, without even looking around.

Millie needed to talk to Charles about her sons, to apologize for them again, for interrogating him. But now that the entire class, plus a couple of extras with Victoria and someone else's friend, had arrived, it was time to begin the cooking lesson.

She returned to the island where Theresa and Kim had already set out the ingredients for Chicken Thighs with Wine. "Okay," Millie said, "the sooner we start the lesson, the sooner we can eat."

Since the recipe took some time, she'd already prepared what they would eat after the lesson. The kitchen smelled delicious with the aroma of chicken and herbs wafting from the stoves.

First she read the recipe aloud to them since Mr.

Lindstrom's cataracts made reading a little difficult for him. "This recipe is courtesy of Judy Sausto, or Dame Judy, and came out of the *Red Hat Society Cookbook*."

"My wife belongs to the Red Hat Society, but she never cooks," a guy toward the back grumbled, as he began cutting up the garlic cloves. "She makes me take her out to eat every night."

"Smart woman," Theresa whispered. "I'd like to go out to eat every night."

"I'd rather have a man cook for me," Kim commented, with a dreamy expression softening her brown eyes and lifting her lips into a little smile.

"So Mrs. Ryers was right again," Theresa said, her frustration over the busybody knowing her friend's business before she did evident in the narrowing of her blue eyes.

"It's just a rumor," Kim defended herself.

What rumor? Millie had been too concerned about the way she'd spoken to her sons to listen to any gossip.

"Oh, Mr. Lindstrom needs me," Kim said, rushing away from her friends to where the little old man held a knife in his shaking hand.

"She's in trouble," Theresa said, probably not referring to Kim being in danger of getting cut while Mr. Lindstrom tried to chop celery.

Millie ignored Theresa's comment about Kim and demonstrated how to cut the vegetables. "The recipe indicates finely chopped vegetables. A trick to do this would be to use a food processor—"

"Now you tell us," someone grumbled. For once, it wasn't one of her boys.

"But since we don't have enough of those available for everyone, we're using sharp knives. So be careful. Once you have cut some chunks of carrots, celery, onions and garlic, you can hold the knife like this." She two-handed the top of the knife, careful to avoid the blade. "And press down on the vegetables, chopping them against the cutting board."

"Cutting board?" someone questioned.

Millie held in a groan. That might have been Steven. And now they'd have a scarred pub table to fix. "Everybody has cutting boards?" she asked Theresa.

But her friend's head was turned toward where Wally worked at his cooking station, his head bent as he efficiently cut up the vegetables as Millie had directed.

"Wally's doing great," Millie said. "He's really coming out of himself, too," she added, as he turned to help some of the students around him.

Theresa nodded but didn't say anything. Were his efforts too late to impress her?

At the moment, Millie was more concerned about her sons' efforts. There was no arguing or jostling of shoulders as her sons stood quietly in the back, diligently working the recipe. Had it happened? Had they finally decided to take the class seriously?

She walked toward them but stopped to give instructions or advice to other students. By the time she got to them, Mitchell and Steven had moved on to heating olive oil in the skillet, on their hot plate. Oil spit and sputtered in the overheated pan, splashing onto Steven's bare forearms. He jerked away, knocking some of their crudely chopped vegetables to the floor.

"Sorry, Mom," he said.

"Maybe we should call her Millie," Mitchell suggested, as he stooped to pick the vegetables up in a paper towel. "That way no one will know we're her sons."

"Come on, you two," she cautioned them, as she lowered the heat on the hot plate. She stayed far enough back to avoid spatters. "You know I didn't—"

"What?" Mitchell interrupted. "You didn't mean what you said?"

"No, I meant it," she admitted, but with a smile to soften the sting. "Every word of it. But maybe I could have said it a little more sensitively."

"It had to be said," Steven told her, his dark eyes warm with gratitude. "You were right. It's time we get serious about becoming more independent."

"That's all I really want," she told them, "for you two to get serious."

Steven gestured toward the recipe. "Will it take that long to make it? I have plans to pick Brigitte up for a movie in an hour."

Hope burgeoned, swelling Millie's heart. "I have some already cooked. So you can try that to see how the recipe turns out and leave early."

Despite needing domestic skills, a movie date with his daughter was more important than a cooking lesson.

She assured him, "Kim, Theresa, and I will finish up the rest of the chicken when the class is over." And save the successful efforts for a Red Hat Society luncheon.

Mitchell plopped the chicken into the hot pan, spraying more oil on his brother's arms. Steven flashed him an

angry glance as he wiped off the drops. "It was an accident," Mitchell swore.

Millie believed him. She knew that even though they
promised to take the class seriously now, they would still
have accidents. They were too domestically inept to not
struggle. But now, with their return to class, Millie had
the opportunity to change that, to change them. Excitement and happiness bubbled up inside her. She reached
up on tiptoe, pressing a quick kiss against each son's
cheek.

"Remember to turn the thighs," she said, switching
back to teacher from proud mother. "Don't let the
chicken burn."

"We'll be careful," Steven promised, shooting his
brother a warning glare.

Millie turned to offer her assistance to other students,
but Mitchell, his fingers greasy from the raw chicken
and oil, grabbed the sleeve of her peach-colored cotton
blouse. "Mom, I'm sorry about Charles."

"What?" Embarrassing her in front of him?

"The hot blonde he's with." Mitchell sympathetically
patted her arm, leaving handprints on the peach cotton.
"So who is she?"

"His niece," she told him.

A grin spread across Mitchell's face, and he flashed
his dimples. "Is that right?"

"She's out of your league," Steven taunted him.

Sometimes Millie felt that way about Charles. He
was rich, successful, a lawyer. Victoria was his niece but
he could easily attract a woman of her age, of her beauty.
But it was Millie he'd almost kissed. Twice.

As she looked across the room at him, he glanced up and gave her that wink again . . . the one that had butterflies fluttering around her stomach. Millie carefully closed one eye, returning the gesture.

Thanks for letting me join the class," Victoria said as she cleaned up the workstation. "The chicken was delicious."

Millie glanced to where Charles and Wally talked as they washed dishes at the granite island. He was out of earshot so she dared to speak as openly to his niece as she had her sons. "So did you really come to learn to cook? Or to check me out?" she asked with a smile. She understood. Her sons had done the same to Charles.

Victoria laughed. "No. Not at all. Uncle Charles is a much better judge of character than I am. After all, I was the one who set him up with Ellen."

Millie smiled. "Well, he obviously doesn't hold that against you."

"I'm so grateful for Uncle Charles putting his life on hold to raise me," Victoria began.

Millie patted Victoria's arm like Mitchell had hers, but her hand was clean. "I know he didn't feel that way. He loved every minute of taking care of you."

Victoria blinked hard. "I love him, and I wanted to give him something back. I didn't want him to be alone. So I set him up with this client of mine." She sighed. "Ellen."

"Telling all my secrets?" Charles asked as he joined them at the end of the counter.

Victoria laughed. "You don't miss a thing."

He contorted his handsome, bearded face into a grimace. "I missed the fact that Ellen didn't love me. So I'm not the good judge of character you think I am," he said, confirming that he had overheard their entire conversation.

Victoria turned from him to Millie, looking back and forth between the two of them. "Well, I think that's changed."

"You better hope so since you conned me into going back to work."

Before Millie could ask about that, he turned toward her, putting his hand on her shoulder. "Thanks for letting my niece join up. I failed her when I raised her."

Victoria protested, "Uncle—"

Millie understood the guilt dimming Charles's usually bright eyes. In some ways, she felt the same, that she'd failed her sons.

"No, I did," he insisted. "I should have taught you more things growing up. Or at least made you take a home economics class."

Victoria shook her head. "I preferred debate. And don't worry about the past. You did a great job."

"You're right. That's in the past. But Millie taught me that it's never too late to learn something new," he admitted, then turned to Millie. "The girl needs to learn some housekeeping skills."

Victoria laughed. "Hey, I know the important things, like the numbers for a cleaning service and every takeout restaurant within delivery."

"To the office, not your home."

"What home?" she sassily quipped.

"Exactly," he said, as if he'd won a debate.

Victoria laughed again. "Well, I better get going. I have a mountain of work I need to get through tonight. Thanks again for letting me sit in. I haven't eaten that great a meal in a while."

"See," Charles said, "takeout isn't all it's cracked up to be."

Victoria made a face at him as she grabbed up her purse to leave.

"I'm glad you came to the class," Millie told her. If not, she might not have learned about Charles returning to work. And her sons, despite their efforts, might have reverted to their old ways. They'd behaved, but Millie wondered how much of that was Mitchell trying to impress the new student. As Victoria headed for the door, he caught her, extending his hand as he introduced himself.

"Oh, no," Millie said, not exactly thrilled that her son might get involved with Charles's niece. He didn't have the greatest track record in the romance department. But maybe the classes would help him.

Unlike her, Charles grinned his approval. "I saw that happening," he admitted.

"You were playing matchmaker?"

"No, she really needs the class. I should have taught her more when she was growing up." He sighed. "But you can't teach what you don't know."

Millie narrowed her eyes at him. "You know far more than you admit. And you taught her about the law instead? She's a lawyer like you?"

He nodded, pride beaming in his grin. "Yeah, she took over my practice."

"But you're going back to work?"

"She persuaded me. She needs help, and there are certain clients . . . who would prefer to work with me."

Probably besotted female clients. Millie could definitely relate.

"Not that Vic's giving into the pressure of the chauvinists," he said, dispelling Millie's theory. "She'd tell them to take their business elsewhere. But . . ."

"You want to go back," Millie realized.

He nodded. "I loved law. I miss it. I retired too soon. If I hadn't, I could have avoided the whole mess with Ellen."

So he was going back to work just as Millie was finally retiring her tiara? The implication of that smacked her like a hand upside the head. They'd only exchanged a few winks, a couple of almost-kisses, so she shouldn't be concerned that they had different goals.

But it mattered.

Too much.

# Chapter Fifteen

"Most women set out to change a man, and when they have changed him they do not like him."

—Marlene Dietrich

Hi, Audrey," Millie said over Brigitte's head, surprised when her daughter-in-law followed the teenager into the condo. She released her granddaughter from her arms and reached for Audrey, giving her a quick hug. "It's great to see you both."

Only a couple of weeks had passed since her casserole delivery to their house. But it felt longer. She could only imagine how long it felt for Steven, not living with them anymore. But at least he was seeing Brigitte.

Audrey didn't seem in any particular hurry to drop her and rush off, though. "It's great seeing you, too," Audrey said, but she glanced around the condo, gazing down the hall toward the kitchen, as if looking for someone else.

The romantic in Millie wanted to believe she missed

Steven and wanted to catch at least a glimpse of him. Millie's hope grew when Audrey asked, "So how's your class going? Mitchell and Steven still attending?"

"Yes, they're doing pretty good, too," she said, although they'd never be star students like Charles, or even Wally, who'd shown vast improvement.

"Just pretty good?" Steven asked, as he walked up from the basement. He didn't look at Millie as he asked the question; his gaze was running hungrily over his wife. Like their daughter she wore denim shorts and a tank top, looking almost as young as Brigitte.

"Fantastic," Millie lied, but she doubted he heard her . . . with the intense way he and Audrey were staring at each other.

"Does your friend Kim still have that cat?" Brigitte asked, taking Millie's hand and tugging her toward the door.

Millie got the hint. "Yes. She wanted you to come by and see it the next time you came for a visit. So we better go. You don't want Kim mad at you."

No one protested as she and Brigitte ducked out the door. Maybe Audrey and Steven didn't even notice their leaving.

"Wow," Brigitte breathed, her brown eyes sparkling with excitement. "Did you see the way they were looking at each other?"

Millie's heart raced a bit, too. "Yes. But let's not get ahead of ourselves. Your mom's impressed he's taking the class, but I have to admit that he has a long ways to go."

"But he's trying, really trying," Brigitte said. "I think

that's why she's not as mad as she was." Her face glowed with hopefulness, nearly as bright as the orange tank top she wore.

Millie, although forty years older, had dressed in an outfit similar to her granddaughter's and Audrey's: long denim shorts, but she wore a sleeveless orange sweater instead of a form-fitting tank. She and Brigitte both favored bright, happy colors. And optimism.

"Yes, she's not as mad," Millie agreed. And maybe she'd missed him as much as he had her.

"We can really go see the cat," Brigitte said, as they walked the sidewalk downhill toward Kim's condo.

"I'm thinking about getting a dog, myself," Millie shared. "Would you take care of it when I go away?"

Brigitte stopped on the sidewalk and whirled toward her. "Where are you going?" she asked, a bit panicked.

"Nowhere right now," she assured her.

"But when things are back to normal, you want to go somewhere?" Brigitte guessed. "Where do you want to go?"

"I don't know," Millie realized. "I'm thinking about taking a cruise."

Funny how it didn't hold as much appeal now that she knew she'd be doing it alone. But since the trips she intended to take were planned tours, other people would be along. Red Hatters. Hilltop residents. But there'd be couples. And then her.

Alone.

"You're going to wait until you're done with the class first, though, right?" Brigitte double-checked. Her parents' problems had brought out an insecurity that the usually confident teenager had never had before.

Millie nodded. "Of course I will. We have a lot more to teach yet."

"Is it only guys?"

"No," Millie admitted. "A friend's niece joined."

"Is she my age?"

"No, more like Uncle Mitchell's." In age, career, and domestic ineptness. She didn't know if it was promising that they had so much in common or not. Maybe Mitchell had a better chance of keeping a Suzy Homemaker type even though he was drawn to the high-powered career women.

Why was Charles drawn to her? She knew he was; he'd almost kissed her too many times to not be drawn to her. If he was drawn to the domestic goddess, Millie didn't intend to be one much longer. She was determined to retire her tiara. But her plan to travel didn't sound quite as appealing as it once had . . .

"Grandma?" Brigitte called her, as if she'd called her before. Even though they stood just feet apart on the sidewalk Millie hadn't heard her. "Would that be okay then?"

"Would what be okay, honey?" she asked, contrite over not listening to her granddaughter. Whatever Brigitte wanted, Millie wasn't likely to refuse.

"If I joined the class, too."

"What?" she asked, caught off guard by the teenager's request. She'd expected a request to see an R-rated movie or the purchase of a parental guidance CD.

"Yeah, I want to learn how to help out around the

house, too. I'm old enough. I know you took over taking care of Grandpop when you were younger than me, when your mom died. I can do more around the house than I do," she said, guilt heavy in her young voice. "Then Mom wouldn't be so stressed . . ."

And she might take her dad back. Millie was touched by her granddaughter's reasoning and her sacrifice. What teenager actually wanted to do chores?

Only very special ones. She put her arm around her granddaughter's thin shoulders, and they resumed walking toward Kim's that way, their arms around each other, their hips bumping. "I'd love to have you in class. And if your mom is too busy to drop you off, I could pick you up."

Brigitte shook her head. "It might be better if Dad picked me up."

The little schemer. "Yeah, it might," Millie agreed, as she knocked on Kim's door.

Only a few seconds passed before her friend flung it open. At first disappointment flickered through Kim's dark eyes, but she blinked it away with a bright smile for Brigitte. "Hey, kid! Man, you get prettier every time I see you."

"Thanks," Brigitte said, blushing a little. "I look like my grandma."

"Good genes," Kim agreed.

Because she was blushing now, Millie stated the reason for their visit. "We came to play with the cat."

"Good, you can have him," Kim offered, as she gestured them through her foyer. Her condo looked a lot like Millie's, with its earth tones and hardwood floors, but while Millie's walls were a more neutral tan, Kim's were a rich chocolate. "He's been really surly lately."

"Well, you know how pets start acting like their owners," Millie teased.

"I'm not his owner," Kim was quick to deny, then grumbled something about the cat acting like it owned *her.*

Now Millie understood why she wanted to get rid of it so badly. Kim couldn't handle anyone acting like they owned her. Millie hoped her friend's new neighbor was aware of that.

"I couldn't have a cat anyways," Brigitte said, "between school and practice and now taking Grandma's class, I'll never be home."

"Another student?" Kim nodded her approval. "Good."

"Maybe we should have your neighbor join, too," Millie said, following Kim as she looked under the couch and behind the curtains for the cat.

"He doesn't need any more talents," she remarked offhandedly, then blushed when Millie gasped. "I'm not talking about . . ." She sighed. "We're not going to talk about him. There's enough going around about us already."

"Any of it true?"

"Don't I wish," she muttered again, as she leaned over the railing to the basement stairs. "No, I don't mean that. Where is that dang cat?"

"It's okay," Brigitte assured her. "We really didn't come over to see the cat. We just had to get out of Grandma's condo to leave my mom and dad alone. They were looking at each other."

When Kim didn't react, Brigitte said it again, "You know, looking at each other."

Kim nodded. "Yeah, I know. Unfortunately."

"No, that's a good thing. That means that they're not going to get a divorce."

"Don't get your hopes up," Millie cautioned her.

"Hmmm," Kim mused, "where could she get that eternally optimistic attitude from?"

A smile tugged at Millie's mouth. "I don't know."

So everyone brought their vacuum cleaner?" Millie asked, looking around the class. They'd moved from the kitchen to the open area of the community center where they held Movie Night. They'd moved the assorted recliners to one side of the room, near the sliders that opened onto the deck like the ones in the kitchen did. Sunlight flooded the room, making the carpet appear more cream than deep tan.

Maybe they should have waited until after Movie Night to vacuum; then they would have had popcorn kernels and potato chip crumbs to pick up. But Millie had brought along some dirt . . . in a bag and a bottle of ketchup to squirt on the floor. Theresa had ground up some crackers, and Kim bustled into the room carrying the picnic basket she'd borrowed from Millie.

"What was she supposed to bring again?" Theresa asked.

"Cat hair?" Millie asked, glimpsing gray fur through the basket weave.

"You brought the cat?" Theresa asked, glancing down

herself at the white linen capris she wore with a silk blouse, probably imagining cat hair on them.

"I—it doesn't seem quite right," Kim said. "I didn't want to leave it home."

"You're worried about it," Theresa said, in that *ah-ha* voice, with a teasing smile.

Kim shook her head but didn't deny it. She set the basket on the seat of a recliner. "Okay, we can get started . . ."

Mitchell already had, swinging his vacuum cleaner close to Victoria's as he flashed her his dimpled grin. The boy thought he was irresistible, but Millie wasn't sure that Victoria agreed with him. She seemed more intent on picking up the dirt with her Hoover; then Millie caught her sneaking a peek at him from under her lashes.

Charles caught Millie watching them and flashed her that knee-weakening smile of his. He thought his matchmaking was successful. Did he really wish a slob like Mitchell on his niece? But then by the time Millie was done with her baby, he wouldn't be.

Steven was smiling at a girl, too: his daughter, as she worked alongside him. Millie wished she had thought of having Brigitte join. If she'd been in the class from the first, Steven might have tried harder. He was trying now, but maybe his talk with Audrey had provided the motivation. He'd never said what they'd discussed, but he seemed happier than he had since he'd moved in with Millie, more hopeful. Catching his lower lip between his teeth, he concentrated on picking up all the dirt.

Wally wielded his machine with skill equal to or greater than Charles's effortless motions. While Theresa hovered around him, she couldn't offer any critique. Her blue eyes clouded with thoughtfulness. Hopefully she was impressed by how hard her husband worked, not for domestic expertise, but for her.

As usual, Kim was helping Mr. Lindstrom, shouting out instructions above the droning of all the machines. His hearing aid screeched, either from the racket or her yelling. Then as he pushed the cleaner, the cat jumped out of the basket into the path of the vacuum's head. Before it could move, Mr. Lindstrom sucked up its tail. Its yowl curled Millie's toes.

Kim reacted fast, pulling the cord on the vacuum to cut off its power supply. Millie rushed to help her friend but hesitated reaching for the hissing animal. It slashed its claws across Kim's hand, drawing blood, but she quickly freed its tail. "I'm sorry, Millie, but I have to leave. I need to bring it home," she said.

"I understand." The cat mattered to Kim. Despite all her protests to the contrary, she'd become attached to it.

"I didn't see it," Mr. Lindstrom said. "It came out of nowhere. Did I hurt the poor thing?"

Millie patted his thin arm. "It wasn't your fault, Mr. Lindstrom." But at least they knew he could pick up cat hair. "We'll move on to emptying the bag or bagless canister on your cleaners and some general maintenance, like replacing belts." She imagined Mr. Lindstrom's machine would need a new one after sucking up a cat.

Since there was no cooking, the class was a short one. In addition to vacuuming, they covered mopping. Although these were probably Millie's least favorite housekeeping duties, her class seemed to enjoy them, judging by their laughter.

"Will your friend's cat be okay?" Brigitte asked Millie as the class wrapped up.

Millie nodded. "Kim will take care of it. Don't worry. So what did you think of the class?"

"It was fun. I really like hanging out with Dad and Uncle Mitchell. And Victoria's funny. So is Mr. Moelker."

"Good."

"But the best part is you, Grandma," Brigitte said, giving Millie a quick hug. "You make cleaning fun. You're pretty cool."

Cool was not old-fashioned at all. Millie loved it.

"So do you need me to drop you home?"

"I'm going to do it," Steven said, as he walked up behind his daughter and put his arm around her thin shoulders. Either the class or stress had dropped a few pounds off his frame, so that his belly didn't strain at the buttons of his shirt anymore, and his jeans were looser. "I love hanging with my best girl," he said.

"Dad," Brigitte protested, as if embarrassed. But her eyes were bright and she smiled. Happy. Hopeful. Like Millie, she probably suspected that Brigitte wasn't the only girl he wanted to hang with tonight since he was going home.

Not for good. Not yet. But Millie hoped it would happen. "What's your brother doing?" Coming over to her house to mooch another meal?

"He talked Victoria into going out with him," Brigitte revealed, as if sharing a salacious secret.

But since Mitchell and Victoria walked out together, it was hardly a clandestine affair.

"It's just coffee," Steven said. "But still, I thought she was too smart to be taken in by his questionable charm," he added, shaking his head in mock disappointment.

Millie wondered if Steven didn't live a bit vicariously through his single brother. Didn't he see that *that* life could be lonely? Millie could tell him that. She was lonely, especially so as she watched everyone leave the community center in pairs. Even Mr. Lindstrom had someone helping him home. But Charles wasn't gone yet. As usual, he was helping to pick up.

"So what do you think about Mitchell taking your niece to coffee?" she asked, figuring he'd either whoop over the success of his matchmaking or admit he'd changed his mind about them.

"I think it's a great idea," he said, with a wide grin. "Want to join me for coffee?"

Millie shook her head. "If we showed up at the café, too, they'd think we're spying on them."

"We don't have to go out," he said. "Remember, I know how to make coffee. I make a pretty good cup, if I say so myself. How about coming back to my place?"

She might have agreed, if she really believed they'd just drink coffee. But he might finally manage a kiss before someone interrupted them. And Millie knew that was all it would take for her to change the plans she'd made.

If she were true to her plan, she wouldn't be a domestic goddess much longer. So she had to figure out exactly what that left her. She needed to learn that for herself, before she could begin a relationship with anyone.

"I can't," she begged off. "I have to start planning the next class." She restrained a flinch over her lie. The lessons were all planned out and carefully labeled in her binder.

Charles stared at her, his brow wrinkled as if he were trying to find the pieces to a puzzle. She had to be confusing him, blowing hot and cold. Heck, she was confusing herself. But his returning to work had changed her plan, reminding her of the nights when she'd waited on Bruce hand and foot when he'd come home after a long day at the office. She'd had his meal waiting, warm in the oven; she'd even brought his slippers, not like a dog but like a dutiful wife. She didn't resent or regret any of those years.

He'd worked insurance; she'd worked the home. But she didn't want to work anymore.

"Millie . . ."

"Charles, I'm sorry. This class is keeping me so busy."

"It's a success," he praised her. "Being successful at anything takes time."

That was what she was afraid of; he'd be spending long days at the office. She'd be just as alone with him as she was now. "Yes," she agreed. "You understand."

He shook his head. "I didn't say that. Maybe next time?"

Millie nodded. Maybe by then she would have figured out exactly what she wanted.

The travel, the cruises, or Charles.

# Chapter Sixteen

"I would be content being a housewife if I could find
the kind of man who wouldn't treat me like one."
—*Terry McMillan*

Knuckles rapped against the glass of the patio door.
Kim glanced up, instantly recognizing the shadow outside her walkout basement. She gestured for George to
come inside.

"Different welcome from last time," he remarked, as
he closed the door behind himself, "when you knocked
me over and held a gun on me."

"You fell over," she felt obliged to remind him, "and
Harry's not a real gun."

"Where is Harry?" he asked, glancing around. "I
haven't seen him around in a while."

"I don't need Harry anymore," she said. "I've got
you." Then realizing what she'd revealed, she sputtered,
"I mean, who needs a fake gun when you have a cop living next door with a real one—a real gun?"

He puffed out his chest, still clad in his navy blue

uniform, and faked a deeper baritone. "That's me, I live to serve and protect."

He might have said it as if in jest, but she knew he meant it. He was like her dad; it was the motto by which he lived.

"So serve," she said, giving in to the worry she'd been fighting since the class.

"You, gladly. You up for my after-shift snack?"

"No, not me. I know someone with a problem."

"And they need a cop? Are they in trouble?" he asked, instantly on duty.

Kim shook her head. "We don't need a cop. But we could use your advice."

"About what?"

She nodded toward the cat sitting on the floor near her yoga mat.

"Are you still trying to pawn that cat off on me?" he asked with a deep chuckle.

"No." She could admit it, at least to herself—she didn't want to get rid of the cat. And she didn't want to lose it. "I think it's sick."

"Sick?"

"Hurt. Maybe."

"What's wrong with it?" he asked, bending over to look at it more closely.

"Well, Mr. Lindstrom sucked its tail into a vacuum cleaner tonight."

"What—oh, your class. Vacuum lesson," he surmised. "Do you think it's broken?"

"It can move. So I don't think so. But even before the vacuum, it was acting strange. Quiet. Hiding. I think it's sick. Really sick." She waited for him to mock her, to call her on her concern for the cat.

"Put it back in that basket," he said, pointing to Millie's picnic basket on the floor near the cat. "I'll change out of my uniform and be right back."

"What are you going to do?"

"Take the two of you to an emergency vet clinic," he said with soothing logic.

She watched as he ducked back out the slider and into the night. As he did, her heart moved, as if to follow him. It belonged to him now. Just that simply, she'd fallen for him. She should be mad; this was something that had happened beyond her control.

A short time later, as she sat in the car next to him, he reached across the console between them and touched her hand. The scratch shone in the dim lights from the dash, an angry red gash. "It got you pretty good. Are you all right?"

No, she wasn't.

"You said the cat was being quiet. It's not the only one. You're really worried."

Yes, she was.

"This is a great vet."

"You don't have any animals," she reminded him, wondering if the vet was someone he'd dated after his divorce.

"Not anymore. I had a dog, though."

"Had? I take it the dog didn't make it. Are you sure this is a good vet?" she asked a bit anxiously, as she tightened her arms around the picnic basket on her lap.

He smiled. "Ollie died from old age," he assured her. "Still broke my son's heart, though."

"Your son?" She'd thought he didn't have any kids. She'd never seen any weekend visitors at his place.

"Yeah, he's away at college now," he answered her unspoken question. "Great kid. Smart, confident. Loves to work out. He'd love you."

"College," she said, still trying to wrap her mind around George being a father. "What's he going for?"

"Criminal justice. He wants to be a cop."

"Like his old man," she said, expecting his smile to beam with pride.

But he was frowning instead. "That's what his mother says."

Kim had a feeling it wasn't a compliment. "Is she worried he'll get hurt?"

"I'm not sure." He sighed.

"Are you worried about him?"

"No, he's a smart kid. He'd be a good cop. But his mother may succeed yet in talking him out of it."

"He's a smart kid. He'll do what he wants," Kim assured him.

His smile flashed again as they pulled into the brightly lit parking lot of the emergency vet. "You're right. And now that you've made me feel better about my kid, let's see if I can make you feel better about yours."

"This cat is not my kid," she protested, but not too strenuously as she followed him into the clinic.

Fortunately the waiting room was empty and the assistant showed them to an examining room right away. The vet, a quiet young man, had probably chosen animals over people to treat because he lacked any bedside manner. But he thoroughly checked out the gray tiger.

"She's not sick," he said. "She's pregnant."

"She?"

"You didn't know," George laughed. "And you were raised on a farm. What will your dad say?"

"Hey, I thought it was fixed," she defended herself.

"Well, she's not," the vet assured them. "She's got quite a litter in there, too. You're going to have a lot of kittens very soon. I'll get you some vitamins you can put in her food." He rummaged through a cupboard behind his small examining table.

Great, she was going to play midwife to a feline. And she'd become what she'd always been afraid of becoming, an old maid with a bunch of cats for company. The cat lady of Hilltop. She sighed, knowing Mrs. Ryers would have a field day with that. But then she didn't care what anyone else thought. She had, however, come to care about the cat.

"Fine," she said, as she accepted the small bottle.

"You're going to be a grandma," George taunted her.

Grandma to a litter of cats. That was something she would have never expected, like her feelings for George. But she was going to have to find a way to deal with both.

The aroma of rich coffee teased Theresa's nose, waking her from a light sleep. She turned her head to the bedside table, where steam wafted in spirals from a mug emblazoned with cats in Red Hats and purple scarves.

"You're finally up, sleepy head," Wally teased, his voice low as if wary of waking her too abruptly.

She stretched, then scooted up to rest her back against the cushioned leather headboard. "What time is it?"

"Early."

She couldn't stop herself from asking. "What are you doing up then?"

"Early tee-off time."

"You're going golfing?" He hadn't gone in so long; she hadn't even known whether or not he still had his clubs. She'd figured he might have sold them with the business.

He wore a golf shirt in deep green that made his eyes bright, and khakis. He nodded. "Yes, I'm going golfing. Here, try the coffee," he said, handing her the mug.

She would have liked to brush her teeth first, but tempted by the rich aroma, she took a sip. "Mmmm, that is good."

"I'm glad you like it. I tried a new blend."

"You went shopping?"

"Of course."

She thought about asking for his ID, just to make sure he was her husband. But she knew this man, with the sharp eyes and the wide grin, better than she knew the stranger she'd been living with for the last several months. This man bore an uncanny resemblance to the young ambitious man she'd married.

"So are you going golfing with Charles and some of the other guys from class?" Like she'd hoped he would, he had made friends.

He shook his head. "Not today. We've got a golf date for Saturday. Charles is working today."

"That's right. He went back to work." She wondered how Millie felt about that. A man with a job didn't fit with her plan. "So who are you golfing with?"

He grinned. "A couple of guys from the office and an old client."

"From the business?"

"Yeah. This client always insisted on dealing with only me," he said, the pride back as he lifted his chin.

"So you're going back to work?"

"They'd like me to," he said, flashing a really wide grin. "Apparently things don't run as smoothly without the old man."

"You're not an old man," she told him. Not today. Today he had all the fire and determination of the young man she'd fallen in love with. "So what are you going to do?"

"I'm thinking about following Charles's example, put in a couple short days a week, just enough to keep an eye on things. What do you think about that?"

"You worked a long time building your business. I can understand you wanting to keep an eye on things." She understood that more easily than his selling it; it was his baby, like she'd once been.

"So you think it's a good idea?"

"If it'll make you happy, yes."

"I want to make you happy," he told her, then he leaned over her, pressing his lips to hers. His mouth moved softly and sweetly over hers, as his big hand cradled her face.

Theresa's toes curled into the sheets, and she murmured in her throat. But he pulled away, his eyes twinkling, as he told her, "I don't want to be late."

He wasn't.

Not too late for them.

She reached for the Red Hat mug again, her hands not quite steady. "Thanks for the coffee. Coffee in bed, you're going to spoil me."

"That's my intention," he assured her even as he took the cup from her hands and kissed her again.

She pulled slightly back to tease him. "I thought you didn't want to be late."

He groaned as he tore his mouth from hers. "Yeah, yeah, I have to go," he said as he headed toward the door.

She leaned back in bed, smiling. He wasn't leaving, not really. He was finally back.

Chapter Seventeen

"The effect of having other interests beyond those domestic works well. The more one does and sees and feels, the more one is able to do, and the more genuine may be one's appreciation of fundamental things like home, and love, and understanding companionship."
—*Amelia Earhart*

*A*s the wind picked up the paper, Kim caught the photocopy of the page from *The Red Hat Society Cookbook.* "Copying from the bible again?" she teased Millie. "Jalapeño-Stuffed Bacon-Wrapped Grilled Shrimp."

"Great day for grilling," Millie said, as they supervised the heating up of the grills on the community center's expansive deck. Situated as it was near the top of the hill, the deck was suspended off the center, overlooking treetops. The beautiful setting tempted Millie to schedule more grilling lessons. She'd have to look in the "bible" for more grilling recipes, like this favorite of hers. "The shrimp are delicious this way."

"Yes," Kim agreed, "but spicy." Using the recipe, she gestured toward Mr. Lindstrom. He stood at one of the several patio tables on the deck, the umbrella over his head undulating in the wind.

"I didn't get really hot jalapeños," Millie promised, knowing she spoke the truth since her eyes weren't watering and her sons had already complained that they weren't hot enough. She popped a thin piece of pepper into the back of a shrimp and wrapped a slice of bacon around it. "But we have other options," she reminded Kim.

Along with the shrimp, they had fixings for other kebabs: chunks of beef and plenty of vegetables that the students had had to cut up. She'd already shown them what size and how to cut the pieces; finished skewers sat on the table in front of her and Kim, ready for the grill.

"They're doing a great job," Theresa said, as she joined her friends. Even though she said "they", she only watched one student. Wally.

Millie could understand why. The man looked good. His skin, once pale from all his time inside, was now a golden tan. And his eyes were bright again, like Charles's had always been. Millie's gaze strayed from Wally to Charles, where he stood in the middle of her family. Brigitte was totally focused on him, hanging on his every word as he chopped vegetables.

Steven tried to mimic his movements. Mitchell used a little more flair, wielding the knife as if it were a baton. Millie winced, certain he was going to chop off a finger. Maybe he thought it would be worth it if Victoria kissed it to make it better. She stood near him, shaking her head as if exasperated with him, but her smile was wide.

As usual Charles caught Millie watching him . . . and winked. Her knees weakened, and for just a moment she clutched the edge of the table. If the man could make her feel like this with just a wink, what would a kiss do to her?

"So what's going on between you and Charles?" Theresa asked.

Millie wasn't sure if she was asking in general or about the wink. Either way, her answer was the same. "Nothing."

"You can tell me," Theresa coaxed, "I'm not Mrs. Ryers. The whole community won't know your business."

Kim sighed. "That's not what we're worried about. It's the lecture on how men are the root of all evil," she teased, with a gentle nudge to Millie's arm. They shared a quick, amused glance.

"I know I've been a little overly dramatic lately," Theresa admitted, with her usual grace. "I was working through some things."

"Whether or not you wanted to kick Wally to the curb," Kim said, with her usual bluntness.

Pink color rose in Theresa's face. Embarrassment didn't redden and blotch her skin like it did Millie's. Theresa looked pretty; Millie usually looked like she'd been out in a snowstorm and was suffering frostbite.

"I don't know where you get these ideas," Theresa said to Kim, but she didn't deny that she'd considered it.

Kim shrugged. "Doesn't matter—looks like you've decided to keep him."

"Looks like," Theresa agreed with a small, secretive smile reminiscent of the *Mona Lisa.*

Millie wrapped an arm around her friend, gently squeezing her. "I'm so happy for you," she said.

"What about for you?" Theresa asked, squeezing back. "And Charles Moelker?"

Millie shook her head, causing the wind to tousle her curls even more. Her hair was probably standing six inches above her head, like Ronald McDonald's. Maybe she needed to get it cut short, like Kim's.

"There is no me and Charles," she insisted, "except in class. And speaking of the class, we'd better get back to teaching it."

Kim nodded, either letting Millie off the hook or trying to avoid getting on it herself. "Yeah, it looks like Mr. Lindstrom could use some help."

"He thinks you're mad at him over the cat," Millie clued in her friend.

Kim waved off his concern. "She's fine."

"She?"

"Yes, and she's expecting. So you two need to expect a couple kittens each in a few weeks. She's carrying a big litter." Before they could refuse, she rushed off to help their oldest student.

Mr. Lindstrom beamed as she walked up to him, obviously grateful that she didn't hold a grudge. He even reached up to give her a hug, but he'd apparently forgotten he held the grilling fork. Or maybe he hadn't. Either way, he got her with it, in a sensitive area.

Millie tried to smother a laugh, but Theresa didn't

even bother. "She's going to feel that when she sits down," she said, chuckling.

"Okay, everyone, let's put our skewers on the grills," Millie announced, managing to keep from laughing until Theresa muttered, "I hope Mr. Lindstrom doesn't try to put Kim on the grill."

Millie might prefer getting put on the grill herself over Theresa's grilling her about Charles. It would be less uncomfortable because she wouldn't have to say anything. Because about herself and Charles, she had nothing to say.

Charles scoured the grill with a wire brush, cleaning the scraps of meat and veggies off the metal rungs.

"You've done this before," Millie commented on his practiced technique. He wasn't the only one to stay to help this time. Even though Theresa and Wally had left, and Kim as well (probably to go home and sit on an icepack), Millie's family had stayed.

"I use the grill more than I use my stove," Charles admitted. "Well, I did before I joined your class."

"I'm glad you're learning something."

"You've taught me a lot," he insisted.

But was he talking about domestic chores or something else? The way he looked at her, his blue eyes intense, led her to believe it was something else.

Before she could consider what, Brigitte ran up and threw her arms around Millie. "I love your class, Grandma!" she said. "It's fun, and I love the food."

"I'm glad you're enjoying it, honey. So I'm still cool?" That comment meant so much to Millie, like she had come a long way from "old-fashioned."

Brigitte nodded. "You'd be even cooler if we baked cookies next cooking class."

Millie laughed at her granddaughter's bribe. "Well, I don't have cookies planned, but we're going to cover something even sweeter. Theresa, Kim, and I are going to teach you all how to make our favorite desserts."

"Sweet!" Brigitte exclaimed.

"That's the idea," Millie agreed. "So you won't miss the next class then?"

"No way!"

"I'll make sure I'm here, too," Victoria spoke up from behind Brigitte. "Sounds like my kind of class."

"You're happy you joined?" Millie asked, knowing Charles had coerced his niece into the class. Maybe like Brigitte, he had even exercised a little bribery, using his return to the practice as leverage in getting Victoria to join the bachelor's survival course.

But then what could she say about his manipulation when she'd done the same to her sons?

Victoria glanced toward where Mitchell stood next to his brother before she answered Millie's question. "I'm most definitely happy that I joined."

"Ready to go, squirt?" Steven interrupted to ask his daughter.

"You're taking her home again?" Millie asked, trying to control the smile teasing her lips.

Steven didn't fight his; it lit up his eyes, which until

recently had been so sad all the time. Despite the smile, he cautioned her. "Mom . . ."

"I know, I know, I'll back off," she said.

"That'd be a first." But he leaned over to kiss her cheek, then led Brigitte toward where he'd parked in the community center lot.

Before the wind could dry Millie's cheek, Mitchell pressed a kiss to her other one.

"What was that for?" she asked.

"Thanks." He didn't tell her why he expressed his gratitude; he just took Victoria's hand in his as the two of them walked away.

Millie blinked hard, fighting the tears springing to her eyes. Her sons were happier. That was all she'd wanted.

"Are you okay?" Charles asked, as he pressed a handkerchief into her hand.

She nodded. "Yes, better than okay."

"That's why you're almost crying?" he asked, clearly perplexed. He wore that trying-to-find-the-pieces-to-a-jigsaw-puzzle expression again.

She laughed. "I'm okay, really. It just occurred to me that the bachelor survival course is just about over."

"Really?" he asked, his bright eyes dimming with disappointment. "I can't remember how many weeks it was supposed to run."

"Just until my sons didn't need me anymore. And I think that's about now."

"Millie," Charles said sympathetically, putting his arm around her shoulders. "Don't ever think that. They're always going to need you."

"Oh, I hope not," she said, her voice just about a

breathless whisper, not from what she was saying but from being so close to Charles. His arm was heavy across her shoulders, his body hard against hers.

"I don't understand."

"The purpose of the class was so they'd learn to take care of themselves, so that they *wouldn't* need me," she said, sharing her ulterior motive with him. She needed to tell him the rest, too, about her plan to retire and spend more time traveling and having fun.

Before she could broach the subject, he shook his head in confusion. "I thought it was to get Steven back together with his wife."

"That, too. I'd hoped it would work." And she wanted to believe it had, but Steven was still living in her basement.

"It is working, Millie," Charles insisted.

She bit her lip as the tears pooled again, then nodded. She couldn't share her plan with him now, not when she wasn't sure this was what she wanted anymore.

"Then what's wrong?" he asked, his voice deepening with concern.

"They won't need me anymore," she nearly wailed, as her heart contracted painfully. "I know it doesn't make sense, that I wanted this, but I'm so used to them needing me . . . that . . ."

She felt a little lost and never more alone, except that she wasn't alone. Although everyone else had left, Charles was with her on the deck, in such a beautiful setting. Just the two of them. She turned toward him, then reached up to pull his bearded face down to hers. And she kissed him.

Astonished at her own action, she pulled away. But Charles delved his fingers into her curls and kissed her back, his beard soft against her face, his lips hard and passionate. Millie's breath caught in her lungs, and her heart pounded madly.

Finally Charles slid his mouth from hers, breathing hard. "Wow."

"Ummm," Millie murmured, beyond coherent conversation.

"You kissed me," he said, stunned.

"I had to," she said, "you were never going to do it."

"Hey, I've been trying . . ."

"Yes, you have," she agreed, letting the silly grin spread across her face. She didn't care; she was too giddy.

"Hey," he protested, then added, "so let me try again." And he kissed her again. "See . . ." he murmured against her lips.

Laughing, Millie pulled away. "You're getting better."

"I have to impress my teacher," he said, grinning. "She always says practice makes perfect."

"Does she?"

"So you want to go somewhere and practice?" he asked, suggestively wriggling his eyebrows.

Millie giggled now, surprised she could make such a girlish sound. She hadn't been a girl in a long time. But Charles made her feel like one; he made her feel like she had when she'd first fallen in love.

So full of hope.

"Ah, Millie," he said with a sigh. "Your sons might

not need you as much as they did. But I think *I'm* starting to *need* you . . ."

Was that why she was falling for him? Because she
wanted to be needed? She'd wanted her sons to be independent, but did she really want to retire her tiara? Did
she really want for no one to need her?

Before she could go any further with Charles, she had
to figure out exactly what she wanted.

Chapter Eighteen

"At worst, a house unkept cannot be so distressing as a life unlived."　　　　　　　*—Rose Macaulay*

Tonight the community center kitchen was more crowded than usual for class, even since the additional students had joined. Standing against the wall of sliders behind the workstations were spectators—some relatives like Audrey, and a camera crew.

"What's the deal?" Kim asked as she joined Millie and Theresa at the counter.

"I don't know," Theresa said with a shrug.

Millie's nerves jangled. She'd only just gotten comfortable teaching in front of her growing class. She didn't need the added pressure of the camera crew. "This must be a mistake," she insisted.

But the local news reporter, a gorgeous redheaded girl who did the special features, or as some called them, the fluff pieces, was talking to Mr. Lindstrom. She kissed his cheek before walking up to the island. "Hi," she said,

"I'm Candi Brewer from Channel 7. My grandpa told me about this class."

"Mr. Lindstrom?" Kim asked.

Candi nodded. "Yes, he's a sweetheart."

"A real sweetheart," Kim ruefully agreed, rubbing her hip.

A man in his forties with thinning hair like Steven's walked up behind Candi, reaching his hand across the counter. "I'm James Stehouwer," he said, "producer for Channel 7. Hope you don't mind us crashing your class, but it sounded like a great segment for tomorrow's noon broadcast."

Millie glanced toward her friends, hoping for their support in turning down the coverage. But they both shook their heads. "It's no problem," Theresa said.

"Sounds like fun," Kim added.

Millie couldn't say anything as her nerves choked her, rendering her speechless. She couldn't even shake the man's hand; hers was trembling too much.

"So which one of you is the Domestic Goddess?" Stehouwer asked.

"Domestic Goddess?" Millie sputtered, finally finding her voice.

"Grandpa told me one of you is called that," Candi said, explaining how they knew the title.

"How high does he turn up that hearing aid?" Kim wondered aloud, casting a glance his way. He grinned at her, a wide, dentured grin.

"Millie's the domestic goddess," Theresa volunteered. "She's the true expert."

Millie shook her head. "That's really not the case at all," she argued.

"It's her Red Hat name," Kim added. "We all consider her the goddess."

James grinned. "A Red Hatter? Can you wear the hat during the segment? We'd love that."

"So would she," Kim spoke for her, erroneously. "I'll go get it from her condo."

Millie resisted the urge to shout "Traitor!" after her as Kim rushed out. She really wished she had hid her house key in another spot; Kim knew where she kept it, above the trim around the garage door.

"I don't think this class will be exciting enough for your program," she said, hoping they'd change their minds about taping it. "We're just doing some cooking, nothing newsworthy." Unless she passed out from nerves during the class, but that would be hardly newsworthy either.

"We're cooking our favorite desserts," Theresa interjected. "These are recipes from *The Red Hat Society Cookbook*." She handed them a photocopy of each recipe. "My favorite, Chocolate Angel Pie. The blonde Amazon who ran out to get Millie's red hat loves this one, Dreamsicle Cake. And this one is Millie's favorite—"

"Theresa," Millie interrupted, trying to discourage her friend's helpfulness. "We need these for the students." She grabbed up the stack of copies and headed out to the individual workstations.

But no one worked individually. Victoria worked with Mitchell, Brigitte with her dad, and usually Charles and Wally teamed up.

"What's with the cameras?" Wally asked her.

Millie tried to settle the nerves swimming in her stomach, unsure if they were caused by the presence of the television crew or Charles. She hadn't talked to him since that kiss on the deck. She hadn't entirely made up her mind yet about why she was falling for him. The only thing she knew for sure was that she was. And falling hard.

"They're taping us for the noon news tomorrow," Theresa told her husband, as she rushed up behind Millie, excitement flushing her face and brightening her eyes.

"Are you okay with this?" Charles asked Millie, his voice low so only she could hear.

"Nervous," she admitted, pressing a palm against her quivering stomach. She'd worn a purple knit shirt and skirt, which was fortunate since it would go with her red hat.

He squeezed her hand. "Don't be nervous. You're a wonderful teacher. You'll do a great job. Just forget that the cameras are here."

She quickly dragged in a shaky breath. "That's easy for you to say."

"No, it'll be easy for you. Just focus," he said, touching her chin so that she looked up and into his amazing blue eyes, "on me."

Now her stomach flipped as her nerves increased ten-fold. The last thing she needed to focus on was Charles and her growing feelings for him. She'd only get more flustered, and probably flush with embarrassment so that she was as red as her hat, and blotchy, too. Fainting from nerves would be the easy way out.

"That's a bad idea," she told him but with a smile, so that he wasn't hurt.

He grinned. "Too distracting?"

She vehemently nodded. "You'll have me burning my pie. But that might be a good thing. No one will call me a domestic goddess then."

"You'll always be a goddess to me," he said, outrageously flirting.

Flustered and flushing, Millie slapped the recipes down on his workstation and quickly walked away. The man was way too distracting.

"Don't worry," Mitchell told her, as she handed the papers to him and Victoria, "we'll behave. No one will embarrass you on national television."

"Local," she corrected him, as her stomach flipped again with those unrelenting nerves.

Mitchell shook his head. "Just for now. But you'll be such a hit that they'll syndicate you."

"Yeah, right . . ."

Every student said something to that effect, bolstering her ego and increasing the pressure. By the time she'd passed out all the copies, her nerves were so unsettled that she had to swallow them down. And waiting at the island was her red hat, but someone had adorned it . . . with a glittering tiara.

"Cute," she told Kim, shooting her a mock-ferocious glare.

Kim laughed. "Yes, you are," she agreed. "The camera will love you."

"Where's *your* red hat?" Millie asked, then turned toward Theresa. "And yours?"

They shook their heads. "We're sitting this lesson out."

As if she hadn't been nervous enough. "No."

"It's your show," Kim insisted. "It's always been your show."

"It was your idea," Theresa reminded her. "Your inspiration. And you've inspired all these students. You deserve the limelight to yourself."

"But I don't want it," Millie whispered furiously, resisting the urge to wail like Lucille Ball on any episode of *I Love Lucy.* Who loved Millie? How could her friends desert her like this when they'd always been there for each other?

"You're going to do a wonderful job," Theresa assured Millie as she and Kim smiled and backed away, leaving Millie alone . . . in the front of the class with the cameras facing her.

All she had for reinforcement was her red hat. For a second she thought about taking the tiara off it. But it said so much about who she was: the Domestic Goddess.

So she put on her hat and turned toward her class. "This is going to be our most delicious lesson yet," she enthused, surprised that her voice held not even the faintest quaver of nerves. But then she realized her nerves were gone. Maybe it was the red hat and tiara; maybe it was the quick wink Charles sent her. Either way, she knew she was going to be just fine.

"Let's start with my personal favorite," she said, "Brown Bag Apple Pie. That's right—you heard me. Brown bag. That's not at your workstation for packing up leftovers. We need that to bake this delicious cinnamon apple pie. Everyone pick up your recipe."

First they tackled the pie crust, then set about peeling, coring, and slicing the apples. Some students nicked their fingers. Mitchell still wielded his knife with more flash than finesse. Millie, ever the mother, passed out Band-Aids like she'd earlier passed out the recipes.

Then she resumed the lesson without missing a beat. "We'll put your pies in to bake, but first double bag yours. These new bags are thin. This keeps your crust from drying out or burning." That advice was in the recipe as well, courtesy of Princess Knit Wit from the Flashy Sassies Red Hat Society chapter in Motrose, Colorado.

Millie loved using *The Red Hat Society Cookbook* because she felt even more connected to her Red Hat sisters. Because of that connection and their long friendship, she couldn't stay angry with Theresa and Kim. They moved through the students, helping out behind the camera.

The scent of cinnamon and apples already filled the kitchen, as Millie, Kim, and Theresa had prepared pies and put them in the ovens before class began. She pulled out the baked pies, carefully maneuvering them out of their bags. "And this is what yours will look like. When they've cooled a little bit, we'll taste them."

Then she moved on to Kim's favorite dessert, a light and airy Dreamsicle cake. And Theresa, who shared Millie's love of chocolate, loved the Chocolate Angel Pie. Theresa's pie had been prepared before class, too, so that it could set up in the refrigerator. Kim's cake didn't take as long as the apple pie to bake, so they moved onto that.

"This is a long class," she cautioned. "If anyone would like to leave now . . ."

"Not until we eat," someone called out. "I'm not missing out on these desserts."

Millie turned toward the news crew, expecting them to be putting their equipment away. But the cameras were still trained on her; she'd forgotten about them. As she immersed herself in the lessons, she forgot about them again.

When everyone was eating the pre-baked desserts, the producer walked up, wiping cinnamon apple pie juice from his lips. "You really are a domestic goddess," he said.

"These aren't my recipes," she reminded him. "I've taken these from *The Red Hat Society Cookbook*. These women created the recipes, I've only copied them."

"You've done more than that. You taught other people how to follow the recipe without making a mess of them," he said, clearly impressed. "You're a natural. We used to do a cooking segment at noon."

"I remember," she said. "Chef Sheldon. What happened to him?"

"Heart attack."

Millie gasped.

"He's all right," he assured her. "He's just not doing much cooking these days. He's only eating rabbit food."

"Well, that sounds healthy," she said.

"And unexciting. You're exciting. I love the hat. I love the whole package."

Charles came up behind the producer, his attention riveted on them. Millie didn't care if James Stehouwer loved the whole package; she wanted to know if Charles did.

But the other man wasn't done talking yet. "I'd like you to replace Chef Sheldon," he told her. "The domestic goddess could give a quick lesson every noon broadcast."

"Every day?" Millie asked, then shook her head, nearly dislodging her hat. "I don't know . . . that sounds like a full-time job."

"Is it that you haven't worked before?"

"Oh, I've worked." Far harder than if she'd held a nine-to-five job. "But my intention is to retire."

"You're not going to continue your class?"

"This was a one-shot deal, for these students."

"So when the class is over, you'll have time to do a segment for the news," the producer said, as if arranging Millie's life were part of his producing duties.

She shook her head. "My plan is to travel, take a cruise, take it easy. I'm not looking for a job, Mr. Stehouwer, but I'm flattered by the offer."

The man's face fell, his jaw tautening with frustration. "I hope you change your mind. You'd be perfect for our station."

Millie hoped to be perfect for someone else. But Charles wasn't standing nearby anymore. He'd gone back to his workstation. When Millie caught his attention, he didn't wink. His blue eyes were flat with disappointment. She couldn't believe he was upset that she hadn't taken the job; he was upset to learn about her plans.

Because she hadn't told him, or because he didn't want to travel with her?

*M*illie walked through her garage carrying her red hat. Because her attention was focused on the glittering tiara, she almost missed that Steven's trunk gaped open. She flashed back over a month ago, to the first time she'd found his car in her garage with the trunk open.

That had started everything: Her resolve to make him and Mitchell more independent. The class. Her falling for Charles. Or had she started that before then? When she thought his wife had died.

It didn't matter now, not after the way he'd looked at her . . . without the wink . . . like he didn't even know her. And he hadn't. Because she hadn't let him. She hadn't shared her plans with him, and she should have.

"Hey, Mom," Steven said, as he stepped into the garage with an armload of boxes. "Why so sad? I thought you'd be thrilled when I moved out."

"As long as you're moving back home," she qualified, scarcely daring to hope.

Audrey and Brigitte came out of the house behind him, carrying bags. "Yes, he is," Audrey said, "moving back where he belongs."

"I belong there," Steven agreed, "now that I appreciate how hard my wife works." He leaned around the boxes and pressed a kiss against the side of her head. "And I'm determined to help her."

"Me, too," Brigitte said. "I can do a lot now, too. We'll be a team."

"Team Truman!" Steven shouted, as he dumped the boxes into his trunk. Then he wrapped an arm around each of his girls.

Millie blinked hard, clearing tears from her eyes.

"Mom, are you all right?" Steven asked, letting go of his girls to put his hands on her shoulders.

"I'm happy," she said. "I hoped for this for you."

"You did more than hope," Brigitte said, "you made it happen, just like you promised." Her granddaughter wrapped her arms around Millie, squeezing tight. "Thank you so much!"

Audrey stepped close, too, pressing a kiss against Millie's cheek. "Thanks, Mom."

Millie had to blink hard again but still she couldn't stop one tear from slipping free and rolling down her cheek. "Don't thank me. You all worked hard. And I'm sure if I hadn't interfered, you would have gotten back together."

"Maybe," Audrey agreed. "But it wouldn't have happened this quickly or this completely. We're closer now than ever, more of a partnership than just a marriage." She blinked back some tears of her own, obviously emotional over the reconciliation. Then she smiled. "I can't wait for Steven's cooking."

"Or mine," Brigitte reminded her mom. "I can cook, too. But there's still a lot I want to learn. Grandma, you're going to keep the class going?"

Millie glanced toward Steven's open trunk, nearly full now with his belongings. Her intention had been to end the class when he went home. "I hadn't planned on it . . ."

She'd planned so much other stuff. Not in any great detail, though. She didn't have itineraries prepared or a cruise booked. Like Audrey, she hadn't expected her boys to learn so much so quickly. She hadn't thought she'd be able to retire this soon. Now she wasn't entirely certain that she really wanted to.

"You should think about it, Mom," Steven advised. "It wouldn't have to meet as often, but I feel like I could learn a lot more, too."

Millie nodded in agreement. "I'm sure you could." But it wasn't entirely his fault, as her old guilt resurfaced. "There's so much I should have taught you long ago."

Then his family never would have hit that rough patch, but maybe that wasn't an entirely bad thing. Because of that, they could appreciate what they had now.

"I could have taught him, too," Audrey said, "but I thought I could do it alone."

"You shouldn't have had to," Steven told her, putting his arm around her shoulders again. He couldn't stop touching her, his dark eyes soft with love as he gazed down at his pretty blond wife.

She smiled up at him, her face glowing. "That's in the past. Things are going to be so much better now."

"Perfect," Steven agreed.

Brigitte caught Millie's gaze, then rolled her eyes. "Grandma, I think I'm going to be spending a lot of time at your house. Or they might make me sick."

Steven laughed. "Smart aleck."

His daughter was a smart girl; she probably knew how empty Millie's house would seem without Steven. When they all left, Millie sat alone at the counter in her kitchen, listening to the silence.

No television blared. No phone rang. She'd once thought she'd wanted this silence. Now she wasn't sure exactly what she wanted.

Chapter Nineteen

"Many husbands today pitch in to help with
household chores—it's called partnership."

—*Dear Abby*

Kim waited until she heard the car pull into the garage
next to hers, then she slipped out of her door. She was
dressed for a run in a white tank top and silky blue running shorts. Sometimes she did run at night, if she
couldn't sleep. She hadn't been sleeping a lot lately because of her handsome neighbor—not because he'd
been over but because he hadn't. Ever since the night
he'd taken her and the cat to the vet, he hadn't been
back.

She extended her leg and bent over, stretching.
Muscles protested, hurting most in the area where Mr.
Lindstrom had got her with the grilling fork. A little
groan slipped unbidden through her lips.

"Are you okay?" George asked as he stepped out of
his garage. Her heart fluttered at the sight of him in his
navy blue uniform.

"Just getting old," she said, her tone flippant, but it did matter to her. She was older than he was; maybe that was why he hadn't been around lately. She couldn't give him everything he might want.

He laughed heartily at her remark. "Impossible. You'll be forever young."

She shook her head slowly, horrified. "God forbid. I wouldn't want that."

"I thought that's what every woman wants," he said. "Eternal youth."

"I'd prefer to be a little older and a lot wiser." And if she were, she had no business waiting for him to come home to ambush him in his driveway.

"That makes a lot of sense," he agreed with a heartfelt sigh.

"At least something does," she said, as she straightened up.

"Something wrong?"

"You tell me."

"What?" he asked, but she had a feeling his innocence was feigned . . . because something sparkled in his eyes, either amusement or vindication.

She struggled with frustration; she hated playing games and hadn't thought he'd be the type to enjoy them either, not after his divorce. "You haven't been around lately."

"I've been around," he insisted. "I live just a wall away."

"You haven't stopped by." Hating how needy she sounded, she added, "to check on the cat."

"How is the little mama doing?" he asked.

"Whiny and needy," she said, like George made her feel. The frustration nagging at her now was with herself.

He chuckled. "I know you hate that," he said, as if he knew how he made her feel.

Maybe he did. "Is that why you haven't been around?" she asked.

He shrugged his shoulders, which looked especially broad in his uniform. Kim's pulse quickened, as if she'd begun her run. "Like I said, I live just a wall away. I figured you were wise enough to know where to find me if you wanted to," he said.

"Playing hard to get?" she asked.

His mouth quirked into a lopsided grin. "Maybe bowing to the competition."

"Competition?"

"Mr. Lindstrom. You seem more willing to let him touch you."

"With a shopping cart and a grill fork?" she asked. "I don't think so."

"A grill fork?" George asked with a laugh. "The old man's kinky, huh?"

"The old man doesn't stand a chance," she told him.

"Against Harry?"

She stepped close to him, sliding her fingers across the shiny badge on his chest. "Against you."

"That's right," he said, sighing raggedly, as her fingers skimmed across his chest. "You don't need Harry anymore. You have me."

"Do I?"

He nodded.

"Are you sure?" she asked, her doubts returning. "I can't give you everything you might want."

"What?" he asked, his forehead creasing in confusion. "What can't you give me?"

"Well, let me put it this way," she said, "my clock's not ticking anymore. It's broken."

"I have my son. I don't want any more children," he insisted, his dark eyes wide with surprise at her confession. "I want a companion, someone who challenges and infuriates and fascinates me."

Kim swallowed hard, as her heart rose to her throat. He was looking at her so intently.

"That's you," he told her. "That's how I feel. How do you feel?"

She stared up into his eyes, letting him see her vulnerability in a way she'd let no one else. "I don't want to run," she said.

His eyes narrowed for a moment before understanding dawned and his smile widened. "You're going to let me catch you?"

"Or chase you down," she said as if accepting a challenge, "if you make me."

"I'll never make you do anything you don't want to do," he assured her, as he looped his arms around her waist. "That's why I stopped coming around."

"You wanted me to come to you?" she guessed.

"I didn't want to pressure you. I wanted you to make your own decision about us," he admitted.

"I have. I've decided you talk too much," she told him as she leaned close, pressing her lips against his. Her pulse raced harder and faster than if she'd taken the night run for which she'd dressed.

He kissed her back, with heat and passion, sliding his mouth across hers. Then he pulled away. "I have to say one more thing," he insisted, almost panting for breath.

She sighed, as if seeking patience with his long-windedness. "Go ahead," she said, long-suffering.

"I love you."

Her chest shuddered as her heart shifted. But that declaration didn't frighten her as it might have in the past. She trusted George. "I love you, too."

After another kiss, this one a long one, she reminded him, "This means you're going to be a grandpa."

"What?"

"To the litter of kittens."

He chuckled. "I can't wait for my son to meet you. He'll love you as much as I do."

Kim would make sure that he did, by showing him how much she loved his father.

"Oh," George said, as if something momentous had just occurred to him.

"What?"

"We're going to break his heart."

She didn't think he was still talking about his son, since she had yet to meet him. "Whose heart?"

"Mr. Lindstrom's."

Kim sighed. "You're right. I feel so bad. Maybe we can't do this."

But George's strong arms resisted her effort to pull away. Then he picked her up. "You're not going anywhere. Mr. Lindstrom's going to have to find his own girl. You're mine."

Once that possessiveness would have bothered Kim, would have had her running. But when George said it, it warmed her heart and excited her. And expressed how she felt about him. "And you're mine."

Theresa drew open the blinds in the family room, bathing it in light. Just a little over a month ago, Wally would have protested, grumping and groaning from his battered leather recliner in the corner of the room. But his chair sat empty today. He'd left early in the morning for a breakfast meeting with an old client.

Wally wasn't old or defeated anymore. He was the man she'd fallen in love with so many years ago. While happiness lifted her heart, it was still a bit heavy . . . with loneliness. She was thrilled that he'd recovered his purpose in life, but she wished he could have found it with her.

Now she was the one looking for the television remote. Of course she wanted to record the news at noon; they were going to be showing the segment they'd shot at the community center. But she couldn't find the remote lying in his recliner or on the glass-topped coffee table. So she opened the espresso-colored entertainment unit, but the armoire was empty. No television sat inside, as it always had.

"Where did it go?" she wondered aloud, worried that they'd been robbed. But the patio doors, through which the sun poured, were unbroken. How had a robber gotten inside? If she and Wally weren't home, they engaged the security system.

"What?" Wally asked, as he descended the stairs to the family room.

She gestured toward the empty armoire, but her focus was on him. He looked handsome in his dark suit, his green eyes bright with excitement. Her pulse skittered with a little excitement of her own, then she remembered his question.

"The television's missing. I think we've been robbed," she said, a feeling of being violated building. She hated the idea that a stranger might have been in their home.

"We haven't been robbed," he assured her. "I know where it is."

"Where? The repair shop?" She wouldn't be surprised if he'd worn it out during those months of inactivity after his retirement.

"No, it's not broken," he told her as he stripped off his suit jacket and loosened his green silk tie. Instead of dropping the jacket on the floor, he draped it over the back of his recliner.

"Did you give our TV away?" she asked.

"I thought about that," he admitted. "But I kept it. We'll watch Millie on the news later. It's set to record."

"Where is it?" Theresa asked again.

"In the storage room." Which was just off the family room. "Along with all the other stuff we only use occasionally."

"We're only going to use our television occasionally?" she asked, shocked.

He nodded vehemently. "Of course. We have better things to do."

He did. She wasn't so sure about herself anymore. She'd had a breakfast meeting, too, with Millie and Kim. The domestic goddess was sticking to her plans . . . with some modifications.

"Such as?" she asked him.

He stepped closer and took her hand. "How about we go for a walk?"

"A walk?"

"Like we used to. I'd walk you home from a date and steal a kiss on your parents' front porch."

Feeling a little giddy, Theresa nodded. "I'd love to take a walk with you."

They ducked out their patio doors, walking around the grounds rather than the streets of Hilltop. The complex was delightfully landscaped, with glorious gardens and small ponds where goldfish swam in the sun-kissed water.

As they walked, the years and the children and grand-children, all of it fell away. They were two teenagers again, crazy in love, their hands trembling as they held each other's.

"I hope you don't mind," he said.

"Walking?" she asked, shaking her head, then leaning close enough to brush her face against his shoulder. "I don't mind at all. In fact I love it."

"Good," he said, squeezing her hand. "But that wasn't what I was referring to."

"You're talking about missing Millie's debut?" she asked. "You taped it. We can watch it later." She wouldn't miss a minute of this time with Wally, not even for her friends.

"Yes, we will," he agreed, "but what I hope you don't mind is that I'll still be around the house a lot. I'm limiting my hours at the office and on the golf course. I'd rather be with you," he told her as they neared the patio where they'd begun their walk. Flowers hung from the deck above; impatiens in hot pink, deep red, and pristine white streamed down.

Theresa's heart softened, moved by his confession. "Oh, Wally . . ."

"That's why I put the TV away. I'd rather watch you than it. You're so beautiful, even more so than the day I met you," he said, cupping her cheek. Then he stole a kiss, just like he had so many years ago.

And like so many years ago, he stole Theresa's heart. Again.

"I love you, Wally. I'll love spending every minute I can with you," she promised him, as she wrapped her arms tight around her husband, ready to hold on for the rest of their lives.

*M*illie glanced at her hair once in the rearview mirror before sliding out of the driver's seat in the garage. She'd had her beautician touch up the cinnamon color. It was probably a good thing she'd worn the red hat for the taping even with the tiara. It had hidden the gray showing at her roots. But the gray was gone now.

As were the helpless men who'd brought it on. Mitchell was getting serious about Victoria; he looked at her the way his father had looked at Millie so many years ago. And Steven was home where he belonged.

Millie grabbed her purse and gathered up the big manila folder lying on the passenger seat. She'd made a stop after the beauty parlor at a travel agency. She'd booked that cruise she'd promised herself as a retirement reward. Giving in to her eternally optimistic nature, she'd bought two tickets. If Charles didn't want to use one, she could always ask Mr. Lindstrom; with Kim serious about her neighbor, he would need a consolation prize.

But Millie didn't want to be anyone's consolation prize, almost as much as she didn't want to be anyone's maid. She would make Charles a pie, though, and bring that over to his place with the tickets. Hopefully the pie would mellow him out enough to listen to her proposal.

Not a marriage proposal, but a traveling proposal.

The scent of cinnamon and apple wafted out of the house. Someone was already baking.

She considered reaching for the feather duster that stood handle up in a milk crate next to the back door. But she doubted she needed it to fend off a robber; it wasn't likely anyone had broken into her house to bake.

"Hello?" she called out, expecting Steven, or maybe Mitchell, although she hadn't seen their cars.

"Brigitte?" Her dad could have dropped her off.

"Don't be disappointed," a deep voice called back, "it's just me."

"Charles?" She walked into her kitchen slowly, as if walking into a strange house and not her own home. It was almost as if she didn't know where she was. Since

Steven had moved out, she'd grown used to her house being quiet and empty again.

"You're not armed," he observed, as he glanced over his shoulder from where he stood at her stove.

"Armed?" She shook her head. "That's Kim who carries Harry, not me."

"I've been warned that you wield a mean feather duster," he said.

She flushed, since she had considered it. "Steven told you. He must have given you the key, too?"

"He would have, but Kim had already told me where you keep it."

Kim, the traitor, had struck again.

Millie glanced toward the dining area, where her good china was set on the white linen tablecloth and candles burned in polished brass holders.

"So you didn't break in to rob me," she surmised.

He chuckled. "I don't want to take anything away from you. I want to give you something."

"What?" she asked, heart pounding as her nerves jumbled around in her stomach.

"For starters," he said, deep voice full of mystery, "I want to give you your favorite meal."

"What's that?" she asked, curious if he knew.

"For an appetizer, Jalapeño-Stuffed Bacon-Wrapped Shrimp. For an entrée, Chicken Thighs with Wine, and for dessert Brown Bag Apple Pie."

"Hmm," she mused, impressed despite how obvious she'd made it for him, "you figured that out from class, huh?"

He grinned. "Yeah, I figured that out." His tone suggested he'd figured out some other things as well. "Go, sit down. I'll serve you."

And he did.

In addition to her favorite recipes, he'd made rolls, wonderful crunchy-on-the-outside, soft-on-the-inside whole wheat rolls, and a salad with fresh strawberries and walnuts.

"This is wonderful," she told him. "You pass."

"What?"

"The class. You get an A."

"I didn't do this for Millie, the teacher," he said. "I did this for Millie, the woman."

Her breath caught in her lungs. "Why?"

"Because I'm falling for her." A ragged breath shuddered out of him on a sigh before he added, "Hard."

"Charles . . ."

He reached across the tablecloth, taking her hand in his. "I should have told you sooner."

"When?"

"When should I have told you or when did I start falling?" he asked, with a teasing glint in his bright blue eyes. "I think I knew when you pulled out of the garage and nearly ran Buddy over."

"Where is Buddy?" she asked, suppressing a smile at the frustration that drew a frown on his handsome face.

"You're asking about Buddy *now?*" he asked, knitting his brows with mock irritation.

"I wouldn't want him to be alone," she teased.

"Don't worry. Vic and Mitch took him roller blading in the park."

"How do they fit the Rollerblades on his paws?"

"Millie!" he said, exasperated. "You're not going to make this easy for me."

She shook her head, not caring that her curls tumbled around her face. "'Fraid not."

He leaned farther over the table and pressed his mouth against hers. When he drew away, her breath shuddered out of her. "Keep talking and I'll have to keep doing that," he threatened, "so you'll stop."

"I don't want to stop—" She couldn't finish because his lips stilled hers.

He pulled back, pressing a finger against her lips instead. "You're too distracting." He shook his head. "What was I saying?"

"That you've fallen for me," she reminded him, with a wistful sigh. "Hard."

"And I should have told you sooner."

She nodded. "That would have been nice. But then I should have told you, too."

"Told me what?" he asked, his blue eyes bright and hopeful.

She gathered her courage in a fortifying breath, then said, "That I'm falling for you, too."

"Ah, Millie," he said, threading his fingers through her curls as he leaned his forehead against hers. "You make me feel things I don't think I've ever felt . . ."

She couldn't say the same. She'd been in love before; she knew its giddy rush. But this was different; she was a woman falling in love, not a girl. She felt deeper and more. "Charles . . ."

"I know you loved your husband a lot, that you probably still miss him, and I'm not trying to take his place. I just want to share your life."

And here was where they ran into problems. "You want to share mine or have me share yours?" she asked. "I loved being married to Bruce, but I don't want to repeat that relationship. It was work. Mine. I want to retire that tiara," she said, gesturing to where her red hat, adorned with the glittery piece of jewelry in question, sat on the counter.

"I don't want you to wait on me," he vehemently insisted, nearly sounding insulted.

"But what about on the days that you work?"

"We'll go out to dinner those nights."

"And on the days when I work?"

"You work? Where?" he asked, his deep voice vibrating with excitement. "At the television station?"

She smiled. "I talked to them today." They'd given her a copy of what they'd shown on the noon news that day. "I can tape segments far ahead of time. I won't be working every day. There. Or teaching the classes. Kim and Theresa and I are going to work out a schedule so that we all get some time off."

"So you can travel?"

She nodded, wondering how he felt about that.

She didn't have to wonder for very long, as he grinned and said, "Good."

"Good? You didn't look too happy when I told the TV producer about my travel plans," she said, calling him on his less-than-enthusiastic reaction.

He nodded. "I reacted without thinking. It took me a little while to remind myself that we're both rational adults. We might have other plans, but we understand compromise. You probably weren't thrilled I went back to work."

She nearly groaned her confession, embarrassed about it. "No . . ."

He sighed. "I should have talked to you about it."

"Why?" she asked. "Until now neither of us has been willing to admit our feelings."

"Maybe we're not as rational as I thought," he acknowledged with a wry chuckle. "But still, I should have told you about it and explained that I'm not going to work that much. I'll still have time to travel with you. If you want me . . ."

She stood up and walked over to the counter where she'd set the manila folder with her purse.

"Millie?" he used her name as a question, his voice deep with concern that maybe she didn't want him.

But Millie turned back to the table. Instead of taking her seat, she settled on his lap and handed the tickets to him. "I want you," she told him.

He pressed a quick kiss to her lips before reaching for the tickets. Then he laughed.

"What? Too presumptuous?" she asked.

He wiggled his knees. "Sitting on my lap? I'm all for that."

"And the cruise?"

He wriggled again on the chair, then reached into his back pocket where he pulled out tickets and handed them to Millie. Now she laughed. "You didn't."

"Great minds think alike," he said.

"Think we can get time off work for two cruises?"

"I think that, together, we can do whatever we want."

She nodded her agreement. "Yes, together, we can."

Charles stood up, then set her on her feet. "Time for dessert," he said.

"Yes," Millie agreed. "But we can skip the pie." And she pulled his head down for another kiss.

Epilogue

"Happy marriages begin when we marry the ones we love, and they blossom when we love the ones we marry."
                                            —*Tom Mullen*

$\mathcal{M}$illie never quite retired her domestic goddess tiara; she was seen wearing it every day at noon in living rooms across America. As Mitchell had predicted, she was picked up for syndication. But she and Charles still found time to travel around her schedule of filming cooking segments for the news and continuing to teach the Bachelor's Survival Course.

Of course she had the help of her best friends, Kim and Theresa, for the class and to plan the many weddings held on the deck of Hilltop's community center.

Kim was the first. Impatient to marry the man she loved, she wore her running shoes with her wedding dress, so she could run down the aisle to him.

Millie hadn't had the heart to tell her friend that although hers was the first wedding, Millie had been the first to marry. She and Charles had wed aboard their first cruise, using their second as their honeymoon. But then they said their vows again, in front of their family, friends, and the rest of the class, on Hilltop's deck where Millie had first kissed Charles.

Mitchell and Victoria also married at Hilltop, in the community center where they had first met and fallen in love. While both were busy, they vowed to always have time for each other. Two couples renewed their vows there, too; Steven and Audrey and Wally and Theresa.

They all lived happily ever after and ate really well. Here are the recipes Millie taught in her Bachelor's Survival course from *The Red Hat Society Cookbook.*

Brown Bag Apple Pie

A fun recipe—make sure everyone is watching when you pull the pie out of the oven. Veteran bakers say new grocery bags are thinner than old-style bags, so double-bag the pie.

CRUST

> 1½ cups flour
> ½ cup vegetable oil
> ¼ cup milk
> Dash of salt

FILLING

> 4 large Granny Smith apples
> ½ cup sugar

3 tablespoons flour
½ teaspoon cinnamon

TOPPING

½ cup sugar
½ cup flour
½ teaspoon cinnamon
1 stick (8 tablespoons) butter or margarine

Preheat the oven to 375°.

For the crust, combine the flour, oil, milk, and salt in a bowl and mix until the dough holds together. Roll about ⅛-inch thick and fit in an 8- or 9-inch pie pan. Bake for 10 minutes.

For the filling, peel, core, and slice the apples. In a large bowl toss the apples with the sugar, flour, and cinnamon. Arrange them in the pie crust.

For the topping, combine the sugar, flour, and cinnamon. Cut in the butter with a pastry blender, two knives, or in a food processor. Spread over the apple mixture, pressing down slightly. Slide the pie into a brown paper grocery bag. Fold the top of the bag to close, and then fasten with paper clips. Bake for 1 hour.

Makes 8 servings.

Peggy Krickbaum
Princess Knit Wit
Flashy Sassies
Motrose, Colorado

Dreamsicle Cake

"Refreshing and cool," "Beautiful icing," "Excellent," "Super cake for a formal party," chirped tasters of this pretty cake.

1 (18-ounce) package orange cake mix
1 (3-ounce) package orange gelatin
1 (5-ounce) package vanilla instant pudding mix
4 eggs
½ cup vegetable oil
1½ cups milk

FROSTING

8 ounces sour cream
1 cup sugar
1 (5-ounce) package vanilla instant pudding mix
1 (12-ounce) can crushed pineapple, drained
1 (6-ounce) package frozen coconut
1 (8-ounce) tub whipped topping

Preheat the oven to 350°. Grease and flour three 9-inch cake pans. In a large bowl combine the cake mix, gelatin, pudding mix, eggs, oil, and milk with an electric mixer for 3 minutes. Pour the batter in the pans and bake for 25 to 30 minutes, or until a toothpick inserted in the cake comes out clean. Cool in the pans for 10 minutes, and then invert onto cooling racks and cool completely before frosting. Cake must be refrigerated.

For the frosting, in a large bowl mix the sour cream,

sugar, and pudding mix together by hand. Stir in the pineapple and coconut. Fold in the whipped topping.

Makes 12 servings.

Debbie Anderson
Lady Scarlett
The Red Hot Flashes
Advance, North Carolina

Chocolate Angel Pie

Meringue stands in for crust in this heavenly creation. The tester thought a decorative drizzle of chocolate syrup would be a nice finish.

½ cup sugar
⅛ teaspoon cream of tartar
2 egg whites
½ cup chopped walnuts
¾ cup chocolate chips
3 tablespoons hot water
1 teaspoon vanilla
1 cup heavy whipping cream, whipped

Preheat the oven to 275°. Stir together the sugar and cream of tartar. Beat the egg whites until stiff but not dry; add the sugar mixture gradually, beating until the meringue is smooth and glossy. Line a well-buttered, 9-inch pie plate with the meringue, keeping the bottom just ¼ inch thick. Sprinkle half the walnuts on top and bake for about 1 hour, or until delicately browned. Let cool.

Melt the chocolate chips in the top of a double boiler

set over simmering water; stir in the hot water and cook until thickened. Cool the mixture slightly, add the vanilla, and fold in the whipped cream. Pour into a pie shell. Sprinkle the remaining walnuts over the top. Chill 2 to 3 hours or until the filling is set.

Makes 6 to 8 servings.

Connie McGrath
Queen of Cabernet
Last of the Red Hat Mammas
Riverside, California

Chicken Thighs with Wine

For the family that prefers dark meat. Testers commented that it tastes like pot roast and suggested adding mushrooms.

flour
8 chicken thighs
5 tablespoons olive oil
4 ounces butter
1 large carrot, finely chopped
¾ onion, finely chopped
1½ celery stalks, finely chopped
3 cloves garlic, finely chopped
1½ cups white wine
½ cup dry Marsala
1 teaspoon dried rosemary
4 basil leaves
1 teaspoon hot pepper oil, optional
½ cup chicken stock

salt and pepper
cooked rice

Coat the chicken in flour. Heat the oil in a skillet over medium-high heat. Add the butter. Fry the flour-coated chicken in the hot oil. Remove the chicken from the skillet and add the carrot, onion, celery, and garlic. Reduce the heat to medium low and sauté for 15 minutes, or until soft. Return the chicken to the skillet and add the wine, Marsala, rosemary, basil, pepper oil if using, chicken stock, and salt and pepper to taste. Cook for 1 hour. Serve the chicken with the sauce over rice.

Makes 4 servings.

Judy Sausto
Dame Judy
Dames with a Par-Tea Hat-titude
Egg Harbor Township, New Jersey

Jalapeño-Stuffed Bacon-Wrapped Grilled Shrimp

Leave the tail on when grilling shrimp—it gives guests a "handle" for eating them.

fresh jalapeño peppers, cut into very thin slices
4 to 5 pounds fresh cleaned shrimp, shelled,
    deveined, tails on
uncooked bacon slices
dash of celery salt
dash of lemon pepper

dash of garlic powder
melted butter, if needed

Place a toothpick-sized sliver of fresh raw jalapeño inside the slit made when shrimp are deveined. Press shut and wrap with a 1- to 2-inch piece of bacon. Run a barbecue skewer through one of the shrimp and then the other, so that each shrimp is well secured on the skewer. Pack several shrimp snugly onto the skewer—this helps hold them in place as they cook. Lay each skewer in a shallow dish, and sprinkle with the celery salt, lemon pepper, and garlic powder.

Grill the shrimp on a medium-hot grill for about 10 to 15 minutes, or until the bacon is crisp. The lower tail sections may blacken; this isn't important. If the shrimp appear to be drying out too much during the grilling, baste the cooking shrimp with the melted butter.

Makes 8 to 10 servings.

Glenda Bonham
Countess of Confusion
Ruby Roadrunners
Fort Stockton, Texas

The Red Hat Society®
isn't done yet!

Please turn this page
for two previews of
Regina Hale Sutherland's
other novels of fun, friendship,
and romance over fifty.

Acting Their Age

and

Queens of Woodlawn Avenue

Acting Their Age

*M*ia MacAfee hated mornings, but at five A.M. on Friday, hers were the first bootprints in the two inches of · sugar-soft snow that had fallen during the night.

It's the best part of the day, Mia, she imagined Dan whispering in her ear. *Why would you want to snooze it away?*

Mia glanced over her shoulder, half expecting to see her husband behind her, a wink from his flashing green eyes, his lopsided smile and crooked front tooth. Instead, she saw only the curved pathway she had carved through the sleeping streets of Muddy Creek. In her mind, she whispered back to him, *Okay, Dan MacAfee, you win. It is beautiful. Peaceful, too. And cozy, in a weird sort of way. But the quilt on our bed is also all those things and it's* warm.

They had these conversations from time to time, Mia and her dead husband, the same intimate banter they'd indulged in when he was alive. The talks kept Mia sane, though she suspected if she told anyone, they might disagree with that assessment of her mental state.

Like every morning, Mia made her way to the Brewed Awakening, the coffee shop she'd opened four years ago with Leanne Chilton, her most unlikely friend, as Dan used to call her. A year ago September, only a couple of weeks before Dan died, she recalled sitting with him in the stands at a football game in Brister where their son coached. When the band marched onto the field, the brass section drowning out everything else, Dan laughed and said that if women were instruments, Leanne would be a trumpet. All brassy and full of sass. "Now *you,* on the other hand," he started, then some kid had dumped a Coke in his lap, ending the conversation. It was one of many talks left incomplete between them, little discussions they probably would've continued at some point, had he lived.

While Mia had no clue what instrument she'd be, her friend Aggie Cobb was another story. Dan hadn't gotten around to Aggie, either, but Mia saw the older woman as a flute. Upbeat, fluttery, happy. Or a bass drum. Steady as a heartbeat, predictable, reliable.

Unlike her friendship with Leanne, Dan understood her friendship with Aggie. So did Mia. Which was why she was up and out this morning so much earlier than usual. Some things in life are more important than an extra hour beneath the covers, Mia thought. Some things can't wait. Some things are so troublesome they have the power to jar even a morning-hater awake before the alarm.

Please, God, please let her be in the kitchen like al-

ways, kneading the sweet roll dough, humming along to Patsy Cline.

Mia shoved her fallen purse strap up to her shoulder then settled one mitten-covered hand atop the stack of clean, folded tablecloths she carried. How old was Aggie's mother when her mind started slipping? Older than Aggie, surely. Much older. Seventy, at least.

Seventy.

A sigh slipped past her lips in a puff of smoky white as Mia remembered that Aggie wasn't much younger than seventy. It didn't seem possible her friend had turned sixty-eight last month. She remembered Aggie's mom, Sally, at seventy as a fragile, defeated old woman. But Aggie sparkled with life and enthusiasm. She had the most positive attitude of anyone Mia knew. Up until last week she had, anyway. Or was it the week before?

Mia couldn't pinpoint the moment the changes started. At first only little things caught her attention. No smiles for the customers. No corny jokes. Long stretches of time unpunctuated by Aggie's usual cheerful chatter. Then, on Tuesday, she burned three batches of sweet rolls, one right after the other. On Wednesday, she forgot to add baking soda to the blueberry muffin batter and the muffins came out rock hard. Aggie blamed the oven for both incidents, complaining that Leanne and Mia bought "cheap" merchandise. Yesterday, Aggie burst into tears when Old Man Miller wished her a Happy New Year. Then she missed a curve in the road on the way home from work and mowed down the decorated spruce tree in Joe and Missy Potter's front yard.

A heartbreaking air of sadness surrounded Aggie

lately. Most of the time, she seemed only physically present, her mind a million miles away. At fifty, both Mia and Leanne were eighteen years younger, but they had always had to stay on their toes to outrun, outsmart, or outwit Aggie. As the only morning person of the three, Aggie volunteered to open the shop every day when they'd hired her to work part-time. Each morning, she arrived by four-thirty to start the baking. Mia normally dragged herself out of bed and joined her an hour and a half later. They unlocked the door for customers at seven. Then, by eight-thirty or nine, Leanne, who was dangerous to talk to before noon, showed up, cranky and grumbling, and Aggie left for home at ten.

Drawing crisp, cold air into her lungs, Mia tried to divert her mind to other, happier things. Cold or not, she loved the snow, as long as the wind didn't blow, which was as rare in Muddy Creek as rain in the Sahara. This particular morning settled around her like a sleeping baby's sigh. The air seemed reluctant to disturb the silence; even the naked trees refused to shiver.

Though already a week into the New Year, a few houses on the side streets off Main still twinkled with Christmas lights. Mia gave thanks that the holidays had ended. This Christmas without Dan hadn't been any easier than last year's. That man did love the season! He used to plunge headfirst into the festivities: the kids singing carols at the school play, the baking, the decorating, the rattling of bright, shiny boxes. Dan's enthusiasm for the holiday had been contagious, and Mia had caught it early in their marriage. But that all ended with his sudden heart attack. Now *Silent Night* and colored lights only made her ache.

As she neared the shop, Mia spied a huddled form at the door, stomping snow from a pair of cowboy boots on the welcome mat and muttering something inaudible.

"Leanne?" she called out.

"You're early." Leanne's groggy voice came from beneath the faux leopard fur-trimmed hood of a fitted coat.

"*I'm* early? This is what time you usually *go* to bed, isn't it? Not get up."

Leanne pulled a ring of keys from her coat pocket. "I couldn't sleep."

"Me either." She glanced into the softly glowing shop window, the only one lit up along Main. "Aggie?"

"Yeah." Fatalism darkened Leanne's quick look, a helplessness at odds with her usual brisk self-assurance. "I'm worried about her."

"Me, too. I've never seen her so down. Or so scatter-brained."

"She chewed me out good yesterday for making a mess and leaving it for her to clean up. Said I reminded her of Jimmy when he was a kid, expecting her to be his maid. I think those are the only harsh words I've ever heard come out of that woman's mouth."

"Other than her comment about our cheap oven, you mean?"

A short, sharp laugh, then, "I forgot about that." Her keys jingled as Leanne searched for the right one. "With Aggie's family history, I can't help wondering if—"

"Don't even think it. We're jumping the gun, worrying about that."

"So, you admit it's crossed your mind, too?"

"Sure it has. But it's an overreaction. Something's bothering her, that's all."

"I hope you're right." Leanne slipped the key into the doorknob and turned it.

The shop's bell tinkled as Leanne opened the door. A swirl of warm, scented air rushed to greet Mia. Cinnamon and yeast. Comfort. Memories. Aggie provided most of the baked-good recipes served at the coffee shop, but the sweet rolls belonged to Mia. She had perfected them through years of cooking for Dan and their three kids, all grown now and gone.

Mia's oldest, Brent, currently lived more than an hour and a half away in Brister with his wife, Sherry, and their two children. Brent had followed Dan's example by becoming a smalltown high school football coach. Trey, Mia's middle child, lived the single life in Dallas, where he worked as some kind of business consultant; she never had figured out exactly what the job entailed.

Then there was Mia's daughter Christy. Twenty-seven and twice divorced, Christy lived in New York City where she waited tables. At least, the last time they'd talked she did. How long had it been? Over six months, at least. And ten long years since they'd seen each other. Mia had tried to reach Christy at Christmas, but her home phone had been disconnected, and she didn't answer her cell or return messages.

And Christy didn't send a card.

"Aggie?" Mia shouted. No response came from the kitchen, and Mia caught Leanne's frown. No country music played on the sound system, no off-key voice sang along, no pans clattered. Something wasn't right. Tension hung in the air, as thick as the yeasty scent of baking dough.

Mia didn't bother taking off her coat or wiping the soles of her snow boots on the entry rug. Nor did Leanne. They hurried through the small dining room, past a hodgepodge collection of wooden chairs and scarred oak tables, around a glass-front counter soon to be filled with rolls, muffins, and pies. Mia placed the stack of tablecloths on it and, with Leanne on her heels, pushed through the swinging doors leading into the kitchen.

They froze.

Five-foot-tall Aggie stood with feet apart, clutching an icing tube in one hand and aiming it toward the closed storage room door. Flour smudged her cheek and dusted the red baker's apron she wore over a loose beige sweater and stretchy double knit black pants. The tube shook like a tambourine.

Mia took a cautious step toward her. "Aggie . . . what—"

"Shhh!" Her gaze intent on the storage room door, Aggie whispered, "Something's in there. Hear it?"

Leaning forward, Mia strained to listen. Paper rustled faintly on the other side of the door. Relief rushed from her lungs.

"Lower your weapon, Annie Oakley," Leanne said with wry sarcasm. "Sounds like we've got ourselves a mouse, that's all." She shrugged out of her coat, revealing a skintight sweater and a tall body still shapely enough to turn the heads of men less than half her age. "I'll have Dale Roby come by later to get rid of it."

"It's too big for a mouse." Aggie's voice wavered, sounding more like a piccolo than a flute or a drum.

Leanne groaned. "Okay, *mice*."

Reddening, Aggie thrust out her jaw. "Tell me this, smarty pants. How many mice would it take to move a step ladder? I swear I heard it scrape across the floor a minute ago."

"Rats, then." Leanne shook out her long mane of bottle-blonde hair, then went to hang her coat next to Aggie's on the rack beside the back door. "Or even a possum."

Mia put her purse aside, took off her mittens and stuffed them into her coat pocket before handing it to Leanne to hang. "It's okay, Aggie. We'll call Dale, like Leanne said."

The tube shook harder. Aggie shuddered, her face as pale as a winter sun. "You know how I hate rodents."

Shaking her head, Leanne asked, "What're you plannin' to do? Shoot it with icing and send it into a sugar coma?"

Mia walked past Aggie and reached for the storage room door handle. "Come on, let's take a look."

"Oh, Lord." Whimpering, Aggie kept the tube poised to squirt.

"No one would ever believe you live on a farm, Ag," Leanne said with a sigh.

The hinges squeaked as Mia pushed the door wide, letting the light from behind seep into the storage room. Blinking, she scanned the small, crowded area stacked high with supplies. As she stepped in, she heard a gasp in the far right corner, a sharp intake of breath.

"Turn on the light, Leanne," Mia whispered. Her heart ticked like an over-wound clock as she peered toward the shadowy corner from where the sound had come. The bare bulb overhead flared, illuminating a pale, frightened face with dark, hollow smudges for eyes. The eyes stared back at Mia.

Aggie screeched, and Mia felt something hit her back. *Icing.*

"Sorry," Aggie murmured. "My finger hit the trigger."

Ignoring the ooze beneath her left shoulder blade, Mia concentrated on the girl crouched on the floor in the corner, hugging dirty, torn, blue-jean-covered knees to her chest. "Hello, there." Mia reached out a hand.

Cringing, the girl scrambled to her feet, her eyeliner-smeared, sleepy brown eyes too big for her face; her short, dark-rooted, white-blonde hair flattened to her head on one side and stuck out in spikes on the other. She appeared too young for makeup and bleached hair. Twelve, maybe. Thirteen at the most. A kaleidoscope of emotions flashed across her face then quickly disappeared behind a stony mask.

"Heavens," Aggie whispered.

Leanne moved up beside Mia as the skinny, shivering girl pressed closer to the wall. "We have a rat, all right. A packrat." She pointed to the nest at the girl's feet: a man's down jacket, a well-worn backpack, two tablecloths bunched into a makeshift bed. A scatter of crumpled paper muffin cups surrounded an empty Brewed Awakening mug. "A packrat with an appetite."

Mia detected a hint of concern in Leanne's tone.

The girl's chin lifted as she blinked the sleep from her eyes then narrowed them into defiance. Mia took another step toward her. "What's your name?"

No answer.

"How'd you get in here?" Leanne crossed her arms, one cowboy boot tapping out her impatience. "You better check the safe, Aggie. Make sure our little packrat isn't a thief, too."

"No one could crack that thing," Aggie scoffed.

"Are you okay?" Mia asked the girl in a careful voice. No use frightening her more than she was already.

"You would'a been smarter to break in to the beauty shop down the street," Leanne said. "Betty hates a cold shop in the mornings. She leaves the heater running full blast all night."

Aggie squeezed in on Mia's other side. "Talk to us, sugar. We don't want to hurt you. But we can't help you, either, if you won't tell us who you are."

When the front bell jingled, the girl jumped, her gaze darting toward the door.

"Well, damn," Leanne huffed. "Don't people know by now we're not open this early?" She called, "Just a sec!" then backed out of the storage room for a moment before poking her head back in. "It's the sheriff. I swear, Mia, the man gets earlier every day." Her half-grin brimmed with insinuation. "Guess he can't stand not seeing your smiling face first thing in the morning."

For once, Mia welcomed Sheriff Cade Sloan's daily visit, instead of dreading it. She'd known him most of her life, did the sports booster club thing and PTA with him and his ex-wife, Jill, before they divorced. Years back, she and Dan had even socialized with them some. Then, a couple of months ago, Cade started flirting. Now, just the sight of him made her as nervous and self-conscious as a girl at her first school dance. Especially since Leanne and Aggie insisted he had a "thing" for her.

Mia wasn't convinced of that. Like Leanne, Cade was a tease and always had been. At one time or another, every woman in town had been the recipient of his playful joking. Now it was her turn, that was all.

But the looks he gave her lately still made her heart skip a beat. Though she'd never admit it to Leanne or Aggie, Mia feared *she* was the one with a "thing" for *Cade,* not the other way around. "Tell him to come back here," she said.

"No!" The girl stepped toward the three women, one arm thrust out, trembling. "Don't tell him I'm here."

Mia's heart beat too fast. Why did this child seem so familiar?

"Please," the girl whispered. "Just give me a chance."

And then, at once, Mia knew. Her eyes had a different shape. The color was wrong, too; brown rather than blue. But the flash of desperation, the lost look in them, was identical to what she'd glimpsed briefly in her own daughter's eyes before Christy ran away.

Queens of Woodlawn Avenue

$\mathcal{I}$ could smell the pound cake through my closed front door. Vanilla, sugar, butter—luscious scents mingling in a heavenly aroma that promised rapture. Of all things, why did it have to be pound cake—my sugar-addicted Achilles' heel?

"Mrs. Johnston? Ellie? Are you in there?"

The nasal voice reminded me of Gladys Kravitz, the nosy neighbor on *Bewitched*. Unfortunately, I didn't possess Samantha's supernatural powers to rid myself of this unwanted visitor. Which meant that the only way I was going to get the cake and/or make my neighbor go away was to open the door.

Honestly, I'd have had no dilemma at all if it weren't for the pound cake. For the past two weeks, I'd been closeted in the house, safely hidden from the outside world. All I wanted was to lick my wounds, marinate in endless bubble baths of grief and regret, and eat whatever was handy. I had consumed the entire contents of my kitchen. Campbell's chicken noodle soup. Krispy Kreme donuts. Butter pecan Häagen Daz. Betty Crocker brownie mix. No saturated fat or carbohydrate had escaped me, because for the first time in my adult life, I was eating whatever I wanted. Two weeks, though, of consuming my way through the kitchen had yielded a predictable result. Like Old Mother Hubbard, my cupboard was now as bare as my bottom was wide.

I wanted to be left alone to grow old and die in solitude, cut off from the outside world in this tumbledown 1920s Tudor, the symbol of my wretched post-divorce existence. I could keep drifting from room to room, looking glassy-eyed out the windows at my overgrown backyard with a cup of cold coffee in my hand. The drone of late-night infomercials would keep me company during the long, sleepless nights I spent flipping through photo albums of the life I had lost. I could depend on the stray tabby cat that pawed through my garbage can for my social interaction. But if I didn't replenish my food supply soon, I was going to grow old and die much more quickly than I'd planned.

"I made pound cake. To welcome you to the neighborhood." Her temptress's voice, along with the scent of vanilla, slid through the cracks around the edge of the door. My new neighbor was scarily persistent. I had simply ignored her earlier visits, but now I didn't have the luxury. Who would ever have believed it would come to this?

Once, I'd been Mrs. Eleanor Johnston, wife of a successful surgeon and pillar of the Junior League. Now I was nothing but another high-end Nashville divorcée who'd been banished from her 37205 life by her husband's wandering eye. I had become nothing but a cliché, and not a very interesting one at that.

"I think you'll feel better if you eat some of this," the voice said through the door. God, but this woman was not going to give up, was she?

And she did have pound cake.

My hand shook as I reached for the doorknob. The warped wood stuck tight, and I had to give it a strong yank before it gave way, revealing the perky middle-aged woman standing on my front porch.

"There you are." The woman's bright blond hair competed with her paper-white teeth for brilliance. With a start, I recognized her from her advertisements on bus stops all over town. She owned one of the big real estate firms and I had probably even met her at one fund-raiser or another, but I couldn't remember her name.

"I was beginning to worry about you." Uninvited, she stepped across the threshold and into my inner sanctum with the same determination that must have gotten her to the top of the Nashville real estate market. I had the grace to blush at the state of the living room. Twinkie wrappers and empty Coke cans littered the scarred coffee table. The sagging couch that once had done duty in our bonus room—I'd considered it fit only for small children and teenagers—was now the centerpiece of my living room suite. Sadly, it classed up the joint, a strong indication of the general condition of the house.

"I knew you'd open the door eventually," the woman trilled as she brushed past me and headed toward the kitchen as unerringly as if she'd traipsed through the house a million times before. "My pound cake never fails."

I stood rooted to the spot, mouth gaping for several

long moments, before I realized I was supposed to follow her size-2 frame. By the time I caught up with her in
the kitchen, she had placed the cake on my cutting
board, unwrapped the cloth like a priest preparing the
host for the congregation, and was using a lethal-looking
knife to slice off a wedge of the promised ambrosia.

"Got milk?" she chirped.

My mouth watered so heavily I had to swallow twice
before I could form a reply.

"Um, no. I'm out."

"That's okay. We can have coffee instead."

I paused and cleared my throat. "Well, I don't actually have any coffee either."

Her eyebrow arched. "You've gone through it all,
then?"

My stomach twisted. I feigned ignorance. And hau-
teur. "What do you mean, I've gone through it all?"

Her laugh was like silverware clanking in a drawer.
"Honey, I know how it goes when you're newly on your
own. Eating your way through the refrigerator is practically a rite of passage."

"I haven't—" A flush crept up my neck.

"It's nothing to be ashamed of, honey." She placed a
hunk of cake on a paper napkin from the stack on the
counter and thrust it toward me. "And you look like you
need this."

My hand froze, fingertips an eyelash away from the
cake. For a moment, I saw myself through my nosy
neighbor's eyes. Greasy hair that hadn't seen shampoo
in a week. Dressed in my son's cast-off sweat pants and

a paint-stained Vanderbilt sweatshirt. Had I even brushed my teeth that morning?

With a laugh that was two parts humor and ten parts shame, I ran a hand over my hair to smooth down the inevitable bed head. "I don't really . . . That is, I'm sure . . ."

The other woman smiled, this time with no condescension at all. "It's okay, honey. We've all been there."

That got my back up. Because, *pardon me,* not everyone had been where I was now. Not everyone was eating off Chinet while a DD-cup tramp ate off her Haviland china and drank from her Waterford crystal.

"I don't know what you mean." Indignation kept me from reaching for the cake.

"It's no secret, sugar. News travels fast on the Woodlawn Avenue grapevine. We're practically psychic."

Years of good Southern upbringing kept me from making a sharp retort. I didn't need the final humiliation of a public airing of my dirty laundry in my new neighborhood. Wasn't it enough that I could never hold my head up again in Belle Meade? I'd lost everything. My husband. My beautiful home. My place in society. And now I was nothing more than fodder for gossip over the backyard fences of Woodlawn Avenue?

My neighbor remained undaunted by my silence. "I'm Jane, by the way. Jane Mansfield." She laughed, showing off her blinding teeth again. "I know, I know. But you can't pick the last name of the man you fall in love with. Or out of love with, for that matter."

Jane Mansfield. Now I remembered. Her publicity photo on the bus stop ads showed her dressed in fifties attire with a matching bouffant hairdo. She was ten years or so older than me, but at the moment, she looked a decade younger. She probably felt that way, too. Because right then, I must have looked at least a hundred and five.

"It's my birthday," I said, the words falling from my lips of their own volition.

The woman nodded. "Good thing I showed up. Every woman deserves a cake on her birthday."

I nodded, my throat too tight for speech. When was the last time I'd had a birthday cake I hadn't made with my own two hands? Jim had been good with presents but bad with remembering to order something from Becker's Bakery, and none of my children had inherited my homemaking gene. As I'd learned over the years, there was something inherently sad about providing one's own cake.

"I'm Ellie," I finally rallied enough to blurt out. "Ellie Johnston. I mean, Hall. Ellie Hall." Another change that was going to take some adjustment.

One of Jane's perfectly waxed eyebrows arched. "It's final, then, your divorce?"

A lump formed in my throat. "I signed the papers yesterday."

"Hell of a birthday present."

I didn't know whether to laugh or cry at the irony of it all. "Yes. Yes, it was a hell of a present."

Jane stood up straight, all ninety-eight or so pounds of her. "So today's the day you start over. New house, new life, new you."

That point of view had never occurred to me. I'd been so focused on what was coming to an end, I hadn't given much thought to what might be beginning. The very idea made me queasy, so I took a bite of pound cake.

A profusion of flavor exploded on my tongue. "Oh my God," I moaned through the ecstasy melting in my mouth. "I can't believe this cake."

Jane smiled. "Well, there's more where that came from." She reached down and sliced off another piece. "So, Ellie Hall, do you have plans for your birthday?"

I sighed and leaned against the counter. "No. Not really. Since it's Saturday, Oprah and Dr. Phil won't be expecting me."

"Good." Jane took another paper napkin from the pile and brushed the crumbs from the counter into her hand. As casually as if it were her house instead of mine, she opened the cabinet door under the sink and tossed them into the waiting trash can. "We've been waiting for a fourth."

"A fourth? A fourth of what?"

"A fourth for our bridge club."

"Oh. I'm sorry, but I don't play bridge."

Jane smiled. "That's okay, honey. I didn't play either when I moved into my house. But I learned."

The woman might bake heavenly pound cake, but she was clearly a bit loopy. "I'm sorry, but what does your house have to do with a bridge club?"

"Follow me."

Jane stepped around me and led me back through my dining room to the archway that separated it from the living room. The heart-shaped arch had mocked me from the moment my realtor had first shown me the house. But it had been one of the few in this rapidly gentrifying neighborhood south of Vanderbilt University that I could afford. It was as close to Belle Meade as my budget would allow. In time, I could channel my inner Martha Stewart to drywall the offending arch into another shape. A dagger, perhaps, for sticking through Jim's faithless heart.

Jane ran her hand over the curve in the plaster, caressing it. "Didn't you wonder about this when you bought the house?"

I shrugged, not wanting to reveal the depths of my pain or my sensitivity about the arch. "It's important for some reason?"

"All four houses have them. One for each suit."

"All four houses?"

"Built by the original members of the club."

"Someone built houses based on a club?"

"Not just any club. Their bridge club. The Queens of Woodlawn Avenue."

That drew a rare chuckle from me. "Queens of Woodlawn Avenue? You've got to be kidding."

Jane shook her head. "Nope. I'm the Queen of Diamonds. Grace on the other side of you is the Queen of Spades. And Linda, in the Cape Cod on the other side of me, she's the Queen of Clubs. We each have the dining room arch for our suit."

Okay, her pound cake was sinfully good, but this woman was starting to frighten me a little. "Look, I appreciate the invitation, but really, I don't think I'd make very good company right now." Not to mention my complete ineptitude with card games of any variety. While some of my sorority sisters in college had been bitten by the bridge bug, I'd declined to be infected.

Jane waved away my words with a flick of her expensive manicure. "You'll learn. We all did." She stepped back into the living room and I followed like an obedient puppy. "In fact, I think we should meet tonight. You need backup on your birthday."

"Look—" Okay, I was starting to get perturbed. Couldn't this woman see that I just wanted to be left alone?

"Seven o'clock at my house," she said over her shoulder as she tugged open the obstinate front door. "And wear a red hat."

"Wear a what?"

"A red hat."

I sagged against the arm of the sofa. "I'm not sure I own a hat, much less a red one."

Jane smiled, again blinding me. "Then you can borrow one of mine. We never play bridge without our hats. Chapter rules."

Chapter rules? Great. Not only had my husband thrown me over for a Hooters waitress, but I had spent all the money from my divorce settlement on a house in a neighborhood of crazies.

"Bring a dish, too. That's another rule."

"A dish of what?"

"Hors d'oeuvres. Casserole. Dessert. Whatever you feel like."

"But I don't have anything in the house."

Jane smiled again. "Then I guess you'd better run to the grocery store." Her eyes traveled over my sweatshirt and sweatpants. "You might want to change first. In this town, you're going to see someone who will report back to him."

"Report back?"

"To your ex. He'll hear about your every move. So you can decide what kind of report he's going to get. Would you rather be the spurned woman in scruffy sweats or the fabulous divorcée who embraced life and moved on?"

Truthfully, I'd rather be able to dial the clock back nine months so that none of this had ever happened. But she did have a point. Jim was bound to hear about it if I schlepped to the grocery store in our son's castoffs. When it came to demographics, Nashville might be a major metropolitan area, but in all the ways that mattered, it was still a small town. I'd learned never to say anything bad about anyone, because you could count on the fact that the person you were speaking to was somehow related to the person you were disparaging.

"Seven o'clock?" I said weakly, and Jane beamed.

"Good girl. You're going to be okay."

I wanted to believe her, but reason and hard truth were not on her side. I was a fifty-year-old broke divorcée, living in a run-down, eighty-year-old house and wondering how I was going to pay next month's electric bill. But even at my lowest, I still had my pride. It was about all I had, but for the time being, it was going to have to be enough.

Jane waved good-bye and disappeared through the front door, leaving me alone with the pound cake. I straightened my spine, walked to the coffee table, and scooped up the Twinkie wrappers and Coke cans.

Whether I wanted it or not, two things were apparently going to happen.

With or without Jim, life was going to go on.

And much to my consternation, I was going to learn to play bridge.

When love is just around the corner, you can't be over the hill!

The Red Hat Society brings together women across the world for friendship, fun, and laughs. Now, there's a new treat—official Red Hat Society novels about companionship, adventure, and love over 50.

The Red Hat Society's
ACTING THEIR AGE

The Red Hat Society's
QUEENS OF WOODLAWN AVENUE

The Red Hat Society's
DOMESTIC GODDESS

Don't miss out on these red-hot romances!